PRAISE FOR *BROKEN*

"[A] fast-paced thriller" with an "I-totally-didn't-see-it-coming ending."

—*Entertainment Weekly's Shelf Life*

"An intense page-turner. Readers will race to the end to see if Scarlet will uncover the truth about herself and those around her before it's too late."

—*New York Times* bestselling author April Henry

"Laurie Halse Anderson's *Speak* meets Kathy Reichs' *Virals*."

—Jill Moore, Square Books, Jr., Oxford, MS

"A suspenseful thriller laced with medical intrigue and coming-of-age triumph."

—*Booklist*

"A chilling medical suspense story—Lyons' specialty—expertly entwines with teen-oriented family drama and the eye-rolling social hierarchy that is high school."

—*RT Book Reviews,* Top Pick, 4½ Stars

ALSO BY CJ LYONS

Watched

BROKEN

CJ LYONS

sourcebooks fire

Published by Sourcebooks Fire, an imprint of Sourcebooks, Inc.
P.O. Box 4410, Naperville, Illinois 60567-4410
(630) 961-3900
Fax: (630) 961-2168
www.sourcebooks.com

Library of Congress Cataloging-in-Publication data is on file with the publisher.

Printed and bound in the United States of America.
VP 10 9 8 7 6 5 4 3 2 1

To Abby.
Despite Long QT, your heart is too big
and generous to ever be broken.

MONDAY

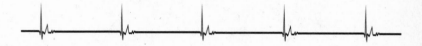

1

If you want to get noticed fast, try starting high school three weeks late as the girl who almost died.

Unfortunately, attention is the last thing I crave. Give me anonymity anytime. Every time.

I just want to be a normal girl. No one special.

Saw a movie once, don't remember what channel, but it was in the dark hours of the night when it was just me and the TV. My favorite time of day.

It starred John Travolta back when he was young. The kid was so sick he lived in this plastic bubble and he was so excited when he got to leave it.

Me? When I saw the boy leave his bubble, I wanted it for myself. Coveted it.

God, how I'd die for a cozy little bubble to live my life in, safe from the outside world.

Only I'd paint my bubble black so no one could see me inside.

2

There are two metal detectors inside the main doors of Smithfield High and 337 students plus one trying to crowd through them. I'm the plus one. Not sure which line to stand in or if there's even a real line at all hidden somewhere in this mass of humanity. It's the largest crowd I've ever been in.

The school lobby echoes with voices and the stamping of feet. We're herded like a bunch of cows headed for slaughter. All that's missing are the cowboys and the branding irons.

No one else is nervous about this. They don't care about the metal detectors or what's in their bags or even the two guards manning the operation. They're not worried about being trampled or that there isn't enough oxygen or how many billions—no, trillions—of bacteria and viruses are wafting through the air, microscopic time bombs searching for a new home.

All they care about is me. The stranger in their midst. They shuffle around me uneasily, quickly sniffing out that I don't belong.

A girl with a pierced nose and heavy eyeliner looks at me like I'm a tacky rhinestone necklace on display at a pawnshop counter. She hides her mouth behind her hand as she whispers something to her friend with the purple streak in her hair.

A guy wearing a white and orange Smithfield Wildcats letterman jacket trips over the backpack I wheel behind me, almost smash-ing into a wall before he catches himself. "Out of my way, loser."

His snarl is accompanied by a sneer. He stares down at me—he's huge, at least six feet tall, with shoulders that block my view. "I said, move it." I try to steer my backpack, but his feet get tangled as he zigs the same direction I'm zagging. "You don't want to piss me off. Understand?"

The crowd pushes him even closer so all I can hear is his voice. My heart booms in response, sending up its own distress call. His name is on his letterman jacket, embroidered above the wildcat with the long, sharp fangs. *Mitch Kowlaski. Football.* I shrink against the wall, making myself even smaller than my usual five feet two, and pull my backpack between my legs, giving him room to cut in front of me.

He joins a cluster of football players and continues to stare at me. His look is easy to read: what kind of loser brings a wheeled backpack to high school?

Not cool. Neither are my virgin-white, just-out-of-the-box-this-morning sneakers that a guy in a pair of work boots stomps on. And why didn't I think to put on at least a little lip gloss this morning?

I scan the crowd, searching for the normal kids—and fail. Seems like being normal is out of style this season. You have to be "someone," create an alter ego: a jock, a church girl, a rebel, a loser.

Even I understand the danger of that last label.

I'm too skinny, too pale; my hair's all wrong; I should've tried to figure out makeup (as if Mom would ever let me!), shouldn't have worn this jacket (but I love my faded, soft, frayed denim jacket; my dad gave it to me). It's out of style and doesn't go with the new-blue of my jeans that everyone can tell are a last minute buy from K-Mart, because who needs clothes when you live in a hospital and—

An elbow nudges my back. My turn at the metal detector.

I roll my backpack—heavier than any other student's—over to the guard. He hefts it onto his examination table and zips it open. "What's this?"

"My AED." I try to sound hip and casual, like doesn't every kid carry their own advanced life support resuscitation equipment?

The guard snatches his hand away from my bag. "An IED?"

Now everyone is staring. At me.

"New kid has a bomb in there," Mitch, the guy I accidentally tripped earlier, shouts in mock dismay. His voice booms through the crowded space louder than a real IED going off.

Not everyone thinks it's a joke. A gasp goes up behind me, traveling down the line of waiting students faster than a roller coaster. I'm imagining that last part—I've never been on a roller coaster. Their stares push me forward.

"No. It's an *A*ED." Sweat trickling down the back of my neck, I rush to explain before I'm branded a terrorist or, worse, a freak. Too late. Mitch and his group of football players are snickering and pointing at me. "Automated External Defibrillator. I need it for my heart."

Actually, I hope I never need it, but even though the school has an AED in the gym, Mom convinced the insurance company that I should have my own, smaller model to carry with me at all times. Just in case.

Story of my life in three words: Just In Case.

Just in case my heart does a backflip at the sight of a cute guy and lands on its ass, unable to spring back on its own.

Just in case the fire alarm goes off and startles me, releasing adrenaline, shocking my heart into quivering, cowardly surrender.

Just in case I'm too hot or too cold or eat the wrong thing or forget to take my meds and my heart decides today is the day to go galloping out of control, leaving me lying there on the floor for guys like Mitch Kowlaski to walk over while everyone else points and laughs at the girl who finally died…

Mom has a thousand and one Just In Cases. Like she keeps reminding me, if I were a cat, I'd already have used up more than nine lives.

Swallowing my pride and the chance that I'll ever be accepted here—who am I kidding? I never had a chance, only a hope—I pull my Philips HeartStart AED free from its case and show it to the guard.

He stares from the AED to me, taking in my way-too-skinny frame, paler-than-vampire complexion, sunken eyes, and brittle hair, and nods wordlessly. "Humor the girl-freak before she does something crazy" kind of nodding.

"See? Here's how you use it, it talks you through everything," I prattle on, trying desperately to sound nonchalant. Normal. I call the defibrillator Phil for short. The perfect accessory for any fifteen-year-old girl, right? The bright-blue plastic case matches my eyes, can't you see?

"Aw, look. Freakazoid has a broken heart," Mitch says. "Waiting for Dr. Frankenstein to shock some life into you, sweetheart? I got everything you need right here."

"Shut it, Kowlaski," the other guard yells at him. He turns to me. "You must be Scarlet Killian."

I now realize that the second line has also stopped to witness the end of my short career as a normal high school sophomore. Everyone now knows my name. Knows my heart is broken. Knows I'm a freak.

"Your mom told us to be on the lookout for you. Go ahead through."

Our hands collide as we both reach to return Phil to my pack. He jerks away. Reluctant to touch the complicated machine—or the girl whose life it's meant to save?

Why does everyone assume dying is contagious?

I shove Phil back in, zip the pack shut, slip through the metal detector without anything exploding, and bolt.

The football players, including Mitch, are crowded together on the other side, forcing me to push past them. "Must be tough having a heart ready to go tick, tick, boom!" Mitch laughs. His friends must think it's funny because they join in.

Totally embarrassed and certain everyone is staring, I keep my head down and walk away, hauling Phil behind me. My heart is beating so fast spots appear before my vision. Not a Near Miss, just plain, old-fashioned, let-me-crawl-in-a-hole-and-die mortification.

Time spent in high school: three minutes, forty-two seconds.

Time spent as a normal sophomore girl before being outed as the freak with the bum heart: fifty-five seconds.

Time remaining in my high school career as a freak: 5,183,718 seconds.

Maybe less if the doctors' predictions are right and I get lucky and drop dead.

3

So this is high school. I stroll down the hall, pulling Phil behind me, taking in everything. Feeling a bit like a kid at the zoo—only I'm the specimen on display.

There are large banners plastered onto the walls above the rows of lockers, exhorting us to "Chew up the Raiders!" We have a home football game on Friday against the Bellefonte Red Raiders. The Wildcats lost the first two games of the season—I actually listened to them, one from my hospital bed and one from home. It was so cool to have a team of my own to cheer for. Especially since, around here, people live and die for high school football. There's just not much else to do in a small Pennsylvania town like Smithfield, not since the steel mill shut down.

The other students, even the freshmen, already know where they're going; they've had three weeks to practice. They walk down the corridor in pairs or triads, the occasional singleton or clump of four or five. I've studied online maps of the school and try to look like I know where I'm going as I translate my mental image into reality. But it's hard not to be distracted. The vast majority of my social interactions have been me and Mom facing a doctor or nurse, with the occasional intern or med student thrown in.

Nothing in my life has prepared me for this. The hallway becomes claustrophobic, crowded by the frenzied movements of the students, studied glances and postures, scented hair products that tickle my nose…and the noise. Voices high and low, loud and gruff, shrill and dour—everyone seems to have something to say, but I'm not sure if anyone is actually listening. They just keep talking, like a machine-gunner hoping the more bullets he fires the more chance of hitting something sooner or later—whether or not it's his target.

The first bell rings and the hall is flooded with a sudden influx through the front doors. I'm shoved and jostled by kids long gone by the time I look around. People swear as they trip over Phil and I try to keep him closer to me, but it doesn't help.

They've given me an upper locker in the main corridor. No way am I going to be able to ditch Phil in there. I twist the combination open and peer inside. Not that there's any room. Whoever I'm sharing it with has already made himself at home.

I'm guessing "him" since it's crammed full with a gym bag that reeks of Axe and sweaty socks, a very large pair of soccer cleats, plus a teetering stack of notebooks and ragged paperbacks, mostly way-old science fiction with covers of busty blonds and lusty monsters, all guarded by a picture pasted to the inside of the door: something ripped out of a *Sports Illustrated* Swimsuit edition. Minus the swimsuit. The girl is naked from the waist up, hands strategically spread over her breasts, mouth half-open in a sultry pout.

Narrowly avoiding an avalanche of books and papers, I shove

my jacket in. By the end of the day, it'll stink of Axe and testosterone. The smell makes my head swim, but isn't as bad as I first thought. Kinda nice, warm and spicy, like a guy's arms wrapped around you. I glance at the picture again, a surge of jealousy filling me. Which is silly. How can I be jealous of a model?

Even more irrational is the sudden fantasy of wanting a guy I've never met to put his arms around me—based solely on his scent. Hormones, pheromones, frontal lobe excitation. That's all it is. No guy would ever want me, the half-dead girl.

But I'm only fifteen and never been kissed and have no defense against hormones. Or hope.

Angry at myself, I slam the door so hard the metal rings out like a call to prayer. Or maybe a prayer answered.

Because there *he* is. Very real, very solid, very GUY.

He slouches against the wall of lockers, his gaze directed at my feet. His eyes, the color of the burnt coffee that somehow makes hospital cafeterias smell like home, roam slowly up my legs, taking in the "skinny jeans" that hang loosely on my bony-thin hipless frame.

A blink and the jeans are whisked away, leaving a red-hot trail behind as his gaze continues ravaging my body. Another blink and the vintage Nirvana tee I'd hidden from my Mom under my denim jacket and Bongo cardi vanish as well. But somehow I'm not wearing my cotton sports bra and panties anymore. Instead I feel as naked as his swimsuit model, and my mouth opens and closes as I try to figure out how to pout like she does.

And end up burbling like a fish snared on a hook. At least

that's what I imagine as his eyes finally make it to my mouth and sunken cheeks and barren, naked eyes. My ears pop as my fantasy bursts.

Suddenly he's just a guy, shoulders and neck hunched as if he isn't sure how tall he's meant to be, navy T-shirt with a frayed collar revealing chiseled arms, single zit marring the perfect line of his jaw, dark eyes staring at me with the same morbid curiosity everyone else has—judging me a freak.

"That's my locker," he says, not moving anything but his lips.

It must take a lot of energy to stand that still, look that non-chalant. Then I realize: the word has spread. Everyone's heard about me and my broken heart. He's afraid to get too close. I might be contagious.

"Mine too, I guess," I stammer, hormones fanning warm embers in my stomach. "They assigned it to me. I'm Scarlet Killian."

Infinitesimal nod. The movement releases a lock of his hair and it falls into his eyes. He doesn't shake it free or even blink as strands curl across his impossibly long eyelashes. I can't stop staring. My fingers itch with a desire to reach across the space separating us and brush it back.

"Jordan. Summers." He adds the last like I should already know his name. As if his reputation had preceded him.

Reputation for what, I have no idea, but again hope blossoms in me. Maybe he's the kind of guy who doesn't care what a girl looks like or if she's too bony or has to carry her own AED and would probably die if they tried to ever kiss or, God forbid, fool around.

I might not make it that long. Not with the way my heart is banging against its cage, desperate for escape. How sad would that be? Dying before a first kiss?

Not sad in a tragic, melancholy, write a sonnet way. Sad as in desperate. Loser. Freak.

My cheeks heat with a blush. I grab the handle to my backpack, hoping my sweaty palm won't slip. "Guess I'd better go."

But I can't move, too busy reveling in the fact that the toe of Jordan's hiking boot is touching my left foot.

Then, miracle of miracles, Jordan touches my elbow. I dare to glance up, my head rushing in sync with the bass line of my heartbeat.

"Hey," he says. "I think that's your mom."

He nods over my shoulder to the tall blond in the nurse's uniform rushing down the hall as if there was a life-and-death emergency waiting for her, a pill bottle held aloft.

"Scarlet," Mom calls in a rush, her voice loud, so loud everyone looks away, embarrassed for me.

Before she can reach me, so fast I think maybe I'm imagining things, Jordan breathes into my ear, "I like your shirt."

Then he escapes the spotlight of pity, leaving me to burn alone in my hell on earth.

"You forgot to take your pill this morning. Are you okay? You look flushed." Mom's hand expertly feels my forehead, searing me with its coolness. I cringe, search for an escape, but there is none, my back to the lockers. "I think you should come to my office, lie down. Let me check you out."

Her words douse embers of hormonal flames into a soggy, muddy mess, inking my insides with soot that tastes of burnt toast, like what Mom gave me once to make me throw up after I ate Something Bad.

Silly me, letting hormones expose me to hope—I have no immunity. I need John Travolta's plastic bubble to shield me until I can build a resistance.

In the meantime, I release my backpack and let my mom—well, stepmom actually, but she's the only mom I've ever known—Nurse Killian, drag it and me down to the school nurse's office.

Accepting the fact that this won't be the last time, I vow to let my hair grow longer than the shoulder-length bob it's in now, the better to shield my face as I hang my head. Shame and embarrassment wage a war, both declaring victory while my insides curl up in a fetal position and surrender without even a whimper.

4

When you've spent more time in a hospital bed than at home, and your mom is constantly taking you to new, better, top-flight teaching hospitals, and you have an obscure diagnosis, you get used to med students, residents, and consultants coming in and stripping you naked, their clinical gazes as cold as their hands and stethoscopes.

I'm numb to it, barely notice being touched anymore. By anyone.

Until that one brush of Jordan Summers's hand against my elbow. Staring at my mom's Nurse Mates, following the little red hearts on their heels, I cradle my elbow where he touched me, a smile breaking through. No one can see my smile. Which makes it all the more special.

This was why I fought my parents so hard about coming to high school. All this special and exciting and secret stuff. Things you can't learn from TV or books. Things you have to feel for yourself if you want to know what it means to live.

Really live, not just outlast a doctor's prognostication.

Goose bumps pepper my arms. Being a real girl—okay, *pretending* to be a real girl, a normal girl—is intoxicating. Worth putting up with the humiliation of facing guys like Mitch Kowlaski and his friends this morning.

I don't want this giddy feeling to end. But, just like Cinderella, I'm on a strict deadline. I only have this week to prove I can be normal, attend school without killing myself.

That's hyperbole—but it's also exactly what my folks are most frightened of. After all these years of shielding me from danger, they think a few days of acting like a normal girl will be the death of me. Or at least trigger another Set Back.

It's up to me to prove them wrong.

Mom leads me into her office and closes the door. She sits me down in the student chair, stretching my arm along the desktop as she takes my pulse. It's fluttering in such disarray I wonder if my heart has learned Morse code. I imagine it tapping out J-O-R-D-A-N over and over again.

I don't look Mom in the eyes—I know exactly what I'll see and I'm not ready for it.

But I can't escape her voice.

"Scarlet, I think we've made a mistake, letting you try school. I'm sending you home."

5

Mom sees any deviation from my baseline as a Symptom. I see it as cause for celebration.

Now that I'm actually at school, instead of lying in a bed imagining what life in high school would be like, I feel great. A little light-headed—but not the headachy, nauseating vertigo that means I'm getting ready to have a Set Back. Or worse, a Near Miss.

More like lighthearted.

Who ever thought my heart, so broken and damaged, could feel so light?

I don't tell Mom any of this, of course. She'd be on the phone to Dr. Richter or Dr. Frenzatta or Dr. Cho before I could finish my sentence. Convince them to rescind my school privileges, sentence me to more mindless, boring bed rest.

Bed rest. Now there's an oxymoron for you. I can sleep in bed—when I'm not in the hospital being poked and prodded every twenty minutes. But I can't *rest* in one. How can you rest when your body is cramping with pain and all you can taste is rust and your head is pounding and your heart feels like it's ready to explode?

Much less the times in between when you're being steered—on

your bed—from one test to another or waiting for the next brainiac expert to weigh in with his theory of why your body is trying so very hard to kill you.

If you have to lie there, *resting*, another second, you know you'll go insane…

But I guess it's different for most kids. And most moms.

Mom bustles around the front part of her examination area, grabbing her stethoscope and BP cuff. It's the first time I've been here in her place of work. I think about all the kids parading in and out, asking her for help, trying to ditch classes or maybe seriously sick or injured, and she's there for them.

It's not a very distinguished area to be saving lives in. Same moss-green walls as the hallway, bulletin board with sports physical schedules and immunization info and warnings about teen pregnancy, proclaiming the marvels of abstaining. "You'll feel great if you just wait!" a perky church-girl squeals with glee.

There's an examination bed on the other side of the curtain from me and behind that a second curtain, office desk, chairs, and a built-in double-door cabinet in the far wall. Small dorm fridge in the corner. Outside the door, the nonstop shuffle of students provides background noise, punctuated by the clang of lockers and murmur of voices.

I take a breath from my belly and hold it a few seconds, feeling my heart slow in response. My pulse steadies. By the time Mom gets her blood pressure cuff and the oxygen monitor on me, my vitals are 100 percemt normal, All-American girl.

I say nothing, knowing she really doesn't want me here, that she's scared Something Bad will happen, that I'm taking a huge Risk.

That's what moms are meant to do: worry. I feel bad because I've made my mom worry a thousand times more than any mom should ever have to.

But I can't help it. This is my one and only chance to be normal, and I'm not giving up. Not yet. They promised me a week to prove myself. Today's only Monday.

Protesting will only make things worse. Better to let her change her own mind than try to change it for her.

"Hmm," she says, frowning at the monitor. "Everything looks good. Still…what's next on your schedule?"

As if she doesn't have my schedule memorized. "Meeting with the counselor, Mr. Thorne, and the peer support group."

"Right. PMS."

I cringe at her use of the acronym. The school has assigned me "peer mentors." Two kids in my grade and a junior to oversee us along with the guidance counselor. They say it's something they do for every student with "special needs" and that it's meant to help me "acclimate to Smithfield High's academic and social life."

Of course, in their infinite wisdom, they named it Peer Mentoring and Support: PMS. Exactly the kind of label any kid with "special needs" who needs extra help to "acclimate" wants. Sometimes I wonder how adults got to be in charge of anything, much less my life.

Mom's mouth does a little wiggle-dance, like that witch on that old TV show. I hold my breath, waiting for the magic. "Okay. I guess you can go. But take an extra vitamin just in case."

She hands me one of the wheat-colored horse pills from a bottle in her purse—my mom is always prepared. For anything. That's why she's so good at her job. Nothing surprises her.

As she turns to get me a glass of water, I palm the pill. I hate the damn things; they get caught in my throat and if I take too many of them, I feel flushed and dizzy. I looked up the side effects of the ingredients—multivitamins with extra doses of stress vitamins and antioxidants—and figured out that the high niacin content was probably causing it.

Mom doesn't know about my cheating. Refusing to take my vitamins is my one and only act of rebellion. How pathetic.

I pretend to swallow and hop to my feet, grabbing Phil.

"I'm here all day," she calls after me. "Anything goes wrong, I'll be right here waiting."

She can't see my smile stretching so wide it hurts. Now that we're past Mom's opening-day jitters, I'm certain nothing will stop me from lasting to the end of the week and proving to my folks that I'm healthy enough to stay in school.

The bell rings. I join the crush of kids in the hallway, letting the tide carry me to the library where I'm meeting with Mr. Thorne and my peer support group. My new friends. Truth be told, my first friends outside a hospital.

Phil rolls over someone's foot. "Watch it, freak."

Mitch Kowlaski. Just my luck that we seem to be on the same trajectory as we follow our schedules. I press back against a row of lockers, hoping he'll keep walking.

"Sorry," I mumble.

His foot looks fine; there's not even a mark on his white and orange Nikes. But he doesn't care. He's obviously figured out I'm an easy target: no friends to defend me, no defenses of my own. He smiles and leans in, caging me between his arms. "You talking to me? That's not how it works around here, little girl. Freaks don't talk. They just get the hell out of my way."

One of his football buddies stops, watches us for a beat. He's taller and skinner than Mitch but still muscular. He grins at me and I'm waiting for him to join in on the torture-the-new-kid fun. Then he surprises me by punching Mitch in the arm. "Ditch the bitch, Mitch. We're gonna be late."

Mitch's scowl packs almost as much force as his bad breath. Stale coffee and garlic. He spins on his heel and turns away. Just as I dare to step back out into the corridor, this time keeping Phil close by my feet, he jumps back at me, raising his arms fast like he's going to hit me or grab me, and shouts, "Boo!"

His buddy laughs as I startle. I trip over Phil and bounce off the lockers before skittering away, hiding in the crowd.

That plastic bubble of John Travolta's is looking better and better.

6

One thing living in a hospital has taught me is that you can survive anything, even the worst news imaginable. Once you know what you're up against, you can start to fight.

It's uncertainty that will kill you.

The not knowing.

Is this a symptom or not? Am I imagining that twinge or is it a harbinger of worse to come?

Is this real or am I crazy?

That's why I—we, Mom and Dad and I—embraced my broken heart.

Long QT Syndrome is the real name. The calcium pumps in my heart are genetically faulty, letting my heart hop, skip, and run headlong off a cliff like Wile E. Coyote, legs still pumping hard even as he plummets into the abyss.

These abnormal rhythms will kill me. Twenty percent chance of dying at any moment in any day. Just like that, dropping dead.

Nothing I can do about it—except fight to have a normal life. At least until my crazy, broken heart decides to spaz out on me.

I'd much rather fight against the Long QT than put up with frustrated doctors ordering yet another test or pill or surgery, like they did before we found it. They'd look at me like I was playing some kind of game, making things up just to annoy them or get attention or because I'm nuts.

Finally getting my death sentence freed me from those labels. I'm no longer the crazy sick girl, looking for attention. Now I'm the dying girl, certain—unlike almost everyone else—of exactly how I'll go. I might not know when, but I know how.

And I know how I want to live until the end. I'm not letting the odds or jerks like Mitch Kowlaski stand in my way.

Wrestling with fog, that's what it felt like all those years of not knowing.

Now I've got something to push back against. And it feels good.

7

Kids fill the hall from wall to wall. Despite the unfamiliar press of bodies, I don't panic. Instead, I let them steer me, like running with a herd of wild, untamed horses. At the end of the corridor, the herd separates into two, leaving me alone in front of a high glass wall.

The library.

Footsteps and lockers banging and voices colliding barrage me. Then I open the door, cross over, and step inside. I'm greeted not by silence, but instead by a hushed burble, relaxing, like the sound of a water fountain. I stand, enjoying the sensations, and take a breath.

School smells so much better than the hospital. And the library smells the best of all. To me, a good book is hot cocoa on a stormy winter day, sleet battering the window while you sit inside, nestled in a quilt.

A room filled with books?

I inhale deeply, a junkie taking her first hit. Sweet, musty paper. Ebony ink so crisp it threatens to rise off the pages and singe my nostrils. Glue and leather and cloth all mixed together in a *ménage à trois* of decadence.

Another breath and I'm drunk with possibilities. Words and

stories and people and places so far from here that Planet Earth is a mere dust mote dancing in my rearview mirror.

Hugging myself, containing my glee, I pivot, taking in books stacked two stories high, couches and chairs strategically positioned to catch the light from tall windows lining both sides of the corner, like the bridge of a battle cruiser, broad, high, supremely confident, and comforting. In here, I dare to imagine that I might just survive high school after all.

"Can I help you?" the student manning the desk asks.

"I'm supposed to meet Mr. Thorne here?"

"Upstairs, first room on the left."

"Thanks." I follow her finger to where she points to two flights of lovely wooden steps, Frank Lloyd Wright-inspired. Not too steep—but that meant there were more of them. "Can I leave my bag down here for you to watch?"

She pushes her glasses up with an ink-smeared thumb. "No. I'm not allowed. But there's a handicap elevator behind the stacks."

"Thanks, I'm fine." I haul my bag to the base of the steps, eager to meet my peers who also have "special needs." I've never mentored anyone before. I hope I'm good at it, can help them.

Tugging my bag up the first step, there's a loud thump as the wheels hit the riser. So much for doing things the easy way. Collapsing the handle, I grab on tight and haul it up. I barely clear each step, but my gasping is quieter than the thumping.

C'mon, I try to psych myself up. This is what you've been training for, sneaking into the kitchen and lifting those water jugs when Mom wasn't looking.

Mom doesn't approve of physical therapy—in the hospital she always refused PT, worried they'd push me too far and give me one of my dreaded Set Backs. But I knew the more I lay around, the weaker I'd feel and I'd never make it through a school day, so I started doing stuff on my own. Push-ups, sit-ups, hauling gallon jugs, going up and down the steps even though I'm not supposed to.

It paid off, because before I know it, I'm standing in the door-way of a small conference room, winded but alive.

Three kids sitting at the table look up when I arrive. A black girl with the figure of a fashion model and clothes to match. The girl beside her is kind of plump, with long, dark hair caught in a simple braid curled up in the hood of her gray sweatshirt like a cat napping. And Jordan Summers.

I'm surprised to see him. Guess it must've shown, either that or I was more out of breath than I thought, because next thing I know, Jordan is guiding me into a chair, while the plump girl is taking Phil from me, and the black girl jumps up and skitters back and forth, watching but not really doing anything to help.

"Hey, are you okay?" Jordan asks. My heart is tap-dancing his name again.

"I'm fine." I manage a smile. At least I hope it's a smile. Maybe not, because he looks panicked.

"I'll grab you some water." He rushes out of the room.

The second girl hauls my backpack over to me. "What's in this?" she asks as she takes the chair beside me. "You on the bowling team?"

Up close, I see that, if you look past the layers of gray clothing, she's actually beautiful. Exotic looking. Hers is a true tropical golden complexion, unlike my sun-neglected sallow one. High cheekbones, gorgeous deep-brown eyes.

She catches my stare and turns her face away, dropping Phil between our chairs, hunching her shoulders like a turtle pulling into its shell. "Sorry, shouldn't be touching your stuff."

"No," I protest. "It's fine. Thank you." Didn't I just say that? A blush singes my face. Hoards of doctors and nurses I can deal with. But I am totally unprepared for small-group dynamics or, even worse, small talk. I try again. "Hi. I'm Scarlet. Scarlet Killian."

"We know." The black girl bounces into her chair. "You're late. Like weeks late. Gonna upset our balance of power."

I have no idea what she's talking about. Jordan returns with water in a paper cup and presses it into my palm. Reveling in his touch, I gulp it down, just to fill the silence as everyone stares at me.

"This is Nessa Woodring," he introduces the black girl who waggles her fingers at me. Each fingernail is a good half-inch long and adorned with a different color, jewel, or picture. Watching her wave them is like watching a Pixar animation. "And Celina Price. They're sophomores, like you."

Celina just nods, still not making eye contact.

"Hi," I say again, totally lame, but I have no idea what else to say.

Nessa flounces the top half of her body across the narrow table as if prostrating herself on an altar. "So, Scarlet." She draws out my name into three syllables. "What's it like to die?"

8

Nessa flattens her hand on top of mine, pinning me to the table. "Seriously. What was it like? Was there a bright light? Did it hurt?"

"Nessa!" Jordan snaps. "Leave her alone."

The intensity of Nessa's gaze pushes me back. If we had swords, she would have won the duel. I have the feeling Nessa doesn't often lose.

Finally, she blinks and releases me. She settles back in her chair, pulling her knees up and balancing her chin on them, suddenly smiling, a smile that would be at home on a portrait of an angel. The light brushes her hair, sparking off it as if she wears a halo. "Sorry. My mom says I have problems with being too bold and brash, or is it brusque? Probably all three. And my dad, well, he tosses around words like 'oppositional' and 'defiant' and 'impulse control,' but he's a shrink, so who really listens anyway?"

I find myself nodding in agreement, but I'm not sure who I'm agreeing with: her mom, her dad, or her dismissal of them both. It's easy to see why she might need a little mentoring and support. Something about her feels bright yet jagged, a broken mirror glinting in the sun. But her smile is genuine and I can't help but smile in return.

"Anyway," Nessa continues, turning a palm up as if offering a gift, "since you're starting late, let me fill you in. Jordan, he's supposed to be our mentor—the M in PMS, if you will—but mainly he sits around and says nothing. That's probably because I do all the talking, but I've got a lot to process—you'll hear all about that later." She pauses as if expecting me to interrupt and tell her I already know who she is, but all I can do is sit there and nod as the words pour out of her faster than a freight train.

I'm thinking her dad was right on all three accounts, but I can't help but like Nessa. When she smiles at you, it's with her whole body, like you're the most important person in the world—except herself, of course. Still, there's just this spark to her. Charisma, that's the word for it.

Jordan slides his hand along the tabletop. Trying to distract her long enough to get a word in. "How about if we give her some practical info instead of the *Gossip Girl* sound bite?"

Nessa doesn't even take a breath as she makes a conversational 180. "Sure. You should know that Celina here is the smartest kid in our grade. She can help you catch up. Last year, she held the ninth-grade academic achievement honor."

"Not for the whole year," Celina murmurs, retreating from my nod and smile of appreciation. "Besides, things are different now, especially with my mom gone so much."

"But you can help, can't you?" Nessa bounds from her chair again. Even gravity can't restrain her for long. "And we can all introduce Scarlet to all the right folks, get her on track. Peer mentoring, support, isn't that what we're all here for?"

She sounds ready to leap onto the table and lead us all in a cheer.

Jordan sighs. He's obviously used to having to rein her in. "I'm meant to be the mentor, remember?"

Nessa freezes in midstride. Slowly she pivots to face Jordan. From the look she gives him, it's clear they know each other well. Jealousy stabs my gut as I wonder exactly how well.

"Well, Mr. Junior-big-shot-mentor, if you're so smart, then why didn't you save—"

Celina jumps up, slapping her palm down between the two of them. "Stop it, both of you. Just stop it."

Nessa heaves in a breath as if the air in the room is suddenly too heavy. Jordan doesn't look so good either, blinking furiously like he has something in his eyes, but he doesn't take his gaze off Nessa, as if he's worried she'll vanish.

I have no idea what they're talking about, but it's clear that it's painful and very, very personal. Just as it's obvious that beneath Nessa's incessant chatter lies a deep well of anger and sadness. Suddenly I wonder if I have any support to offer that would be helpful. Not like I have much experience with, well, anything outside of hospitals.

Celina sits back down and says in a calm voice, "It's Scarlet's first day. We should be focused on her, not on—not on things we can't change."

Jordan pulls his gaze away from Nessa and gives Celina a small nod and even smaller smile, which surprises me because she's doing his job, taking control of the situation and playing the peacekeeper. But it works. Nessa relaxes and beams at Celina in another abrupt shift of emotion.

Me, I just sit there, clueless. And fascinated.

As I take them all in, practically seeing the delicate threads of power and pain connecting and interlacing in an intricate web, I realize how woefully unprepared the hospital has left me for the drama that is high school.

Forget algebra and chemistry. I need a remedial course on people.

9

Before anyone can move or say anything, the door opens and a man enters. He's thirty-something, cute in an older-guy kinda way, reminds me of one of my consultants, a specialist in cardiac electrophysiology. Genius but so caught up in his life of chaotic cardiac electrical impulses that he walked around oblivious to the rest of the world. His hands were the coldest and clammiest of them all—he never looked me in the eyes once. If he could have cut out my heart and taken it with him to study, not bothering with the inconvenient body surrounding it, he would have.

"Oh good, you got started without me," the man says with a wide smile, plopping himself down in the chair at the head of the narrow table and leaning it so far back I'm worried it's about to tip.

He wears a dress shirt, tie, suit trousers, but has red socks and a pair of canvas sneakers on, also red. Like he's watched too many *Dr. Who* reruns. His accent isn't English, but it's not ragged central Pennsylvania either. Instead it's flat, like he's washed it clean of any trace evidence. "And, Scarlet, welcome, welcome! Have you all introduced yourselves?"

The others nod. The man doesn't seem to realize that he hasn't introduced himself to me, but I'm not dumb. This must be Mr. Thorne, the counselor who's meant to guide me through the labyrinth of my sophomore year.

Thorne fiddles with his pen, clicking it and twirling it, beaming his smile at each of us in turn as if assessing the weather.

Cloudy with a chance of thunderstorms is my assessment. Thorne bounces his chair, tipping ever farther back, making me catch my breath as I wonder if I should say something, and his smile grows wider. Cocky, even.

"Let me catch you up, Scarlet," he says, and I realize that although I was clueless, Nessa had actually been mimicking him earlier. And doing a pretty good job of it. "These groups are carefully composed, members chosen to help address certain strengths and weaknesses that came to light when I reviewed the incoming sophomores' records. Our job here, together, is to bolster those strengths and work on those weaknesses. Bring everything out in the open, explore them, together, in a non-judgmental, honest fashion."

I stare at him, certain he's joking. His expression is the same as the nurses who'd tell me shoving a honking feeding tube down my nose "won't hurt a bit" while they pin me down and force it in.

"From your record, I see that you've been homeschooled since third grade—most recently via the cyber academy. Your grades are excellent, your test scores very impressive." Celina glances up at that. "But," Mr. Thorne continues, "given all the time spent in the hospital—oh, did you have a chance to tell the others about your unfortunate condition?" He pauses dramatically, waiting for me.

I shift in my seat, one hand going to Phil's handle. Giving it a squeeze, just in case my heart needs a jump-start anytime soon.

"No," Nessa answers for me. I have the feeling she answers for everyone. A lot. "She hasn't."

They all swivel to stare at me.

Talking about everything that's wrong with me is my mom's job. She has it down to a science—can fill in a new doctor or nurse in less time than it takes for a commercial break on TV. And I'm damn sure everything Mr. Thorne needs to know is right there in my records. Besides, half the school saw what happened this morning when the security guard unveiled Phil for the world. By now they would have texted or told the other half. There might even be videos up on YouTube, who knew?

Yet still Mr. Thorne waits. "Go on, Scarlet. This is a safe environment. You can talk about anything."

Why don't I believe him? Probably because of the way none of the others have looked him in the eye since he arrived.

I'd much rather talk about more interesting things—like what the hell was going on between Nessa and Jordan—but I nod and give them the CliffsNotes version. "I've been pretty sick all my life, but the doctors finally figured out it's a genetic defect that makes my heart not beat right, so sometimes parts of my body don't get enough oxygen. No big deal."

There's a long and awkward moment of silence. Great. Been here ten minutes and I've already blown it.

Then Celina leans forward and covers my hand with hers. "But it is a big deal. Scarlet, it could kill you someday."

Nessa adds her hand on top of Celina's. Like we're the three musketeers or something. Their touch spreads warmth through my body—I'm used to being poked and prodded with cold hands and colder stethoscopes, not this. "We're here to help, Scarlet."

Jordan watches from across the table, gives me a small smile and nod. Accepting me into the fold. The moment passes and the girls lean back, but I can still feel their touch, as if they've left something behind.

Is this what friendship feels like? But they don't know me, not at all.

Mr. Thorne clears his throat. "Thank you for sharing, Scarlet." He pulls some papers from a folder and distributes them. "I've updated everyone's class schedule and contact info to include Scarlet's. I think there's enough overlap that we should be able to act as a safety net if she needs anything. And of course, Scarlet, feel free to come see me anytime."

I glance at each of them while they're studying the schedules and programming my number into their phones. Just like that, these people are now part of my life. My safety net. Like I'm walking some kind of death-defying high wire.

The way Mom talks about me coming to school, trying to have a normal life, maybe I am. Defying death.

I smile. I like the idea.

10

"You have English next, right?" Nessa burbles as we three walk down the steps together.

Thanks to her and Celina, we *do* feel together. As if we've always been together, were meant to be together.

I'm glad Celina is carrying my bag because I'm giddy again and would have dropped it for sure.

"You'll love Mrs. Gentry, she's the best," Nessa continues as if I'd answered. "We just started *The Glass Menagerie,* Tennessee Williams. It's so cool, all despair and desperation. My dad, he just loves old Tennessee Williams. Any of those suicidal poets and playwrights and novelists, they all turn him on, big time."

"Kinda like Mr. Thorne? Talk about your psychic vampires, thriving on our pain." I hope it's the right thing to say. I don't want to risk breaking the spell surrounding us.

They both stop. I swallow, sending the spinning giddy feeling plummeting from my head down to my toes. I've screwed up.

But then they exchange a glance, smile in unison, and laugh.

"You catch on fast," Nessa says in approval. She links our arms together. "Don't worry. We'll protect you from old Thorny."

Us against the world. Feels good. I've never had anyone on my side before except my mom and dad. I decide to push things a step farther. "Can I ask, what was all that between you and Jordan?"

Celina's eyes tighten as she meets my gaze and shakes her head. Nessa grabs my arm tighter and hustles me through the door of a classroom as if she didn't hear me. Maybe it's for the best.

Nessa releases me and heads for her desk. Celina leans close and whispers, "I'll tell you later."

Mystery, intrigue, drama—and I haven't even had my first official class yet. High school is so much more fun than the hospital.

11

My first high school class. It isn't what I expect. Oh, the kids lined up in rows of chair-desks, some sleeping, some whispering, some taking notes, some texting—even though phones aren't allowed in school—teacher at the blackboard, that's all just like it is on TV.

But TV doesn't show the really cool stuff. The ideas and discussion and way that, even if you're too shy to raise your hand, you can still feel good when you know the answer. I'd read *The Glass Menagerie* a few years ago and remember enough that I know most of the answers to Mrs. Gentry's questions.

Celina and Nessa surprise me. Nessa doesn't say a word the entire class. Instead, she's focused on writing in her notebook and I don't think it has anything to do with Tennessee Williams. Her forehead is creased and her lips are tugged down in a frown.

And Celina? She's suddenly all sparkly, raising her hand, shouting out answers when the discussion gets going, even challenging Mrs. Gentry, debating the brother's motives in bringing the Gentleman Caller home to meet his sister.

Me? I just watch, mesmerized, too chicken to risk raising my hand or answering anything.

Then Mrs. Gentry winds down the debate and says, "Tennessee

Williams calls *The Glass Menagerie* a memory play. He purposely gives directions for the set to be minimalistic, the same with the costumes. He even uses the unreliability of memory as an excuse for the suggestion that everything in the play is wrong. So the assignment this week is for you to each keep a memory journal. Write down your memories, going back as far as you can. Then try to verify them by interviewing primary sources. Who are primary sources?"

"People who actually witnessed an event," Celina answers.

"Right. Now, memories are tricky things, especially ones from when you're young. To help you, I want you all to close your eyes. That's right, close them. Now breathe deep, in and out. Send your mind back. Past junior high, past first grade, what's the first thing you can remember?"

She drones on and on, helping us to relax and visualize our pasts. Her voice is calm and soothing. I sneak my eyes open a crack. The boy beside me has fallen asleep with soft snores. Everyone else is relaxed, heads nodding in time to Mrs. Gentry's voice.

Not me. I'm panicking. Heart thrumming like a hummingbird in a cage, palms sweaty, fingers curled into numb, dead claws. Even my mouth has gone dead. I can't feel my lips or face. A knot tightens my throat, and I can't swallow.

My eyes pop open wide, searching for an escape. Mrs. Gentry is walking up and down the rows and her back is to me. Everyone else still has their eyes closed. No one sees me. No one can save me.

Blackness curls like smoke over my vision. I'm trapped.

12

The bell rings. Everyone else pops out of their chairs, animated after their restful trips down memory lane, while I sit there working hard to remember how to breathe, trying to swim free of the tsunami of panic that has swamped me.

"Scarlet, are you okay?" Mrs. Gentry asks. "It wasn't too much for you, first day here and all?"

I hide my shaking hands by clenching them around the handle of my backpack. As I work my mouth, my face feels like a pincushion, prickling needles stabbing my skin where it's gone numb. "No, Mrs. Gentry. *The Glass Menagerie* is one of my favorite plays. Great discussion."

My feet are still frozen solid, unfeeling blocks of ice, but somehow I drag them across the room and to the door where Celina and Nessa wait.

"Suck up," Nessa says in a stage whisper. I'm mortified, but she's smiling, and I decide she's just teasing. My mom is the only person who teases me and I never know for sure when she's doing it either. "My dad doesn't believe in memory regression, but that was still kinda cool. So, what did you remember?"

I duck my head, hoping she'll keep talking before she realizes I haven't answered. Now that my panic is over, I'm ashamed.

Why don't I have any memories? Why can't I for once just be normal?

"What's next on your schedule?" Celina asks, saving me.

Hordes of kids stampede around us, making me feel breathless and claustrophobic, but neither of them seems to mind at all, recklessly swerving through the herd as we head down the hallway. "Trig."

"Ugh, another brainiac. Have fun. We have chemistry." Nessa waves and they're swallowed by the crowd, a wall of broad-shouldered, very tall guys wearing Smithfield Wildcat letterman jackets blocking them from my view. Suddenly I feel like a gazelle alone on the Serengeti, facing a pride of lions. I pull Phil close to my side and scurry to the math wing.

Trigonometry is easy. Not just because I'd already covered the material in cyberschool over the summer before I went back into the hospital, but because numbers don't lie. They don't need interpretation.

I make it through the class on autopilot, filling my notebook not with proofs or formulas but with a backward accounting of my life, trying to come up with a real memory. All I can produce is a chronology of hospital stays, medical procedures, and anonymous doctors' faces.

Taking a different tactic, I try focusing on holidays, but there aren't many I can actually account for. Holidays and summers are prime times for my Set Backs. Funny, I never noticed it before. Must be the stress.

Then I try gifts. The tee I'm wearing came from my dad—he

actually saw Kurt Cobain in concert, way back in 1991. And my denim jacket, I stole it from him, but he doesn't mind. He lets me get away with so much more than Mom.

I let my eyes drift shut, finally a memory. It's only from last year, but it's a start. Dad wearing his denim jacket, raking leaves. I'm watching him through my window. He piles them as high as his head, waves to me, holds his nose, runs like hell, and does a cannonball into them. I laugh and tap on the window, pleading for more. He rakes them all over again until Mom comes out and asks him why he isn't finished yet and did he expect her to do everything around there?

I love both my mom and dad, but sometimes I'm not so sure they love each other. Maybe that's why Dad doesn't seem to mind being away so much—he's a sales rep for Academic Supplies and travels from one school district to another; that's how he met my stepmom. My real mother died when I was just a few days old, so I guess by the time I was three, he was pretty tired trying to take care of me all on his own. And who better to take care of a sick kid than a nurse, so that worked out great for everyone.

Nowadays with the economy and layoffs, he's having to cover more territory than ever and is gone most of the time. He says he doesn't mind, since it makes sure my health insurance is covered, and anyway, he hates coming home to an empty house when I'm in the hospital.

When I was little, he used to come visit me in the hospital, but I'd always have a Set Back during his visits—my mom said the excitement was too much for me. Dad hates hospitals, so I think he was relieved when she finally asked him to stop coming.

No one asked me.

And that's it. My only halfway normal memory. I try and try but can't remember anything important from when I was young—certainly nothing as far back as Mrs. Gentry wants us to go. Every time I close my eyes and concentrate on the past, my throat chokes up and my heart stampedes into overdrive.

I wonder if I *am* crazy. Not for the first time. Maybe one of those Near Misses rotted my brain and now it's all Swiss-cheesed like the pictures you see of the brains of people with Alzheimer's or drug addicts. But then why can I remember everything else? Books I read years ago, things like algebra and geometry, even history—although I admit, I get fuzzy on some of the presidents like Taft and Harding and whatshisname, McKinley.

It's my own life that's a blur.

13

Homeroom is next. Fifteen minutes of boring announcements over the intercom and TV screens. The only one that sounds at all interesting is that there's a pep rally scheduled for Thursday, last period. Sounds like fun to me. The rest of the kids groan as if mandatory peppiness and school spirit is too much to ask—some kind of cruel and unusual punishment.

I'm excited and answer with a perky "here" when the teacher calls my name, but everyone else just grunts or makes a monosyllabic acknowledgment. Terminal boredom.

I don't feel sorry for them. Not at all. They have no idea what boredom really is—not until you've spent years of your life drifting between hospital rooms and your house, barely ever going out in public. If they only knew, they'd be as excited by the prospect of being in school as I am.

The fifteen minutes is over and we're all sprung. I meet up with Nessa and Celina outside the cafeteria. First lunch is pretty much mostly sophomores, Nessa informs me. "But some of the other cool kids eat now as well, so it's not too bad."

Celina rolls her eyes and reminds Nessa, "We *are* sophomores."

I'm not paying too much attention. I'm starving. Usually I'm never hungry, so I see this as a good thing. Mom would probably argue otherwise, shove some reflux meds down me, and order me to rest until the rumbles in my stomach subside.

They lead me into the cafeteria and it's like walking into a Category Five hurricane. The sounds are overwhelming—add to them the smells of chili mac, French fries, corn syrup served a dozen ways from Friday, plus body odor, not to mention the bustle of a hundred kids pushing their way through the lines, jockeying for table space, and establishing their social hierarchy.

It almost makes me long for the comparative quiet of my hospital room (although hospitals are actually very noisy and never peaceful—so much for a "healing" environment). Once I get past the initial shockwave, it's kind of fascinating.

"What's Jordan doing here?" I ask, spotting him sitting alone at the end of a table near the windows. Prime real estate, but since he's a junior here at the sophomore lunch period, I guess he's top of the food chain.

"Poor guy," Celina says.

"It's all our fault," Nessa adds. "He might just as well be wearing scarlet letters."

I realize that everyone ignores Jordan, and they've left space around him. Space enough for three at least.

"It's because of the peer support?"

"Yep. Thorne has single-handedly destroyed all of our social lives and condemned us to the freak table. And where we go, Jordan goes as well."

"Couldn't he ask to mentor another group?"

They exchange glances. "You don't get it, do you?" Nessa grabs a tray, hands it to me, then gets her own. "Mentoring us is Jordan's punishment."

"Punishment? For what?"

Suddenly Nessa is preoccupied, trying to decide between the spongy brown slop that's labeled green beans and the green mess that's meant to be dill carrots. I can't eat any of this—no way am I going to even try to be adventurous with my diet and risk getting sick on my first day. All I get is a bottle of V8. Liquid vitamins, yummy.

Celina and I pass Nessa. While we're waiting to pay, Celina finally fills me in. "Nessa's sister, Yvonne, killed herself last year. Jumped off the gym roof."

That explained what I'd seen earlier—the eruption of emotions, anger and I wasn't sure what else tangled together, when Nessa lashed out at Jordan. "Why is Jordan being Nessa's peer mentor a punishment?"

"Jordan was dating Yvonne last year. Before she—" She fills in the blank with a sad look and a shrug.

"So everyone blames him? That's not fair—I mean, did she leave a note or something saying he was the reason why she killed herself?" I can't imagine Jordan doing anything to hurt someone that badly. Suddenly I find myself judging Nessa's sister as unstable, crazy, and I know nothing about her.

Celina shakes her head, leading me through the maze of tables, sidestepping a puddle of unidentifiable brown and yellow mush. "No note. In fact, Nessa's still convinced Yvonne didn't kill herself. Sometimes she even talks like someone might have killed her—"

"No. Really?" My voice jumps and people are looking. Celina throws me a glare that says quiet down, so I do. "Why would anyone—"

"They wouldn't. But it makes her feel better."

Denial. That I understand.

Kinda like a girl with a busted heart trying to come to school and act normal.

"Jordan actually volunteered to mentor Nessa," Celina continues. "He thought since the two of them knew Vonnie better than anyone, maybe he could get through to her, help her. But sometimes all she does is lash out. He figures it's better she hurt him than herself."

Wow. Makes me appreciate Jordan all the more. And wonder at Celina's relationship with him—it was her he looked to when Nessa lost it this morning during the counseling session.

We pass a table of girls who all look like college students. My main impression is pearls, perfect posture, and portrait-ready painted faces.

"Divas," Celina whispers. "The popular girls. They run everything." She looks over her shoulder and I realize she's not whispering because this is some kind of secret but because she doesn't want Nessa to hear. "Nessa's sister was the only sophomore Diva last year and Nessa was a shoo-in to join them this year. Until…"

Nessa catches up to us, one finger caressing her Pandora necklace as we walk past the Divas. They studiously ignore us as if we're less than dirt beneath their fingernails. I never thought the act of ignoring someone could be so very dramatic.

Drama Queens. Like the diabetic I had to room with back when I was thirteen—that was the Year of Nothing Good.

Deena was her name and she could make her blood sugar bottom out, sending her into seizures and a coma, or she'd make it rocket so high she'd be barfing and in danger of her brain swelling. She did it to manipulate her parents, who'd finally had her admitted when they couldn't control her tantrums anymore. The doctors told them to stop visiting because they were "reinforcing Deena's borderline personality."

That's doctor-talk for "this chick is so damn crazy, if she was stable we'd send her to psych, and you're just as crazy and are only making things worse."

My mom loved Deena. Have to admit, Deena, like every other Drama Queen I've ever met, had something compelling about her. Charisma, I guess you'd call it. Some kind of energy field that grabbed you and sucked you into her whirlwind and made you care more about her than yourself.

Mom watched over Deena even more closely than she did me. Alerting the nurses when her sugar went bonkers, holding her hair back when she vomited, teaching her how to adjust her insulin and take control of her diabetes.

The doctors and nurses all said if it wasn't for Mom ("the patience of a saint!"), Deena probably would have died or been admitted to a long-term psych facility.

Mom saved her. They all said.

Back then, at thirteen, during the Year of Nothing Good, I hated Mom. So I rolled my eyes, shrugged, and ignored them. Just like I'd ignored Deena.

Who knew it'd turn out that the Deenas of the world ruled high school?

14

We make it to our table. Jordan manages a smile as I plop down across from him, Celina beside him, and Nessa beside me. I like him even more for that smile. With the sunlight streaming through the window, warming my face, and Jordan across from me, smiling, his hair flopping along his eyelashes again, defying gravity, I can pretend we're on a picnic or someplace fun.

Until the first spitwad hits me between the eyes and slides down onto my T-shirt.

"Losers," an anonymous voice sings out.

"Summers found some fresh meat," a guy from the table of football players beside us says loudly. Someone kicks my pack and it hits the ground with a thud. I grab it and tuck it between me and the window.

Everyone else is studiously ignoring us, yet I'm very aware that they're also focused on us at the same time. It's a weird feeling. Reminds me of waiting for the anesthesia to start working, hoping it kicks in before the surgeon starts cutting, but also kinda hoping someone's gonna rush into the room, say it was all a mistake, and call the whole thing off after all.

My stomach knots with the tension, so tight my hand has to flick the spitball twice before I'm able to knock it to the floor.

Jordan straightens, looking around, and I see he's ready to defend us—defend me. But even I know what the cost would be. I place a hand over his.

He jerks, his gaze slamming into mine. Too much, too familiar.

I try to act casual, sliding my hand away from his. "Those fries look good." They don't. They look like they're ready to melt into a soggy puddle of lard. "Can I have one?"

He says nothing, as if it takes extra long for my voice to penetrate his hearing. Nessa is chattering to Celina about homecoming, even though it's still three weeks away, talking about signing up for the decorating committee so she'll have an excuse to go even if she can't get a date, and should she ask some boy or should she wait and see. They've both missed the entire spitball incident—or ignored it…ah, the power of denial. Handy tool to deal with high school, I'm learning.

So it's just me and Jordan. My skin feels hot all over.

Jordan nods to his plate of fries. "Sure. Help yourself."

I stretch my hand out, thinking one fry can't hurt.

"Scarlet!" Mom's voice cuts through the clamor of students yapping.

My stomach drops to my knees, begging for this to not be happening.

"Scarlet, there you are."

It's happening.

Mom stands at the end of our table, holding an insulated lunch box aloft. "You forgot to stop by my office to get your lunch. Are you sure you're feeling okay?"

I reach across Nessa for the bag, but Mom holds it out of reach. "Aren't you going to introduce me to your friends?"

Swallowing my sigh, I introduce her. She shakes Nessa's hand. "I knew your sister, such a wonderful girl. I'm so sorry for your loss. Let me know if you ever want to talk."

Nessa nods and ducks her head. Mom turns her attention to Jordan. "Mr. Summers. I trust you're keeping a good eye out for these ladies?"

"Yes, Nurse Killian." I can't tell if Jordan is serious or joking or making fun of her, he's that good. I make a note to take lessons from him. A poker face like that could come in handy.

"And Celina Price. Hmmm." Mom makes that nursing noise of hers, the one that makes you want to start planning funerals. "When's your next free period? You need to stop by my office."

Celina's face grows so gray it blends into the gray wall behind her, like she's trying to fade away, vanish. "Peer support takes up all my free periods," she mumbles.

Mom doesn't miss a beat. "Okay, then I'll be waiting before first period tomorrow. Seven forty-five a.m. Sharp."

Celina looks down, smushing her food around her plate in a death spiral.

Finally, Mom hands me my lunch and focuses on me. She steps into the aisle so she can feel my cheeks and forehead.

The guys at the next table laugh. They're jocks, wearing Wildcats letterman jackets—the fluorescent orange snarling outline of the wildcat lunging off the white wool like a hyena stalking its prey. No matter where I move, those hyena eyes follow me.

Mom doesn't seem to notice. "Are you certain you're feeling okay? Maybe you should go home?" She takes my pulse. Her eyes narrow, revealing her worry wrinkles. She really is concerned, doesn't think I can make it all day, much less to the end of the week.

"I'm fine."

She doesn't believe me. "Hmm...okay. Well, take another vitamin, just to keep your strength up." As if by magic, one of her horse pills appears in her hand. She dangles it above my mouth. "Open up."

My face burns as I feel every single person in the cafeteria suddenly stop eating, stop talking, and start staring. At me.

I have no choice but to get this over with fast. I open my mouth and let my mom pop the pill in like feeding a baby bird who's too weak to do anything for itself. Baby birds—quick snacks for hyenas. The vision pops in and out of my mind like a hiccup. And once there, it's just as hard to get rid of.

"Drink. Let me see you swallow it." I obey. "Good girl." She brushes her palms together as if finishing an arduous task and smiles at us. "Nice to see you all." Then she kisses me on the forehead. I'm surprised she doesn't feel how hot it is, burning with humiliation. "Love ya, bye now."

Mom leaves, everyone's eyes following her through the maze of tables as she leaves. Silence reigns. Except for the pounding of my pulse in my temples, ringing out my embarrassment.

My face buried in my hands, I tell myself that the worst is over, nothing else could possibly go wrong today.

I hate being wrong.

15

When I was thirteen, the Year of Nothing Good, I decided my mom was trying to kill me.

It was April. I was feeling tired but okay, just out of the hospital. Another frustrating stay where the doctors did everything except cut me open, which they'd get around to later that summer, costing me a trip to the beach Make-a-Wish had organized—I still have never seen the ocean. Despite all their tests, they had no explanation for my symptoms, so they'd decided to monitor me off all meds, in case I was having an "idiosyncratic" reaction to one of them.

Somehow the idea that maybe I didn't need *any* of the medicine Mom gave me got warped into a suspicion that Mom was behind *all* my symptoms.

After all, I'd pretty much been sick my entire life and she'd been around almost that long, pushing pills down my throat, hauling me from doctor to doctor. It just didn't make sense, one little girl having so many symptoms that all those smart doctors couldn't figure out. And, if Mom was the cause, then as soon as I proved it, for the first time ever, I'd have a chance at being a normal girl.

Don't get me wrong. I love my Mom. I really, really didn't want her to be the one making me sick.

After all, our entire family revolves around her taking care of me, Dad heading out on the road earning a living and keeping us—me—well insured, and me being sick.

I can't imagine what our family would be like without me being sick. What would we talk about? How would we plan our time, arrange family vacations except around trips to specialists and hospital stays?

But that year, the Year of Nothing Good, all I wanted was not to be sick. Not too much for a thirteen-year-old girl to ask, is it?

Of course, like all thirteen-year-old girls, my hormone-fueled imagination ran amok. I became one of those Drama Queens I so despised when I met them in the hospital.

Back then, I kept a journal. Here's what I wrote:

I am going to kill her.

If you're a police officer and reading this, it means I've failed. If you're anyone else, then why are you being a sneaky perv prying into a girl's private thoughts?

But you'll keep reading. Just to see what happens. If I really mean what I say.

I do.

You'll read about my life and delude yourself that this isn't real, that no one you know could have this happen to them, that no one you love could be suffering like I am.

You're wrong.

Even as you uncover my secrets, you won't believe. You'll dismiss me as an angst-ridden, melodramatic, typical teenage girl. You won't do anything about what's happening to me.

That's okay. No one else did anything to help either.

Because I've tried, believe me, I've tried everything. No one believes me.

Despite the life of lies I'm forced to live, I'm determined to tell the truth here. No matter how shameful it is.

And the truth is: I must kill her.

Before she kills me.

Crazy, right? Told you, *total* Drama Queen.

So, home from the hospital, I refused to eat or drink anything that came from Mom. The first day or so, before Mom noticed I was avoiding the food she cooked, I felt fine. But then things went downhill fast. Despite avoiding Mom.

I wouldn't even drink a glass of water that she got me from the tap as I watched. Instead, I'd retreat to my room, drinking only Ensure and vitaminwater, leaving her in tears and Dad yelling when he got home that week.

That wasn't even the worst. Turns out it wasn't Mom making me sick. Or the medicines the doctors had her give me. Turns out everything was all my fault. Me and my stupid genes making my heart run amok.

I ended up back in the hospital, worse than ever. A Major Set Back. They almost lost me. Again.

If it wasn't for Mom, worried and checking on me in the middle of the night, they would have. She saved my life. Again.

Then they found my journal. Shit hit the you know what.

Only good thing that came of it was that my Near Miss finally gave the doctors the clue they needed to figure out what was really wrong with me—my heart was broken.

So broken that it tried to kill me with potentially fatal rhythms. Nothing to do with Mom or the meds. It was *me* trying to kill myself. Which of course made me feel even worse for blaming Mom when all she was trying to do was keep me alive.

Once I was out of the ICU, they made me talk to a shrink. He decided my quasi-homicidal delusions were normal teen rebellion coupled with a high-stress, codependent, mother-daughter dyad.

In other words, I was a perfectly normal thirteen-year-old. At least as far as my psyche was concerned.

Dad made me apologize to Mom and she cried and I cried and everything was fine after that. Except, of course, for my broken heart.

After that there were no more suspicions, no more acts of rebellion…until now.

I am very aware that I'm taking my life in my hands by coming to school. Being normal might just kill me.

But it's my life. If I can't have a say in it, then what's the point anyway?

Might as well be dead.

Of course, with Mom hovering like she is, trying so hard to keep me alive, I might die of embarrassment before my messed-up heart ever gets the chance to kill me.

16

An awful silence fills the cafeteria as my mom walks out. The kind of silence that happens in horror movies, just waiting to be filled with blood and guts and screams when the characters turn their backs on the killer hiding behind the curtain.

Or maybe it's the silence of the Serengeti on a nature documentary…right before the stalking hyena pounces on the baby gazelle or giraffe or girl…I look up, half expecting to see one of the Wildcats leap from a varsity jacket onto our table.

Instead, I'm pelted by a tampon. Still wrapped, thank you, God.

"Not again," Nessa groans as the barrage of feminine hygiene products continue.

No one hears her over the chants of "freak, freak" and catcalls swelling through the room. Jordan springs to his feet and leaps to the front of the table—Errol Flynn had nothing on his moves; too bad Jordan didn't have a sword—placing his body between us and the rest of crowd. Pizza crusts and partially eaten hamburger rolls and banana peels fly through the air.

"Leave them alone," he shouts. His voice goes nowhere, bouncing off the noise of feet stamping and fists pounding tables. "They didn't do anything."

"Whatcha gonna do about it, lover boy?" The largest

Wildcat from the next table stands face to face with Jordan. It's Mitch Kowlaski. Great. Of course he had the same lunch as I did, because the universe—well, my universe—always works that way.

Jordan's just as tall as him but Mitch is twice as wide. He leans closer, spittle flying into Jordan's face with every word. "You gonna hit me, Summers? I'm just exercising my free speech. You can't do anything about that—unless you want to fight like a man. Go on, hit me!"

The chants morph from "freak" to "fight." Mr. Thorne and another male teacher push through the doors, shoving their way through the crowd toward us. Mitch spots them and pivots to grab his tray.

"Looks like lover boy doesn't have the guts to defend his ladies." He says the last with a sneer directed at us.

Nessa is holding one of Jordan's arms with both her hands. I can't tell if she's holding on because she's scared or if she's holding him back. Celina has closed down, hoodie up to shield her face, ponytail fallen into her tray and she doesn't notice, fingers clenched into fists as she rocks slightly, like she's being buffeted by a storm.

And me? I have no idea what to do. I'm as frozen as that baby bird trapped by the hyena's paw. The other football players stand up, grabbing their trays as well. I see what they're going to do. It's all so clear from the grins they exchange and their body language. If they could communicate as well on the playing field, maybe we'd have won a game already.

Jordan has his back to our table, focusing on Mitch and the rest of the crowd. He doesn't see what's coming. But I do.

I know I should just run and hide, let the events play out. Stay out of the spotlight, not draw attention and put myself in the predator's line of sight.

That would be the smart thing to do. The way to survive.

It's what a normal girl would do.

Just as Mitch is getting ready to swing back around with his tray, dumping it all over Jordan and giving the signal for his comrades to do the same with their trays, I roll Phil between his feet.

He's caught off balance and trips, jostling his tray. Instead of landing on Jordan or Celina who are in the line of fire, it dumps into his chest, smearing an open packet of ketchup and fries over the virgin white wool of his jacket.

He howls in fury as his teammates chortle. We're forgotten—except for me. I now stand alone in the spotlight.

Laughter crescendos around me, but for once it's not aimed at me. Rather at Mitch as he turns and drops his tray on the other table.

"Way to go, Kowlaski," one of his teammates sings out just as Mr. Thorne arrives at our little soiree.

"Problem here, gentlemen?" he asks. "Mr. Summers, care to explain?"

"It's my fault," I pipe up, trying to deflect attention from Jordan. "My backpack got in his way. I'm sorry."

From the glare Mitch shoots me, it's clear my apology is

meaningless. I now understand what the phrase "murder in his eyes" means.

Jordan folds his hand over my shoulder, steadying me. Suddenly both Celina and Nessa are on either side of me. I don't feel alone or vulnerable. Not even scared.

Instead, I feel safe. Like I am, for the first time in my life, a part of something…a team.

It feels good. Better than any of the drugs they give you at the hospital, better than sneaking a piece of forbidden chocolate (it's on my list of Bad Foods), or sitting with my mom and dad and watching a movie on our couch at home, fire going in the fireplace, winter locked out for the night, no doctors or nurses or symptoms in sight.

I like this feeling. At the same time, it frightens me. It fills me up, warming empty places I didn't even know I had inside of me. Addictive.

But for right now, I stand up straight. My friends surrounding me—I never even had friends before. Not ones that lasted longer than a stay in the hospital.

No plastic bubble or sterile dressings or flimsy patient gown between me and the rest of the world. The center of attention.

I'm surprised how much I love it.

17

After lunch is art. I opted out of music since I can't tell a waltz from a samba. Escorted by Jordan, Celina, and Nessa, I thread my way through the halls, feeling nauseous and achy. I decide to blame it on the extra vitamin Mom made me take. That's better than admitting it's fear of Mitch retaliating, anxiety over embarrassing Jordan in front of half the school, or just plain old fatigue.

I'm not about to give up, tell my folks they were right, I can't last a whole day. Quit and go home. Not with my two favorite subjects coming up: biology and world cultures. Last period is Spanish, which I couldn't care less about. I promise myself I'll nap in Spanish class if I have to.

I make it to art. The door is open and the scent of paint and turpentine and something greasy—pastels?—wafts through the door, making my stomach feel even more queasy. The others linger as long as they can. Nessa jokes about some TV show I've never seen. Celina halfheartedly chimes in, but at least her hoodie is back down and she's trying. Jordan says nothing, just scowls, watching the other students as they pass like they're suspects in a police lineup.

"I'll be fine," I finally say, their concern making me more nervous than any potential retribution from Mitch or his cohorts.

My cheeks burn with a permanent flush made worse every time someone in the hall stops and points at me, usually with a nod and jeer or laugh. "Really, you can go now."

"Just remember," Nessa says, touching my arm and looking me in the eye, "it's only high school."

Celina shakes her head, her ponytail twitching. "Yeah, only three years to go before graduation. Easy time."

Jordan says nothing, simply squeezes my elbow as if sharing his strength. I inhale deeply, trying to ward off a headache and failing, then enter the classroom.

The art teacher, Mr. Yan, is an Asian-American hippie, with a bald pate fringed by long, dark hair that brushes his shoulders, thick glasses that make his face twist in a permanent squint, and a constant smile.

Seems like no one can do wrong in this class as long as they have a reason for what they do. We work on textures and collages, "exploring the power of sensations," and it would have been fun except the glue smell makes my headache worse.

By the end of class, my stomach is churning like water sloshing in a goldfish bowl. My headache almost drums out the sound of the bell ringing.

I make it to life sciences on my own. It's a junior-level course and of the four of us, I'm the only one taking it. The biology room doesn't have desks. Instead, it's lab tables with sinks and an outlet for a Bunsen burner and lights with magnifying lamps. The room smells of matches and damp earth and sulfur. As if mysterious and magical things happen here.

The only empty seats are in the back. I'm alone at the table. The second bell rings and still no partner. I don't mind, more fun for me. My headache eases off a bit as I explore the drawers and discover safety goggles—we're going to be doing stuff dangerous enough to need safety goggles? How cool is that!—and a Bunsen burner and Petri dishes and tons of cool glass containers and measuring apparatus and tongs and wire stands and...

"What are you doing here, freak?" Mitch Kowlaski takes the stool beside me. He still has his jacket on, but now the stain is worse. He tried to blot it and instead he just spread it so bad that the Wildcat looks like he's a werewolf, blood gushing from his fangs.

If I point this out to him, will it appease him or make him madder? He jostles my stool as he slings his bag up, almost knocking me off. From his smile, he did it on purpose. Great. My favorite subject and he's going to ruin it.

Sliding my stool as far from him as possible, I take out my notebook and wonder what cool experiments we'll be doing today. I lean over the table so my back's to Mitch, hoping he'll take the hint and leave me alone.

No such luck. He hits me with a spitball, right at the nape of my neck so it splats wet against my skin and then slides down beneath my shirt when I try to grab it.

"Stop it." I glare at him. My headache's back, thanks to Mitch.

His smile widens and he assumes a fake mad-scientist accent, pretending the straw in his hand is a cigarette. "The freak speaks. Maybe we should dissect it, see what makes it tick."

"You sure you're in the right place? I thought you were a senior. This is *junior* biology."

Wrong thing to say. Red flushes his face. I watch his hands, worried about those big fists. They could pound the crap out of me before the teacher has a chance to make it back here.

"Shut up, freak." He's starting to resemble the wild animal on his jacket.

I decide to take his advice.

The teacher, Ms. Blakely, is talking about genetic drift and adaptation. "If adaptation to increase potential offspring's survival is an external force on an organism's genetic code, what other forces could lead to a change in DNA?"

"Environmental changes," one student calls out without raising his hand. Looks like Ms. Blakely is pretty informal—maybe it's the lab benches, giving the group a more collegial feel, or maybe it's because it's a junior-level class.

Mitch pokes me in the back, nudging me to look at the doodles he's creating on a stack of torn-up graph paper. "Thought you'd like to see what I have in mind for you," he whispers, sliding the top sheet toward me. "Just how weak is that heart of yours anyway?"

He keeps whispering, threats that grow more specific and explicit—not to mention anatomically impossible—the more I ignore him. His drawings show a bit of artistic talent, although his repertoire seems limited to pornographic images, spurting blood, and wicked-looking knifes.

I turn on my stool, leaning over my notebook to block any view of him or his doodles, trying to concentrate despite a rushing in my brain that's drowning out both Mitch and Ms. Blakely.

"Okay, now we've got some external pressures, what about some internal genetic pressures?" Silence. "Anyone?"

Timidly, I raise my hand.

"Scarlet?"

The rest of the class turns to look and I pull my hand back down, flushing furiously at my gaffe. "Viruses and bacteria can insert their genetic material into our DNA when they infect us. That's also the basis for gene therapy."

Ms. Blakely looks surprised. She beams and nods and turns to the board to sketch a short length of DNA. A few of the other kids also look at me before turning away. I can't help my smile.

The boy in the bubble—the real one, not John Travolta—suffered from an inherited disease called severe combined immunodeficiency. I looked it up, excited that such a terrible disease could be fixed by bone marrow transplant. For a little while, I hoped that since Long QT is also caused by a genetic defect, the doctors might be able to do the same: cleanse my bad genes with radiation and pump in healthy new ones to mend my broken heart.

Unfortunately, for me, the damage is done—my broken heart can't be fixed so easily. Other than the daily meds I take, the only treatment is one I keep refusing, despite my parents' urgings: surgery to implant an internal defibrillator that will shock my heart whenever it runs amok.

I already have enough scars. Not to mention the thought of

having a machine inside me, shocking me whenever it feels like it, terrifies me.

Especially as one of the major side effects of the internal defibrillator is random shocks. They don't damage the heart, but patients have gone insane from the anxiety and anticipation. Waiting for a bolt of lightning to shock you from inside your own body? No, thank you. I'm freak enough already.

My mind drifts, my headache pounding and my stomach tumbling to the same beat when suddenly I smell something burning.

Pain sears through my arm and I jerk back to see there's a small bonfire beside my arm and my sweater is smoldering. A lock of my hair that had been dangling down as I rested my chin in my hand is now smoking. I reach for my hair first, smothering it with my palm, the hair breaking away in an ugly clump.

The smoke and smell and my yelp are enough to alert the others. Tiny flames dance along the surface of my sweater. I jerk loose, turning it inside out and dropping it to the floor before stomping on it. Mitch laughs, scattering the ashes of his pornographic threats as he pretends to help me.

"Scarlet, are you all right?" Ms. Blakely is at my side, examining my arm. It's red and throbbing but no blisters. Not yet anyway. She picks up my cardi. It's ruined. Then she turns to Mitch. The idiot is still holding the flint striker.

"Sorry, Ms. Blakely," he says with a sincere frown worthy of any budding sociopath. "I have no idea how that happened."

"Give me that." She yanks the striker from him, her hands streaked with soot from my sweater. "Scarlet, I think you should go see your mother. And, Mitchell, you're going to the principal's office."

"Maybe I should help Scarlet," Mitch says sweetly. "She doesn't look so good. Her heart, you know."

He's right about one thing. I don't feel good. The room is spinning and the stench of burnt hair fills my nose and mouth, gagging me. My heart is doing a weird jangly two-step and I'm gasping, trying to get enough air. I steady myself with one hand on the lab bench and one hip against the stool.

"Anthony," she calls to another student. "Help Scarlet down to the nurse's office."

All I see in my blurry vision is a bunch of black spots bouncing in time with my heart, a boy's legs clad in jeans, and a pair of black Reeboks. Right before I puke all over them.

18

Thankfully, the other kid, Anthony, has great reflexes. He dodges most of the vomit. Unfortunately, the rest of the class begins to gag—nice to know they have such empathy. Anthony half carries me out of the lab, down the hall, and around the corner to the nurse's office. Then he leaves, before I even get a chance to thank him. Probably doesn't want to risk the chance of seeing me puke again.

So here I am. Me and Mom, each taking our inevitable roles: careless and caregiver.

I brace myself against her reaction. Is she going to be cool and efficient, Mrs. Professional Nurse? Hysterical and angry at the risk I took insisting on attending school? Or a frenzied dynamo, saving me, calling 911, giving the medics report, revealing my sordid medical history like a magician unraveling a mile-long length of ladies' silk underwear from his sleeve?

I lie on the examination table. It's much too hard to be called a bed. They probably do that on purpose to keep kids from staying here long, faking. I watch warily as Ms. Blakely explains what happened, hauling Mitch in with her on their way down to the office. Mitch leans against the open door, leering at me, making rude gestures behind the adults' backs.

"Maybe I should sue," he says when Ms. Blakely finishes.

My mom spins to glare at him. He seems immune. In fact, the smile he gives her in return borders on seductive—or creepy, hard to tell with Mitch. I can see why he'd be attracted to Mom; it happens all the time, especially to hospital interns. With her long blond hair and a figure like a movie star, she's pretty glamorous. That's how folks know she's not my biological mother, not with me and my Plain Jane flat chest and skinny hips.

"This school has faulty equipment. I had no idea it would start a fire. You all"—Mitch's tone grows indignant—"placed me in danger."

Mom's mouth opens and shuts again as she swallows whatever she was about to say. She stands rigid but I see wrinkles form around her lips—a sure sign that a storm's gonna hit.

Ms. Blakely isn't so controlled. "You didn't know a fire starter might start a fire?"

"No, ma'am." Mitch manages to look innocent, injured, and insolent all at once.

She shakes her head and gets a faraway look in her eyes as if counting the days until the weekend or end of school or her retirement. Or maybe she's counting the millennia since Prometheus discovered fire, wondering how Mitch eluded all those generations of human evolution.

"Come with me, Mitchell," she says, her words ending with a sigh of exasperation. "Sorry, Cindy," she murmurs to my mom as she hauls Mitch away.

To my surprise, my mom stands there saying nothing as she

watches them leave. I can't tell what she's thinking, but she's thinking hard. Then she heaves her shoulders as if getting ready to lift something heavy and turns to me. I know that look.

"I'm not going to the ER." I launch a preemptive strike. "I feel better. And my arm is fine, see?"

She looks at my arm. It's not even red anymore, no blisters, no singed hair. My wool sweater took most of the damage. Thank God I wasn't wearing polyester. Too bad I wasn't wearing a wool cap. I string my fingers through my hair, the burnt ends crispy and snapping off.

"Still, you almost fainted."

"I stood up too fast and it smelled so bad and—" I shut up. Fast. But she lasered in on my admission.

"And what?"

"And I didn't eat all my lunch." Didn't eat any of it, actually. I was too busy ruining Mitch's jacket and, apparently, my future.

She blows out her breath in that long-suffering exhalation mothers master. "Scarlet. How can I trust you if you won't take care of yourself? Coming to school was a bad idea. You should stay home. The deal's off."

"No!" My shout surprises even me. "Mom, no. Please. It won't happen again. I promise."

She turns away without answering, raiding her stash of emergency rations, giving me a gluten-free almond butter protein bar and a bottle of orange juice. I dutifully chew as she takes my pulse and blood pressure, monitors my oxygen level, listens to my heart. Finally, she pulls her stool up and sits down across from me.

"You really want this, don't you?"

"More than anything," I answer between chews. I'm afraid to say more; sometimes the more you push Mom, the more she digs in.

"Well, you are closer to me here than you would be at home."

I nod, watching her expression warily.

She rolls up her stethoscope, shoves it into the pocket of her lab jacket. "If you're going to stay in school," she finally says, "we need some ground rules."

I nod again, a wad of almond butter getting stuck in my throat. I don't want to gag, but I can't spit it out, so all I can do is keep swallowing over and over, trying to get it down. Mom doesn't seem to notice. Like for once, she's actually treating me like an adult.

The thought terrifies me. Even though I've been through more and seen more than most kids, I know nothing about the world outside the hospital or my home. One day here in high school and even Mom is acting like I've changed.

My mouth goes dry and the mouthful of almond butter is growing to the size of a small mountain range. It won't budge. I begin to wonder if maybe I'm allergic to almonds, even though I've never had problems before.

"First, I need you to stop by here after lunch, let me check you—" Check to see if I've eaten, she means. Since my meals usually consist of hypoallergenic protein supplements mixed in with baby food and the occasional high-fiber, gluten-free cracker on the side, she's probably smart to do this. I've been cheating a little on my diet at home, even snuck a Pop-Tart the other day, but I don't dare try any of the food I saw on the cafeteria line. I might be going through some kind of adolescent rebellion, but I'm not masochistic.

"And you need to not fight me about taking your meds," Mom continues as I feel my throat closing shut and fight against a swell of panic. I grab the OJ and gulp it down. It burns as it trickles around the almond butter glob.

"That's fine," I manage, my words only slightly garbled by the almond butter. Another sip of OJ and it finally slides down, hitting my stomach with a slosh that echoes through me. I'm surprised she doesn't hear as my intestines grumble in complaint. "I can do that."

I'm lying. After the headache and flushing and nausea from that extra vitamin at lunch today, no way am I going to take more of those. But she doesn't need to know that—not like the doctor even prescribed them; they're just extra protection, like getting a flu shot and drinking echinacea tea when I get a sniffle.

She's looking at me. I try to keep my face blank like Jordan did when the others were teasing him in the cafeteria earlier. Finally I get the seal of approval when she nods.

"And lastly"—Yeah, there's a lastly!—"You need to let me know if you have any symptoms—and I mean *any*—right away, before you get sick. That's a deal breaker. If I can't trust you—"

"No, you can, you can." I don't want to get sick again, be embarrassed in front of everyone like today. And I sure as hell don't want to end up back in the hospital. "I promise."

She smiles and hugs me, back to being my mom instead of my keeper. She kisses my forehead, testing for fever like when I was a baby. "Okay," she says with a sigh. "We'll compromise."

Compromise? I already said I'd do everything she asked. I consider protesting but know better—not when she has that "she who must be obeyed" look. So I sit and wait for her to pronounce my sentence. Will it be life—with my new friends and everything a normal high school girl gets to enjoy?

Or a death of sheer boredom stuck at home doing cyberschool?

19

You may think I'm reckless, stupid even, defying my parents, my doctors, common sense. You probably think I should listen to them, hole up in my safe bubble of a house, take their pills, stay in bed.

I thought that too. Right up until my latest Set Back. The closest I've ever come to dying. Should have died.

Nothing new, I've been close before and Bounced Back, thanks to miracles and my mom. (Not sure why, but it's always Mom and the docs and nurses who get credit for my survival—don't I deserve a little credit?)

But this time, I didn't die. Instead, someone else died. Right in front of me.

She was a nasty, whiny bald girl with a kind of cancer I can't pronounce and who everyone avoided, even the Child Life folks whose job it is to cheer up sick and dying kids.

One day, I caught her trying to steal my iPod and after that we started talking. Turned out she wasn't really nasty and mean; she was lonely.

Her folks lived too far away to visit often and when they did come they spent the entire time crying and fighting and sitting without anything to say as if she were dead already.

Like me, she was dying and knew it—and she was only twelve.

And then she died. Dropped right there in the hall while we were cruising around the nursing station. She was a DNR—do not resuscitate—so the nurses and doctors came and went quickly then put her in her bed and left her alone, waiting for her folks. I snuck in and stayed with her, held her hand until it got too cold, felt gross and clammy.

Mom made a big deal of it—insisting on another psych consult for me and bereavement counseling and threatening to sue the hospital for traumatizing me. Like seeing a slice of reality was more traumatic than being cut open or having a needle drilled into my hip or tubes shoved up and down every orifice.

But really, it was no big deal. Instead, it was as if a curtain had been opened, revealing bright sunlight.

Finally, I understood.

When we're little kids, before we understand Death, we dutifully obey every rule, listen to safety lectures, look both ways.

When we're old enough to understand, we act out. We can't stand the thought of wasting one precious second of life on anything that isn't Important. Real. Vital. We want to create a legacy. Here. Now. Before Death can outrace us.

Somehow I always understood Death, even when I was a child, knew it was coming for me. I accepted it. But after watching Lacey die, I learned something about myself that I hadn't known before.

I want to live. Not just survive. Really Live.

And I'm gonna die trying.

20

Mom stands. I'm still sitting there, waiting for her decision. She grabs her coat and takes her purse from the drawer in her desk where she keeps it locked. Something inside me sinks.

"We're going home," she announces.

I don't get up right away. If my life as a normal girl is already over, I want to treasure every second between here and prison.

"Come along, Scarlet. I want to get you home so I can monitor you properly."

That doesn't even make sense. She has everything she needs right here. I start to tell her that but she silences me with one of her Looks. I slide off the table, grab Phil, and follow her out. She locks the door behind us.

"Is there anything you need from your locker?" she asks.

Hope sparks. A tiny, dim glimmer. "You mean I don't have to empty it? Like I'll be back?"

She glances at me in surprise. "Of course. Your dad and I promised you a week, didn't we? I said I'd compromise. You agreed to my terms. If you're feeling okay by tomorrow, you can come back."

I can't help myself. Phil clatters to the floor as I throw my arms around her and hug her. "I feel better already."

She shrugs me away but she's smiling. "Well, let's not push things. Let me just let the office know what's going on." She hands me her car keys. "You go on out and wait in the car."

I'm practically dancing as I twirl Phil down the empty hall to grab my jacket from my locker and head out to the car. I'll be back tomorrow, I promised the swimsuit model. See you soon, Mr. Metal Detector. And Jordan and Nessa and Celina…I don't even mind the fact that Mitch will be able to torment and bully me some more. Putting up with him is worth it if I get to stay in school.

I get to the car and Mom's just a few minutes behind me. As she steers us out of the parking lot, she asks, "So, was it worth it? Which class did you like best?"

It's strange sitting here with Mom, telling her about my classes so far. I went to elementary school for a few years, but I can't remember most of it—all I remember are the doctors' visits and hospital stays. Until finally Mom figured the best way to keep me from getting sick all the time was for them to homeschool me.

Which translated to days and days and days of boredom and isolation. It never took me long to do my online lessons—which was good, because it made it easy for me to make up any time lost to being in the hospital—and daytime TV was flat-out stupid, rarely with any decent movies on, so I read. Buried myself in books—anything I could get my hands on.

I can't remember ever sitting and talking to Mom about school. Until now. It feels good, like I actually have a life.

Talking to her like this makes me want to stay in school more than ever.

"I don't understand. You couldn't remember anything?" she asks after I tell her about Mrs. Gentry's memory exercise. Her tone makes me think my memory block most definitely is not normal.

"Not really," I hedge. "I remember the doctors and hospitals and stuff, but everything in between is pretty vague."

She turns to face me. Gives me a look like I'm having very strange Symptoms. "Really? Let's try it again. Lie back."

I tilt the seat back, resting my hands on my belly and concentrating on my breathing just like Mrs. Gentry showed us.

"Close your eyes. Relax," Mom says. "Think back, way back. Do you remember the house in Jeanette?" I nod. That's where we lived before moving here eight years ago. "Do you remember the trailer? That's where we lived before then."

Trailer? We lived in a trailer? Why didn't I know that? "No. How old was I?"

"We moved out when you were four. About a year after your dad and I were married. You don't remember? It was in the country, you and your dad used to go fishing—"

"I didn't like putting the worms on my hook, so I used bread." I feel like I'm talking about a character in a book—anybody but myself. "It's no good, I can't remember anything else."

She pats my arm. "Don't worry. It was a long time ago."

We keep driving. The sun hurts my eyes, so I cover my face with my hands. Suddenly I'm drowning in a smell that's worse than the stench of my hair burning. Soap and vomit and sweat, all mixed up with fear. I gag and swallow acid, but keep my eyes closed because in the darkness, I can feel something moving. The sound of laughter fills my mind—not friendly laughter, more like witches cackling.

My vision turns pumpkin-orange then fills with ghastly faces: white with crooked blood-red smiles, too many teeth, black eyes overflowing with evil. It isn't witches laughing. Clowns. Coming at me from every direction, their faces bearing down on me as if they're trying to smother me or suck my life away.

I jerk upright, gasping. As the clowns fade, I see a little blond-haired boy. He's crying. He looks so familiar, I know I should know him, but I don't.

Mom shakes me. I blink my eyes open and realize we're sitting in my driveway. Safe. Home. Only a dream. No witches or clowns or imaginary little boys.

Just me and my crazy, mixed-up brain.

21

My dad's on the road four days a week, so nights around our house are pretty quiet. Usually it's Mom telling me all about the crazy and funny things kids at school did, but tonight I'm the one doing the talking as I drink my evening protein supplement and she relaxes with a glass of wine and Chinese takeout. It smells awesome, and as always I try to psych my taste buds into thinking they're savoring General Tso's chicken instead of artificial vanilla. But after what happened in biology, we're Playing It Safe.

I'm lucky Mom didn't decide to go with a clear liquid diet until she was sure my stomach had settled. I lied and told her I felt fine, even though I still had a pounding headache and my heart was doing crazy zigzags, speeding up and slowing down. Just excitement, I tell myself. My vitals are normal enough that Mom's okay with me drinking a shake for dinner.

Then the doorbell rings. We both look up, our gazes meeting across the kitchen table. "Who could that be?" Mom says as she gets up to answer the door.

I follow behind, equally curious. No one ever visits our house. At least not since I've been old enough to stay home alone. Before then, Mom would always have to arrange for a sitter who knew

CPR and how to handle an Emergency or Set Back—this was before we had Phil or knew my heart was behind all my vomiting and stomach cramps and headaches and breathing problems— which basically boiled down to one or two of her nurse friends. Somehow I'd always get sick while they were here, making them have to call Mom home early. They'd never come back to sit for me again. Mom said she couldn't Risk It.

She opens the door, the evening air breezing in and making me smile as its rich scents wash over me. Then I hear a boy's voice and my smile grows wider.

"Good evening, Mrs. Killian," he says. For a moment I think it's Jordan and my heart does a flutter kick. I move around Mom to see and realize it's not Jordan. It's Anthony, the kid who rescued me in biology class.

"Anthony Carrera. What are you doing here so late?" Mom asks. I'm wondering the same thing.

"Sorry I couldn't make it sooner. I had soccer practice." He's talking to Mom like they're equals. For the first time, I realize how tall he is. Taller than my dad even. Then he turns to me. "Hi, Scarlet. Are you feeling better?"

I nod, suddenly my mouth is dry. "Yes, thanks."

"You left your bio text and notebook in class." Right. Ms. Blakely had grabbed my pack with Phil when she brought Mitch to Mom's office. I hadn't looked inside to see if all my books were there.

"Thanks." I take the books. Our fingers touch. He waits, smiling at me. I know I should say something more but my mind is a black hole, sucking down all intelligent thought or conversation.

Mom is staring at me staring at him. "We appreciate you going out of your way, Anthony—"

"Oh, it's not out of my way," he interrupts, ignoring Mom's scowl. She hates being interrupted. By anyone. "I live just around the block. And please, call me Tony."

"Be that as it may, Anthony, but Scarlet is in the middle of her dinner."

"I finished," I pipe up, realizing this might be my first and last opportunity to invite a boy inside my house. "Tony, could you fill me in on what I missed in bio? It's okay," I say to Mom, drawing on Tony's confidence for inspiration. "You go ahead and finish your dinner."

The way her eyebrows collide as she wrinkles her forehead and frowns is a major warning sign but I ignore it. Something about Tony's smile gives me the courage to usher him inside, past her. It must be the cold air rushing in, carrying with it the crisp perfume of autumn leaves and wood fires. I feel brave, bold, exhilarated—just like I had at lunch after I thwarted Mitch and his cohorts.

"Five minutes," Mom finally says, flipping on the living room lights and nodding to the clock over the fireplace.

I close the door behind Tony. He flops down in my dad's favorite armchair, appearing relaxed and confident as if it were his own house. He was like that in bio as well when he rushed to rescue me. Cool in a crisis. Mom stares at him for a long beat then crosses the foyer back to the kitchen. There are no doors between the kitchen, dining room, and living room, so she'll hear everything we say, but I don't care.

I settle onto the couch across from Tony, trying to match his nonchalance. I have no idea if I succeed on the outside, but my insides dance the jitterbug, torn between excitement, nervousness, and curiosity.

"Thank you for helping me in biology." Damn, didn't I already say that?

He stretches out his long legs until they reach past the coffee table and almost touch my feet. He's not as muscled as Jordan, but is definitely trim, like a runner. His hair's a strange color, reddish gold. Or brownish red. Maybe brownish gold. No mistaking the color of his eyes though. Hazel.

I realize I'm staring and feel a flush coming on. He smiles and my embarrassment flees, replaced by the warm feeling you get when you roast marshmallows in the fireplace—a secret ritual my dad and I have on nights when Mom has meetings or is out late.

Still he says nothing. He's worse than Jordan. Is this how all boys are? Or is it something about me that triggers their selective mutism?

"So." I break the silence. "Biology?"

"Right. We have a project due Monday." He somehow finds room for his feet and legs under the chair and leans forward as he opens his notebook on the table between us. "Ms. Blakely said I could be your partner."

"What'd you do to piss her off?" Too late I realize I've said it out loud.

He looks startled. "Nothing. I asked to have you as a partner."

"Aren't you afraid I'll barf all over you? Or that maybe you'll

85

catch what I have?" I don't know if it's because it's the end of the day and I'm tired or if there's something about Tony, but suddenly I'm not worried about acting normal, I'm just being myself. Snippy and argumentative and suspicious whenever someone's nice to me, because it usually means they're holding a needle or scalpel or want to harvest some piece of my anatomy.

He's silent, his mouth moving like he's not sure if I'm joking or for real.

"You do know who I am, right?"

"Sure. You're the girl who stood up to Mitch Kowlaski not once but twice in one day. That makes you my hero."

My eyes bug then I blink, reining them back in and giving myself time to do a quick reality check. Nope, not dreaming. Heart galloping nice and steady, so it's not a Near Miss. But I seem to have forgotten how to breathe. I haul in some air, close and open my eyes, slowly this time.

Tony's still there, and he's decided to smile.

"I'm nobody's hero," I mutter. He doesn't stop smiling. "What's this big project?"

"It'll be easy." He flips a page in his notebook, revealing a rough diagram of a family tree. "Ms. Blakely wants each team to trace back a medical family history and identify any possible genetic traits then analyze them."

I stare at him, mouth open. "She wants a medical family history?"

He nods. "I know. How cool is that? I heard your heart thing—"

"Long QT Syndrome."

"Long QT, I heard it was genetic, right? So I figure we're certain to get an A."

Rolling my head back, I stare at the ceiling. The universe has spoken. Not only does it want me to stay in school, it's actually inspired a teacher to create a project that makes me a desirable partner rather than an outcast.

Very cool indeed.

22

Mom doesn't agree. A full minute shy of our allotted five minutes, she marches in, brushing her hands together like she's squashing a bug. "I'm sorry, you'll have to go now, Anthony. Scarlet needs her rest. And please tell Ms. Blakely to find you a new partner as I'm not sure that Scarlet will be well enough to complete your project."

All I can do is jump to my feet and stare as she hustles Tony out the front door. He turns to give me one last look and a sad shrug. Then she shuts the door and he's gone.

"Why'd you do that?" I ask. "I feel fine."

She puts her hands on her hips and gives me one of her Looks. I shut up, swallowing the rest of my protest.

"You had a rough day, young lady. Who knows if you'll make it all the way through the day tomorrow? Do you really think it's fair for Anthony to be counting on your help with a project? You wouldn't want him to get a failing grade because of you, would you?"

I haul in a breath but swallow my sigh. "No. Of course not."

"Good girl. It's about time you think of someone other than yourself. Now you'd better get some sleep."

"But I'm going to school tomorrow?" I want to make it a

statement of fact, defiant. But I know better, so I twist it into a question at the end.

She purses her lips in thought. I cross my fingers, praying for a little magic. "We'll see how you feel in the morning."

Good enough. I race to my room before she can change her mind.

Ever since the Year of Nothing Good when my folks almost Lost Me not once but twice, my room has been here on the main floor of our house. At first I missed my room upstairs with its gable and window seat, but Dad worked really hard on my new room while Mom stayed in the hospital with me. He calls it the "every girl's dream come true fairy princess room."

Sometimes I think he thinks I'm still five instead of fifteen. But the look on his face when I came home from the hospital as he carried me from the car and inside the room that used to be his study—he was so excited, so proud. How could I say anything, do anything, except smile and thank him?

This is my room…imagine a wad of bright-pink strawberry Bubblicious gum. Blow the biggest bubble you can. And pow! It bursts all over a room stinking of pipe tobacco, with pine paneling stained so it's more rust-orange than brown and olive-green carpet. Then add pink lace curtains, a dresser painted— one guess—Pepto-Bismol-princess pink, and a hospital bed disguised by pink fluffy pillows and comforters with lace trim (that itches anytime it touches your skin) covered with pink roses.

Yes, it's hideous. But know what? I love it. I really do. My dad might be color-blind, but every time he comes into my room, his smile makes his eyes crinkle and blink fast, like he's holding back tears. It breaks my heart, the way he feels that he can never help me the way Mom does. He's as powerless as I am against my Long QT and he hates it.

So it's easy to keep the lights low and ignore what my room looks like or the fact that I can still smell Dad's pipe every time I walk in. Instead, I concentrate on the love he put into it.

Hoping for the best, that I'll be in English class tomorrow, I finish the last of my homework, my memory journal entry. I give Mrs. Gentry one of my hospital memories since I can't remember anything from my real life that far back. It's a good story, though. The time when I was five and had diarrhea so bad they had to drill a needle into a bone in my leg to give me fluids. Mom tells the story a lot, especially in the summer when I have shorts on and you can see the scar left behind from where the bone got infected after.

One of my many Near Misses. I hope Mrs. Gentry doesn't mind a little gore and pus with her memories—sometimes I forget all this stuff isn't normal for everyone.

The good thing about using this story is I don't have to bother Mom since I already have her first-hand account (have heard it so many times I can recite her version from memory—my own version is a little foggier since I was so damn sick), so that counts as a primary reference source as well.

I'm a little disappointed I haven't been able to remember something that doesn't have to do with being sick. Not because of the homework assignment, but because I'm afraid it's not because I can't remember, but because nothing memorable has ever happened to me *except* being sick.

How pathetic is that?

TUESDAY

23

I have a hard time sleeping. Images of Jordan and Tony. The way both of them went out of their way to help me. Thoughts of Nessa and Celina, wondering if they really like me or if it's just part of the peer mentoring, hanging out with me.

I decide that I think they do like me. All four of them. And I want to keep it that way.

Tuesday morning, Mom and I go in early so she can meet with Celina. I don't mind; arriving early means I get into school before any lines form at the metal detector. The only other kids here at this hour are the athletes with early practice and kids taking remedial classes during zero period.

I want to go to the library—especially as my first period is study hall—but Mom decides she wants to keep an eye on me, so she sets me up in the far corner of her office, behind the privacy screen.

She keeps checking her watch, obviously upset that Celina hasn't arrived on time. Another ten minutes goes by and she goes from upset to angry. Then first bell rings and she throws up her hands.

"That girl. You try and try to help her—"

I look up from where I'm reading the notes Tony brought me from bio. "Is there anything I can do?"

Thanks to Celina, I know Nessa and Jordan are in peer support because of Nessa's sister killing herself, but I have no clue why Celina needs mentoring or support. In fact, yesterday she seemed more of a leader than Jordan.

"No. I'm sure she failed to show up for her appointment because of her little sister." She rolls her eyes in disdain. Which surprises me. What could a little kid do to get on Mom's bad side?

Mom answers the question before I can ask it. "You have no idea about her sister. That girl once bit me."

"She bit you? When?"

"Six years ago." Mom's memory could outlast an elephant's. "I was doing the flu clinic for the district. They sent me to do the special needs kids since I'm most experienced. Didn't have any trouble at all until it was Cari's turn. She threw a fit but I got the shot in her. Then she calmed down, turned around, smiled, and sunk her teeth right in me." Mom's voice changes to a tone I've only heard her use about doctors and nurses who let her down or mess up my care. More than angry. Bitter.

"How old was she?"

"Six. Old enough to know better."

"But if she's special needs?"

"Having autism is no excuse. She knew exactly what she was doing." Again with the voice.

It's funny, but when Mom gets mad at people, bad things tend to happen to them. Like this nurse who wouldn't listen to Mom about my IV—she ended up accidentally overdosing another patient on potassium. Would have killed them if Mom hadn't recognized the symptoms and called the code. And an intern who refused to get the attending to come when Mom was sure I was having Bad Symptoms; two days later someone broke into his car. Karma, she calls it. What goes around comes around.

Still, it's spooky. Makes me kinda glad Celina isn't here. Not when Mom's in this kind of mood.

I go back to bio while she closes the privacy curtain and begins her day. I try not to listen, but it's hard in such a small office. At first it's kids wanting to skip a class or sit out in gym without a note from their parents. Mom makes quick work of them, checking their vitals, asking them questions, and sending all but one back to class. The one, a girl whose voice I don't recognize, sits with Mom, and they begin to talk.

Fascinated, I listen shamelessly as Mom slowly unwinds the girl's story. Her boyfriend is jealous, texted her all night so she got no sleep, and it wasn't the first time. The girl begins sobbing as Mom comforts her and gives her advice about handling the boyfriend as well as making an appointment to talk with her more. She leaves after thanking my mom for her help.

When I was a kid, I was embarrassed by the way my mom always inserted herself into other people's problems. Then, during the Year of Nothing Good, I flat out hated her for it. Here I was, almost dying, and she was focusing all her attention on other dying kids. Not that I actually wanted her overly involved in my life, but that didn't stop me from resenting the fact that I wasn't the center of her world.

But now I understand why Mom does what she does. What

CJ LYONS

I think of as meddling, she sees as helping. Like if she can help someone else with their problems, maybe she doesn't have to worry so much about her own kid. That whole karma thing again.

In a warped way, it's showing me how much she loves me.

Figuring that out makes me proud she's my mom.

More kids come and go and I focus on my work. But then I hear a familiar voice. Jordan.

"I just don't know what to do, Mrs. Killian," he's saying. "When I volunteered for peer mentoring, I figured they'd pair me with other guys, maybe spend my time convincing them not to use drugs or drink too much or help with anger management. But this…" His voice fades. "I'm so worried I'm going to mess up and someone's gonna get hurt. Like before." From the tight edge to his voice, I know he's talking about Nessa's sister, Yvonne.

"It'll be all right, Jordan," my mom says.

"Something's going on with Nessa. She's up all the time and I'm not sure if it's a side effect of grief or an act she's pulling to get people to stop asking her how's she's doing or if she's just in denial and lying to everyone including herself." His words pour out faster than a waterfall.

Wow. This was more than I'd heard Jordan say all day yesterday.

"Is she acting like her sister did? Before—" Concern makes my mom's voice sound like she's caught something in her throat.

"Yeah. Kinda. That's what scares me."

"Jordan." Now Mom sounds serious. "Is Vanessa taking any medication?"

"I don't know. Why?"

"Antidepressants can sometimes unmask mania."

"But her dad's a shrink; wouldn't he know better?" Jordan scrapes his chair back like he can't get comfortable.

"He refused to see what was going on with Yvonne."

"But what can I do? I couldn't help Vonnie. I can't risk messing up with Nessa."

"You can't blame yourself, Jordan. I'll talk with Vanessa's father, see if I can help." She paused. "How's everything else going? With the support group?"

"Scarlet's doing great." I beam, pride filling me with his words. Jordan Summers thought I, the girl freak, was great. I wonder if Mom asked him that just so I could hear the answer. Or has she forgotten all about me back here?

He continues, "But you think she has it bad with Mitch Kowlaski? You should see what poor Celina's going through. I don't know how she does it. I'd transfer out or something if I had to face that every day. She doesn't deserve this shit. I keep telling her that, but it doesn't seem to help. It's like she's shutting out the whole world."

I still have no idea why Celina was in peer support but whatever it was, she was getting bullied worse than being lit on fire by a Neanderthal? Guilt pours over me; it feels cold and clammy, like a spitball hitting my insides. I hadn't even known—hadn't even thought about her much at all, other than being glad when she was there to help me.

My first real friends and I'm failing them.

"I've tried my best to help her," Mom says, an edge to her voice. "But I can't do anything if she doesn't let me."

Back in the hospital, I was pretty good at helping kids with problems. Figuring out how to tell their folks how they really felt about their treatments or finding the right person to tell about a mean nurse or doctor—usually my mom. Maybe I could figure out why Celina was being bullied and help her? After all, I did stand up to Mitch Kowlaski yesterday.

I listen as Mom gives Jordan advice and encouragement, paying attention to how she does it without judging him or talking down to him. See, this is why I need to make it through this week no matter what. If I go back to homeschooling myself, how am I going to learn all this stuff? It's so much more important than learning trig or Spanish.

Friends. Real friends like Jordan and Nessa and Celina and Tony. They'll be much better for me than any medicine the doctors could prescribe.

24

I get to English early. Nessa rushes in just as the bell rings and has to sit all the way across the room from me, but she waves and gives me a smile. Celina comes in a few minutes late, hands Mrs. Gentry a note, and slumps into a seat in the far back.

"Let's talk about the importance of memory—and how it can betray us," Mrs. Gentry says.

I have my memory journal entry all ready to go, but to my disappointment, Mrs. Gentry doesn't actually collect them. Instead, she simply glances to see we've written something, as she circles the room, recapping yesterday's lesson.

"What other media make use of memory as a device?" she asks, moving on to new material.

I can't resist. I raise my hand and answer, "Movies like *Rashomon*. Everyone remembers the same event differently."

"And that difference depends on—" she prompts.

Before I can answer, someone behind me calls out. "Their point of view. Like in *Laura* where the detective falls in love with a murder victim based only on how the other characters remember her."

I twist in my seat. It's Tony. He smiles at me, twirling his pen across his knuckles without looking at it. Show-off.

"Good. Any other movies that are like a memory play? Maybe relying on unreliable narrators?"

"*The Usual Suspects*," both Tony and I chime together. I feel my heart jump when his gaze meets mine. We look at each other, not Mrs. Gentry, as we take turns, trying to top each other.

"*The Man Who Shot Liberty Valance*," I sing out.

"*Casablanca*," he responds.

I roll my eyes; that one's too easy. "*DOA*—the original, not the Johnny Depp remake."

"*Vertigo*," Tony counters.

"Well, if you're talking Hitchcock, then even the camera can be counted as an unreliable point of view," I argue. "He's all about seeing *not* being believing…" I trail off, too late noticing that I've done exactly what I wanted to avoid: I've become the center of attention.

Tony is smiling, bobbing his head in enthusiasm, as is Mrs. Gentry. The rest of the class is half interested, half bored by movies older than they are. But everyone's watching. My flush burns up my neck, scorching everything in its path. I scrunch down in my chair, lower my head, pretending I'm furiously writing notes.

"Well now, seems like we have some cinema aficionados here. But it doesn't have to be classic film. Any medium, from Picasso's *Guernica* to TV to songs, can use memories as a framework to engage the audience. And often those memories bear little resemblance to what really happened."

The sound of pens scratching as we take notes. I slide a glance

102

sideways, through the hair shielding my face, and realize Tony is lounging in his seat, still twirling his pen, still smiling. Then he darts a look at me, his smile widening, like he knows I'm watching him, senses I'm trying to copy his ease and self-confidence. Which of course makes me feel all the less self-confident and more like a dweeb than ever, especially when I drop my pencil and it rolls until he stops it with his foot. He snags it with a lazy swipe of his hand and reaches it forward to me.

Our fingers brush as I accept it. I don't feel anything in my fingers but my face is burning again, a slow burn that seeps down my body until my toes curl like a cat stretching in front of a fire.

The burn smolders, a good feeling even if I have no idea what to do about it. Right up until Mrs. Gentry tells us to partner with someone and together analyze any work of art that is informed by memories. Before I can move, a chair scrapes and Tony pushes himself up against my chair, nudging Phil to the side with a thud.

"Hey there, partner."

Suddenly the day seems a whole lot brighter.

25

The morning goes by in a rush with no problems. I'm actually starting to think maybe I can make it as a normal high school sophomore. Mom makes me eat lunch with her, and I'm afraid she's going to make me go home instead of finishing out the day. But my vitals are fine, so all she does is give me an extra vitamin, watches me swallow it, then lets me leave for world cultures.

On the way, I get lost and have to fight upstream through the throng before finally getting to the classroom just before second bell. Everyone stares at me when I enter, a few of the guys in letterman jackets holding their noses or making gagging motions. As I move down the aisle, searching for an empty seat, the football players and their cheerleader friends edge their seats closer together, blocking my path.

"How's your heart, Killian?" someone behind me calls out in a singsong. I spin around. Now they've pulled their chairs together as well, trapping me in a circle.

My blush burns so badly my scalp feels like it's on fire.

"Hope you're not gonna ralph again, Miss Scarlet." A girl points to my cheeks and I feel sweat edging my upper lip. I'd fought so hard to make it here, but now all I want to do is run back and hide in my mom's office.

"They'd better let Mitch play on Friday," one of the football players says. "If we lose, it'll be all your fault."

"And we won't forget it," chimes in a cheerleader.

"How is it my fault that Mitch set me on fire?" I ask. But no one listens.

There's a crashing noise as someone's book falls to the floor. I whirl around. Make that *is pushed* to the floor. Nessa is there, her smile maniacal as she rocks her hip against one Diva's chair, almost shoving her out of it.

"Whoops. Silly me. Forgot how anorexic you were, Marie. How do you stay on your feet when it's windy?" As she pretends to apologize to one girl, she "accidentally" kicks a football player's messenger bag, sending it sliding across the floor and under another kid's seat. He scrambles for it and we take advantage of the opportunity to push his chair out of the way and finally make it to the last row where Nessa's saved me a spot.

The teacher, Mr. Thibodeaux, rushes in with a dramatic flourish and looks up, expecting to be the center of attention. His expression shifts when he sees he's not, then he sets his sights on me.

"Ah, Ms. Killian. I heard rumors you were actually in attendance today. Thank you for gracing us with your presence." I'm not sure at first if his Southern accent is real or fake. He bows his head in a courtly nod, eliciting a round of laughter from the kids. When he looks up, he's beaming again. He turns and starts writing on the board, enunciating each word as if this wasn't an honors class and we can't read. "His-story is writ-ten by the vic-tors."

As Mr. Thibodeaux turns back and begins a dramatic lesson

on how history would be reinterpreted if told from the point
of view of losers—after the way Mitch and his teammates have
welcomed me to Smithfield High, I'm in total sympathy—Nessa
quietly edges her chair toward me until we're almost touching.
She points with her pen to her notebook and nods.

You OK? Missed you yest.

I shrug and nod in response.

Heard what happened with Mitch, yuck. And your hair!

Almost ruined everything, I write back, self-consciously brushing
the burnt strands that I'd trimmed that morning behind my ear.

Everything???

*Deal with folks—have to make it through Fri without getting sick.
Otherwise no school EVER, grounded FOR LIFE.*

She frowns, gnawing on her pen. *Had no idea. We're here to help.
You need to tell us this stuff!!!*

I shrug, embarrassed.

Nessa scribbles again. *Why didn't you answer my texts???? Texting
you ALL day yesterday!* She taps her pen furiously against the "ALL."

Texting me? No one's ever texted me—I never had anyone who
even called me on my cell except Mom and Dad. My phone is
for Emergencies only. I glance down at my backpack where my
cell is nestled in a pocket beside Phil, waiting for an emergency.

Rules? I write back. The school has a policy of no texting or
cellphone use—which, as I look around, I realize no one actually
follows. Half the class is using their phones beneath their desks,
the other half napping. Isn't anyone listening to the teacher?

Nessa scribbles furiously. *Rules are for fools.*

26

As Mr. Thibodeaux drones on about the French Revolution, I bask in the glow of having friends like Nessa worry about me, breaking the rules to check on me. I guess maybe this whole idea of peer support is a good one. But how can I help them in return?

I scribble a note in the margin of my notebook and angle it toward Nessa. *Is Celina okay?*

No. Bad day with her mom.

Her mom? I thought it was her sister who was the problem. *Her mom?*

Yeah. She's home, dying. Hospice care.

I turn to look at her. I know about hospice care. End of life, palliative treatment the doctors call it. Shame burns through me. Here I am worried about pissing off a few football players or how to fit in so not everyone is constantly staring at me, while Celina has to deal with losing her mother, taking care of an autistic sister, and being tormented by bullies?

I'm so sorry. I didn't know.

Nessa shrugs. *She doesn't like to talk about it.*

Mr. Thibodeaux fixes us with a glare and we both straighten, pretending to care about a world beyond Smithfield High.

27

Last period is Spanish. I've been dreading it, but taking a language is a requirement for graduation. If I'm going to come to school, might as well act like there's a chance I'll live long enough to finish. Too bad, because I suck at languages—I tried teaching myself, everything from French to Russian, but the same tin ear I bring to all things musical, I bring to languages.

As I weave my way through the crowd in the hall, I spot Celina. She's got her hoodie up, head turtled between hunched shoulders, face down as she skirts along the wall. I wave to her then quickly drop my hand as two girls stare at me. No way will she hear me if I call her name—and that's got to be just as uncool as waving—so I try to hurry after her, but she vanishes.

I end up in the wrong hallway and have to backtrack to make it to Spanish. I sneak in just after the second bell only to find that I needn't have worried about being late. The teacher isn't even there. Any students actually interested in Spanish are wearing earphones and droning phrases that sound like they were invented by Dr. Seuss. There are maybe five of them.

Everyone else is talking, goofing off, or doing homework.

Cool. This I can handle, especially at the end of the day.

Turns out Tony is in the class. Earlier, I sat behind him in biology—no sign of Mitch, yeah!—but haven't had a chance to talk to him since our movie geek-out in English.

He smiles and gestures for me to take the seat beside him. Stretching out his long legs—they take up two desk spaces and his feet are big enough to need their own zip code—he brushes his foot against mine. I'm not sure what to do but I'm smart enough to know I should play it cool, despite the way my heart lurches. I fumble in my pack for my Spanish book and try to ignore how close he is.

"That was fun. Talking movies. In English," I say, hoping I'm not making too big a deal out of it. Other than my dad, I never get to talk to anyone about movies—certainly not the way Tony and I had earlier.

"Uh-huh." He's still staring at me but saying nothing. Is it always this much work, getting a guy to talk?

"You know a lot about movies."

He shrugs. "You're not really interested in Spanish?" he finally asks. "Mr. Greenfield is the wrestling coach and he's too busy to be bothered, so everyone gets a B anyway."

"I'm not interested in Spanish," I confess, wondering why he cares.

"Good. Then let's work on our biology project."

For a moment, I wonder if he's only interested in me for my genetic pedigree. But there was a real spark between us in English. I hadn't imagined that—had I?

"I thought you were getting a new partner," I say.

"Nope." He reaches down to grab his notebook. I edge away, uncertain. He pulls out a sheaf of research notes on Long QT.

I'm still uneasy. "But—"

"You think I'm just looking for the easy grade?" He fills in the blanks. I nod. "Let's see, the chance to work with a cute girl who loves the same movies I do and is smart and stands up for herself and her friends…oh yeah, she also probably knows more about genetics than Ms. Blakely does. So hmmm…a chance to get a good grade plus the girl?" He taps his pencil against the side of his head as if thinking hard. "Gee, what do you think I should do?"

His face twists into a parody of confusion. I can't help but smile. But I want to be certain. These feelings…the way he makes me feel is totally different than the way Jordan does and I have no idea if any of them are real or not. Can I trust them? They're too new, too fragile for me to risk it. "You don't even know me."

"Duh. That's the idea." He scrapes his chair closer to me. "If you're worried about your mom, don't. She doesn't scare me."

He's about the only person. Mom pretty much intimidates everyone—even my doctors.

Then Tony looks at me, the full weight of his focus on me. I can't remember anyone ever looking at me like that before—not like I'm a problem patient or a diagnostic dilemma or a freak. More like I'm the only thing in the whole wide world. My heart does a little jig and I take a deep breath to settle it down.

Then his smile wilts. "Unless—do you mind working with me?"

I tilt my head and tap my own temple, scan the ceiling as if looking for heavenly guidance. "Gee, a chance to work with a smart guy who doesn't mind being seen with a girl who has to lug around her own life support equipment? What do you think?"

He blows out his breath in mock relief. "Great. Now that we have the formalities out of the way, let's talk cardiac ion channels and genetic mutations."

28

Spanish is over much too fast. Tony says good-bye; I grab my stuff from my locker and meet my mom at her car. Jordan was nowhere to be seen around our locker, but after spending so much of the day with Tony, in a weird way, I'm kind of relieved.

Mom spends the short drive home fuming about Celina not showing up this morning. "After all I try to do for that girl. I can't believe how disrespectful she is."

"Nessa says her mom's really sick. Maybe that's why she didn't make her meeting with you." I'm trying to stand up for Celina without making Mom think I've taken sides. Juggling friends and parents, I'm discovering, is a tricky thing.

Mom shakes her head in disappointment. "I know she's in peer support with you, but if I were you, Scarlet, I'd steer clear of that girl. She's trouble."

No way am I going to abandon a friend—not when I can count them all on the fingers of one hand. I'm silent. Mom's in no mood to discuss the matter more, but I vow to find some way to help Celina.

"Could you download my medical records onto the home computer so I can use them for our science project?" I ask as we pull into our driveway, hoping that talking medical stuff will brighten Mom's mood.

Dad's Subaru isn't there—he's usually only home Friday nights during the week, but sometimes he surprises us and comes home sooner. I should be used to it, but still it always makes me lonely when I see the empty spot on the driveway. Mom parks her Explorer in the garage and doesn't answer me until we're inside the kitchen.

"What science project?" She's twisting her keys on the metal ring that holds them. Among them is the flash drive shaped like a caduceus that has all my medical files stored on it. Just In Case.

"The one Tony and I told you about last night. Ms. Blakely wants us to do complete medical family histories and then research any genetic predispositions."

Usually she loves talking about my Long QT. She wants my dad to get tested to see if it came from his side of the family, but Dad's afraid of needles and hasn't gone yet. It's not like it changes my situation. She's always telling everyone who'd listen how it's such a relief to finally know what's wrong with me and how it's amazing that such a tiny thing, a tiny misspelling of the DNA on chromosome 11, could potentially kill me.

Tonight she surprises me. Says nothing, merely hangs her coat up and sets her key ring with the flash drive into the small bowl on the countertop beside the door. "We've discussed this before, Scarlet. I know you feel like you're all grown up now that you're in high school, but there are things you're not ready for."

Same old story. When it comes to me and anything to do with my health, I instantly revert to patient. With Mom as decision maker, controller of knowledge, dispenser of wisdom and prescriptions.

We've butted heads over this before. This summer Mom wanted the doctors to implant the internal defibrillator into my heart and I refused. I'd just turned fifteen and knew more about the pathophysiology of my disease than the intern taking care of me, so the doctors agreed. Plus, Dad was on my side. He couldn't bear the thought of me having yet another surgery.

Mom was livid. Didn't speak to me for a week, barely acknowledged my existence other than to hold her hand out with my medicine right on schedule. She gave Dad the cold shoulder as well. Living in the same house with her was like walking around, holding your breath, peeking around corners to make sure you didn't wake the monster.

Not that my mom's a monster; she just knows how to hold a grudge, that's all. The stress was so bad that I had a Set Back—that's why I was three weeks late starting school—and then things went right back to normal. Me in bed, Mom taking care of me, and Dad letting her run the show.

29

You said yourself that I have a responsibility to Tony. It's not fair that he be penalized."

"I also told Anthony to get another partner. This is too much stress on you," she argues.

We stare at each other across the kitchen island.

"This means a lot to you," she finally says with a sigh.

"Part of being a normal student is working with other kids. Besides, there's nothing in those files I haven't lived through."

Her lips tighten and I realize that reminding her of all my Near Misses and the times they Almost Lost me was exactly the wrong thing to say.

"I said no, Scarlet. End of discussion. I'll talk with Ms. Blakely and ask her to assign Tony a new partner and you another project. One that won't require you snooping around sensitive records."

"But they're my records," I protest. I can't lose Tony—despite what he said in Spanish, would he ever talk to me again after I ruined his bio grade?

"I think you've had a long day. Time for bed. Good night, Scarlet." Her tone is one of command.

As always, I surrender. What choice do I have? But as I pass the bowl sitting near the door on the way to my room, I can't help but give the key chain a second glance. I could do it. I could go behind her back, defy her.

But I don't. Instead I creep through the living room and into my room. Sent to bed without my supper. Just like a little kid.

I curl up on my paradise of pinkness bed and sulk. What have I done to deserve this? Being sick my whole life, never making any friends, spending most of my days either in a hospital getting poked and prodded or alone at home, miserable.

The worst thing I've ever done is to hide the vitamins Mom is always giving me—they're really to make her feel better, not me, so I figure I'm not really hurting anyone, right? Except I hate having to do it because I hate lies. Really, really hate them.

Everyone lies. Even my mom lies. A lot. To me.

They aren't nice lies, like "you look good today." Instead she says things like, "this is the last time, I promise," when the nurses are poking me for veins that have collapsed, sticking needles into me over and over, tying the tourniquet so tight and gritting their teeth like they take it personally that I'm a "hard stick."

Or "it's almost done, you're fine, they're almost done," when really they've just begun to shove a tube up or down or inside-out and the real pain is still to come.

Mom's lies are more dangerous than any doctor's dull needle, fat tube, or sharp knife.

My dad lies too. Once Mom was across the state at a school nurse conference and I fainted and it was Dad who found me and rushed me to the ER. He was just like Mom, clenching my hand, biting his lip, telling me over and over that everything would be okay and it wouldn't hurt and last time, I promise.

I was so angry with him. Told Mom I never, ever wanted Dad to take me to the hospital again. She worried he'd messed something up, told the doctors the wrong thing or mixed up my allergies. But no. He'd just broken my heart with his lies.

One of my nurses once told me that all parents tell lies to their kids. Wishful thinking, she said. They hate seeing their kids in pain, so all they can do is hope and pray that it will be over soon. They don't want to tell lies. They want to be telling the truth.

It took me a long time to figure out that she was right. Still didn't make it hurt any less.

But now I'm fifteen—practically an adult, not that I'll ever live long enough to be a real grown-up—and I'm getting ready to do something even worse than lying.

The second worst thing I've ever done doesn't seem so bad, except that keeping secrets feels a lot like lying. Last Christmas when I was in the hospital, Mom thought I was going to die. Guess everyone did because all the churches in town were praying for me and reporters even came to interview my folks about their sitting vigil, hoping for a Christmas miracle. But I didn't die. I lived.

When I got home and Mom was back at work, a package came for me. This happens a lot—usually they're silly get-well cards or stuffed animals or food I can't eat because of my allergies. Mom loves it—she'll have me handwrite thank-you notes while she decides what to do with the loot, doling it out to neighbor kids or taking it to kids we met who are still stuck in the hospital.

But this package was different. It came from a mom whose son had been in the ICU at Children's the same time I was over Christmas. Only he was waiting for a heart transplant that never came and he died on New Year's Day.

He'd gotten an iPad over the holidays but only had the chance to use it a few times before he got sick, she wrote. His name was Nassir and if he'd lived he wanted to become a pediatrician—just like the newspaper article said I wanted to be (I've never remembered saying this to anyone; medicine is definitely an interest of mine, I just know I'll never live long enough to actually become a doctor)—so she hoped I'd accept the gift and think of Nassir as I pursued my studies.

And there it was. My escape route to the world outside. I'd no longer be worried that everyplace I went online and everything I read or wrote would also be read by Mom and Dad. I swear they had the toughest spyware ever installed when I began online homeschooling. Like I was going to waste my days looking at porn or something.

I stared at the iPad and realized two things. First, I was free!

Second, it was the same size as a school notebook, thus easily hidden and camouflaged. It was my secret, something special that belonged to me alone. I could do anything I wanted with it and no one could stop me.

I touched the power button, my wool sweater releasing a spark of static electricity that leapt through me. That feeling of lightning striking stuck with me. I still feel it every time I turn my iPad on and escape from my life.

That was nine months ago. What I'm about to do now is worse than lying or keeping a secret. I think of that key ring, of the flash drive. I listen as Mom climbs the stairs to her room.

A thrill runs through me. I'm going to do it. I'm really going to do it.

I think of Tony, the way he looks at me. My heart skitters. I climb out of bed and creep across the floor to my bedroom door. Open it and listen hard for Mom.

I can't believe it. I'm about to defy my mother for the sake of a boy I've just met. This is not me, not my world. I'm crossing into unexplored territory.

Electricity sings through my veins. It feels good, so very good that it pushes away any guilt. Then I step through my door and head for the kitchen.

30

I stand at the entrance to the kitchen, straining to hear the slightest noise from Mom's room above me, her key chain with the flash drive mocking me from across the room.

After all, it is *my* medical history. Why can't I have it?

Plus, it's not just for me. This project will help both Tony and I get a good grade in bio.

And, if I'm going to be an adult, I should know the truth about my illness. All of the truth. Even the ticking time bomb that is my heart.

A heart that's pounding now. Hard and fast, my pulse jumping along my neck.

All I need is a few minutes—time to upload the files onto the family computer, send them to my top-secret Dropbox account, then erase all traces.

I listen carefully for any sign that Mom's still awake. Nothing.

The family computer is in the dining room since we never use it for eating. That way Mom and sometimes Dad can keep an eye on me when I use it—or so they say. They never use it themselves since Mom has her laptop and Dad has one his work gave him.

I turn back to the dining room and turn on the computer.

Even pull out a notebook from my backpack as if I'm really doing homework. I'm a bit ashamed at how good I am at this sneaking around.

The computer warms up finally (my iPad is soooo much faster!). I get dizzy waiting for Windows to finish loading and realize I'm holding my breath. Then I open a window for my fake homework. Just in case. Behind it I hide my Dropbox, ready and waiting for anything I want to upload.

Now or never.

I creep into the kitchen—only getting a glass of water, honest. I get my glass. Stop and listen. There's a creak overhead. My heart does a somersault and lodges in my throat.

Then the sound of the toilet flushing. I relax, knowing this is my best chance. I grab the key chain, race across the darkened kitchen, and plug it into the computer.

And wait. And wait.

Overhead, from Mom's room, comes the sound of water rushing through the pipes. I hold my breath and listen hard, hoping it will keep going. Maybe she'll take a bath, giving me all the time in the world.

Then it stops. Damn.

Finally the flash drive icon pops up and I open it. I don't have time to take a look at anything; I simply select all and upload them to my Dropbox account.

More creaking upstairs. My mom's on the move.

I keep my hand over the flash drive, ready to snatch it as soon as the light goes out. Mom's bedroom door opens and closes.

Damn!

The drive's light keeps blinking in time with my pulse pounding.

Mom's footsteps start down the steps. There are twelve of them. I hear her come down one, two…

The drive finishes and I yank it out. I can't afford to run back through the kitchen because it will make too much noise.

Counting Mom's steps—six, seven—I replace the drive quietly in the bowl. Eight, she hits the creaky step, nine…I'm halfway across the kitchen, can see the computer—the screen is filled with my Dropbox account!

Ten, eleven, twelve—I make it to the computer and click open the screen with my homework just as Mom rounds the corner from the living room.

"What are you working on?" she asks.

"English. That memory journal I was telling you about."

"For *The Glass Menagerie*, right?"

I nod. She wanders into the kitchen and turns on the light. I panic but force myself to watch her reflection in my computer screen rather than turning around. Does she hesitate when she passes the bowl with her keys? Does she notice that they aren't in the same place? Maybe she memorized how the keys were arranged and is testing me?

No, that's crazy.

But then she stops in front of the bowl. My fingers spasm on the keyboard; I can't even fake typing. Her hand traces the air over the keys.

I suck in my breath. Waiting. She knows, I'm certain.

I manage to close the window of my Dropbox from the icon in the toolbar. But I still need to purge the history from the browser. While she has her back to me, I use the mouse and a few right clicks to do that—have to do it twice, my hand is shaking so bad.

Finally she turns around, raising a teacup in her hand. "I'm going to make some tea. Want any?"

31

Mom drinks tea and watches me do my homework. "I'm sorry about earlier," she says. "But I really think this is a big decision and we should let your dad weigh in on it."

Dad always sides with her, so that's as good as declaring it a done deal. Except I have the files. Will I have the guts to use them? She'll find out sooner or later from Ms. Blakely if I do.

I'm so used to having Mom around to run interference and protect me from Bad Outcomes in the hospital that it never occurred to me that having your mom around all the time at school might not be the greatest thing in the world. Especially when it seems half the school goes to her for counseling and guidance.

Just like she knew everything that went on at the hospital—more than the doctors even—she knows everything that happens at school. No secrets.

Maybe I should erase the records, tell Tony to find another partner.

I take my evening dose of atenolol—the medicine that's meant to slow my heart and keep it beating nice and steady—say good night to Mom and crawl into bed. A trilling noise sounds. It takes me a moment to realize it's my cell phone. I dig it out of my pack.

"Hello?" I ask, sure it's a wrong number. No one has ever called me on my cell phone before—except Dad when I'm in the hospital and he's on the road. And this isn't his number.

"Yeah, so, what's up?"

I blink in surprise. It's Nessa. And—I glance at my clock—it's 10:18 at night.

"Nothing." I'm sure that's not the right answer, but it's better than telling her I'm already in my Hello Kitty pj's.

"Yeah, me neither." Her sigh sings thru the airwaves. "I'm so bored."

I'm not; I'm tired.

"So, how's it feel?" she asks. "Having Jordan and Tony both checking you out?"

Okay, not so tired now. Now I'm wide awake, clenching the phone to my ear as I struggle to act calm. "What do you mean? Did Jordan say something?"

She laughs. "Didn't have to. First time in months I've seen him smile was yesterday at lunch when you took care of Mitch."

"You and him aren't—"

"God no. He was Vonnie's boyfriend. That would just be gross. Besides, we know each other too well to ever hook up. It'd be like kissing your own brother."

"He is cute," I allow, as if I'm not overwhelmed by the thought of Jordan Summers actually being interested in me. The not-quite-dead freaky new girl.

"Oh please. Cute doesn't cut it. Tony Carrera's cute. Jordan's out and out hot."

"Tony's more than cute," I argue. "He's really smart and has tons of great ideas and—"

"I saw how he was staring at you during English. Before you two went all ancient movie history on us."

How did I miss that? "Really?"

"Couldn't take his eyes off you."

I think about that, wince, and ask the question I know I shouldn't ask. I wish I could be certain and confident like Nessa. But instead I'm a mass of self-doubt. "Why? Is it just because the whole school's been talking about me? I'm like the freak flavor of the week. That's all."

"Are you kidding? Scarlet, take a look in the mirror some time. These guys are used to trailer trash and Taylor Swift wannabes— girls who try too hard, pretend to be something they're not. Look at the Divas." She snorts. "Vonnie hated them by second semester, said they were so fake and full of it. You're not like that. You don't put on an act, you're just…you."

Which so didn't answer my question: why would any guy be interested in just plain old me?

But I'm too chicken to ask. Still figure any guy who wants skinny, sallow me is either blind or a loser too. And I'm not about to lump either Tony or Jordan in that category. So instead I say, "You're not upset. About Jordan, I mean, if I—we—"

I can't even finish the thought and feel my cheeks burning just thinking of the idea of me acting on any imaginary attraction Jordan may or may not have for me. Idle chatter, girl talk, that's all this is. Nothing to do with reality.

"Actually, I always thought he and Celina might—"

Oh God, Celina! Shame burns through me as I remember the way she and Jordan sat together at lunch yesterday, the way he's always watching her, like he's measuring something carefully. "You're right. I should just forget it."

"No, no. Jordan's a big boy and Celina has her hands full with her sister and mother and stuff. Last thing she needs is one more complication."

"Doesn't her dad help out?"

"He tries, but with all the hospital bills and stuff, he works two jobs. Does landscaping during the day and works at a convenience store at night. And Celina's sister—she's a handful. Especially with things all topsy-turvy over there. She's twelve but she has autism, and a lot of time Celina's the only one who can calm her down and handle her. Well, Celina and her mom, but with her mom in and out of the hospital—"

And I thought I had a crazy life. "Can't we help? There's got to be something we can do."

"I've tried. So has Jordan. It's hard. Celina loves her sister, but she doesn't really like others to see her. Don't get me wrong, she's not ashamed of her, it's just—"

"Hard." Kinda like carrying your own ICU equipment with you wherever you go. "I get it. But if it's just us, we can make it easy for her. Maybe this weekend we can go over and watch her sister or clean the house or something so she can spend some time with her mom?" I'm totally ad-libbing here. Hoping it doesn't sound too strange, to be so desperate to visit someone else's house, to try to make a difference for them. I want to be able to help, like my mom was able to help Jordan and those other kids this morning.

"Maybe." Her voice upticks and I can tell her mind is buzzing with possibilities. "We can take her to the game Friday night—it's been so long since she's been anywhere except home and school. And then over the weekend, we can return the favor by watching Caridad for them?"

"But who will watch her sister Friday night?" I ask, half thrilled and half terrified by the thought of going to a real live football game.

"Hmm…could your mom? She's a nurse, so there'd be no one better qualified."

Silence thuds between us. I can't tell her my mom doesn't like Celina's little sister. Or that she'll never let me go to a game anyway. "I don't know."

"We have a few days. Work on her." She makes it sound like parents were as easy as homework—give it enough time and effort and you could get any grade you wanted. If only.

32

I lie in bed, so many questions rampaging through my mind that I know I'll never sleep.

Every time I close my eyes, I see Jordan. The way it felt when his hand brushed my arm yesterday. The way he looks at me—through me. And Tony with his goofy smile and the way he talks so fast when he's excited, like he's afraid the future will catch up with him before he finishes explaining his ideas.

Two boys. One makes me burn; the other makes me feel warm and tingly. Is it lust or love or just a crush?

How do you know the difference? Before or after you kiss? Or have sex? Or ever?

The whole sex thing puzzles me. I'm not stupid; I know the mechanics. Despite the parental controls my folks have locked down the computer and cable with, I've seen porn. A little. Once, by accident. It was pretty gross and didn't seem at all real.

Start with kissing. How does that first kiss ever happen? You're standing there, staring into each other's eyes, close enough that every time you breathe out the other person is smelling what you had for lunch, and suddenly you're kissing? Is there some kind of secret signal? How do you know if you should tilt your head to the right or left? How far do you open your mouth? When do you start using tongue? Eyes open or closed—even the romance novels and movies can't agree on that one.

Who decides when to start and stop? Is that something guys know how to do, like leading when they dance? So all I need to do is sit back and enjoy it? But after seeing the guys my age at school, they seem pretty clueless. Women do mature sexually faster than men, so maybe I'm supposed to already know this and be teaching them?

I groan into my pillow, frustrated. Not just by the feelings making every part of my body feel like low-voltage electricity is surging through me, but by the images bombarding my brain. Images of me and Jordan and Tony. But since I'm looking out through my eyes, I can't see what I'm doing or if I'm doing it right. And even if I could visualize it, who's to say my imagination would get it right anyway?

How does anyone make it past that first kiss? Much less what comes after?

It's pretty obvious I'm not getting any sleep tonight, so I might as well get a head start on our bio project. I sit up and throw my pillow to the floor. Sneaking my iPad out, I go online and start reading my medical records. I figure I'll just skim through them, highlight any juicy parts, and we'll plug everything into the slick-looking family history graphic Tony's designing.

The records are sorted in various folders. GI, that must be my food allergies and when I couldn't digest stuff properly, needed a feeding tube and then a central line that went through my chest. I hated that thing. It kept getting infected and once it broke and blood was everywhere—I almost died before Mom fixed it. Believe you me, she was not very happy with the nurses in that pediatric unit. Can't remember now which one it was. I think Philly? Maybe Baltimore. Because Pittsburgh came later, that I remember.

Cardiac, that one's obvious. Urology, ugh, hate those guys; they stuck catheters up my bladder and it turned out there was nothing wrong down there, so all that humiliation for nothing. And Misc, which I guess is everything else.

I click on the Misc folder, scan the dates of the files—and there are tons—searching for the oldest one, dated when I was only a few years old. I open it and start reading.

The first line goes something like this: *Apparent life-threatening event in a twenty-two-month-old white female, full-term product of a twin gestation...*

That's when I stop. The iPad lays on my lap, the only light in the room its ghostly glow. I shiver and wrap a blanket around me before looking at the screen. I want to look, but something in me doesn't want to see, creating a strange tug-of-war inside me. Finally I can't resist. I pull the screen near my face, hiding under the blanket—hiding from what I don't know. Myself, I guess.

I read the words again. They haven't changed.

Twin?

33

Twin! I don't have a twin.

It's impossible, preposterous—surely I'd know if someone shared my mother's womb, was born at the same time as me, was that close…God, wouldn't it be wonderful? If I had a twin, a real-life twin—which I don't, of course, it's ridiculous, the record is wrong. Because if I had a twin, I wouldn't be so all alone. I'd have someone to talk to, someone who understood…

My heart lurches, knocking against my rib cage like someone knocking on the front door, asking to be let in. All I have to do is open it.

I close my eyes and remember the nightmare that's haunted me all my life. The one with the clowns and the little boy crying. He's maybe three or four. His hair is much more fair than mine, almost white, while mine's red. His eyes are blue like mine, but that doesn't prove anything.

He looks familiar—but that doesn't mean he looks like me. Of course he looks familiar. After all, I've been dreaming of him since I was four. I've never told anyone though.

Not even Mom or Dad know about the little boy.

Or maybe I'm wrong about that. Maybe they *do* know.

Maybe I'm the one who doesn't know what's real and what isn't.

What if he's the missing part of me, the reason I've always felt so empty and alone?

My palms sweat so badly I have to wipe them on my comforter before I pick up the iPad again. My twin isn't mentioned again in the first file. I open another record—these are scanned photocopies of handwritten charts, so blurry they're almost impossible to read. I try another tactic: search for the word "twin" in all the files, hoping to find something from a word processor document. Otherwise it will take weeks to decipher all those old scanned files.

I get two more results.

The oldest is from when I was four. A list of symptoms and test results and stuff—it looks like a note my mom wrote to help her remember everything to tell the doctor. It's just a plain text doc, no letterhead or hospital logos. All it says halfway down the list is: *twin?*

I stare a long time at that question mark, wondering what the hell it means.

The other result is my cardiologist's dictation from his initial evaluation during the hospital stay last summer when I almost died and they finally found the Long QT.

Patient is full-term product of an uncomplicated twin gestation. Fraternal twin, a brother, died age three of what was then termed "sudden infant death." Given patient's symptoms and presentation, I suspect this death may have actually been a sudden cardiac event precipitated by Long QT. Genetic testing pending on patient. If she carries one of the Long QT gene mutations, I would recommend testing of her father and any immediate family, since the biological mother died of complications due to childbirth.

The words blur before me as I blink back tears. They keep coming anyway, sneaking beneath my guard. A brother. I have a brother. I wasn't alone—I didn't need to be alone...if it wasn't for our damn genes breaking our hearts and killing us.

I sink back against the pillows.

"I miss you," I say even though I have no idea what his name is. *Was.* Why can't I remember him? More than just how he looked. I want to know him, who he was...who *we* were.

I close my eyes and try, just like Mrs. Gentry taught us.

Darkness dances beneath my eyelids. I try to use it like a blank movie projector screen, flashing memories on it. Lots of white coats and white walls and white sheets...needles and tourniquets and scalpels...pain in my belly, pain in my chest, pain everywhere... the taste of cotton in my mouth as everything turns pumpkin orange...someone crying nearby, a kid, someone else whispering to them to "hush, it's not your turn yet"...can't breathe, overwhelmed by the smell of flowers—artificial like fabric softener or soap—the orange blurs then white blotches rearrange into triangles and circles—the clowns laughing, crying, howling...

The scream chokes me and I wake. I sit up, heart thumping so loud I'm surprised it doesn't make the bed shake. Sweat makes my skin clammy, sheets tangle around me, comforter half off the bed, half on the floor. The clock says it's four thirty-two.

Dried tears scratch at my eyes. As my heartbeat slows from a gallop to a mere canter, all I can think is: *why didn't Dad ever tell me?*

WEDNESDAY

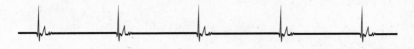

34

I'm just as nervous today as yesterday. Maybe more; after all, my entire life has changed since then. I've made it through a full day of classes, just like a normal girl. According to Nessa, there are two guys who like me—and I like them. Plus, I need to figure out a way to ask my father about my dead brother without admitting to stealing my medical records from my mom.

My brain is fuzzy with everything I have to do today—including navigating school and everything that entails. Who knew being a normal girl was so complicated?

I pick out my clothes carefully, trying to walk the line between looking good for Jordan and Tony, but also not wanting to stand out, grabbing the attention of Mitch and the other jocks.

I settle on a pair of leggings and a soft burgundy V-neck sweater that hugs what little curves I have. I dig around my closet and find a pair of ballet flats I'd forgotten I had. When I look in the mirror, my face still looks too pale—vampire girl, that's me—but unless I want to try to sneak makeup from Mom's room, there's nothing I can do about it.

I'm trying to avoid Mom as best I can. I now understand why she didn't want me to see my records—she was protecting Dad. But there are too many questions that might just break free if I let my guard down and I'm more than a little afraid of the answers. So I bottle them up inside, keep my head down and mouth shut, and we make it to school intact.

I wait in the library for the rest of the peer mentoring group, taking advantage of the privacy of the conference room to glance through my medical records some more. It's slow going. Not only because of the out-of-focus scanned documents, but also because there's a lot I don't understand.

Not the medical terms; those I'm familiar with or can easily look up. It's more the sequence and timing of things—it's not at all the way I remember.

I'm wondering if my brain might be damaged after all. Turns out I've been having Near Misses since I was a little baby—Mom's right, I've already used up a lot more than nine lives.

Nessa and Jordan arrive together. Jordan doesn't even look at me; he just slumps in his chair and stares out the window.

So much for him being interested in me.

Nessa flounces into one chair—the one across from me—then changes her mind and hops to the one beside me. "Whatcha working on?" she asks as I scramble to hide my iPad in its notebook.

"Nothing," I mumble.

She twists her mouth into a pout and sulks.

Celina stumbles in, tripping on the doorsill, never looking up as she slides into her seat and pulls her hoodie up, withdrawing into its protective shell. Her eyes are red and puffy like she's been crying, and she's been biting her lips so hard that at the corner of her mouth there's a speck of blood.

Mr. Thorne practically skips in. He scans our faces and rubs his palms together, eager to dissect our collective adolescent angst.

He leans forward, his chair thumping to the ground, and cradles his chin in his palm, his gaze moving around the table like a roulette wheel before finding a target.

"Celina." He almost purrs her name.

Celina jumps then looks down, studying the tabletop as if it's the Rosetta Stone. Out of sight below the table, her hand taps out a manic jungle beat against her thigh.

"Why don't you tell us all about the chemistry quiz you failed last week? How did you explain that to your mother?"

Silence. Celina swallows so hard her head bobs.

Nessa comes to her rescue. "You know how we were talking about a memorial for my sister, Mr. Thorne? Well, I'm having a hard time processing that. I mean, how do we celebrate her life without glamorizing her death?"

She kicks Jordan beneath the table and he picks up the ball. "Yeah, last thing we want is more kids thinking about jumping off the roof."

All three look up at the ceiling. But not Thorne. He pins Celina in his sights as if reluctant to release his prey.

"What was she like? Your sister?" I leap in without any idea of what I'm getting myself into. It's liberating. Thorne's gaze jumps from Celina to me. "If it's okay to ask."

"Of course it's okay," Thorne says. "This is a safety zone where we can discuss anything." Again with the smile that creeps me out. Like I'm not really human, just a thing labeled "troubled teen," a specimen for him to dissect. A few of my surgeons looked at me that way. Right before they cut me open. "Vanessa, would you like to tell Scarlet about Yvonne?"

Pain twists Nessa's face. Jordan's expression reflects it as well. Clearly, despite her bluster, this is a raw wound. Now I'm sorry about asking—although it got Celina off the hook. Who knew meeting with your guidance counselor involved juggling emotional chainsaws?

"Yvonne was a sophomore. Top of her class." Nessa's face blanks into a mask. But she doesn't look away, stares right at me. "She died the week before school ended last year. Fell off the roof of the gym."

"We've discussed how important honesty is, Vanessa."

"Sorry." Nessa's tone loses all inflection, matching her expression. Flat affect, the doctors call it. "My sister, Yvonne, committed suicide by jumping off the roof." Her words fire in a clipped staccato, aimed at Mr. Thorne. None of them hit their target. He steeples his fingers and nods in approval.

Then Mr. Thorne talks about the stages of grief and he seems genuinely to care about helping Nessa heal. A lot of what he says seems aimed at Jordan and Celina as well. Maybe he's not heartless, just clueless?

By the time the bell rings, I'm totally confused. I don't feel very mentored, much less guided or oriented.

Mr. Thorne leaves first, bounding out of the room like a St. Bernard who's just rescued an entire ski club, leaving the rest of us gathering our things. Jordan touches Nessa's shoulder without saying anything, nods to Celina and me, then he's gone as well. Nessa links her arm with mine. Suddenly she's swung back to smiling and chipper, like the whole past hour was just an act.

35

We get to English too late for me to sit near Tony, but he smiles at me across the room. We spend the class reading scenes from *The Glass Menagerie* aloud and the time passes quickly. The bell rings. Celina stays behind to talk to Mrs. Gentry while Nessa and I are swept out of the classroom in a wave of kids.

I turn, thinking I'll try to go back and find Tony, but it's too late. I walk with Nessa, trying out a new route to trig, when we're stopped by a wall of letterman jackets. Three football players to the front and by the time I pivot to go around them, two more on one side. And the door to the boy's room on the other side. Trapped.

"What do you want?" Nessa snaps, her posture making her seem almost as tall as the guys surrounding us.

"Nothing. This is just a down payment on what we owe you for getting Mitch suspended from playing Friday." One of them yanks Nessa's bag from her shoulder and throws it into the boys' room. Another grabs Phil from me and jumps through the door. "Come and get it, ladies."

"Give that back," Nessa says.

I'm not sure what to do. If anything happens to Phil, my mom will kill me. "Be careful. That's an expensive piece of medical equipment," I shout.

Too late, I realize I've just made things worse. They laugh and crowd us toward the door. "How about we flush it down the toilet?" one of the boys says.

"How about we flush *them* instead?"

"I've got a better idea," a third grabs his crotch. A queasy feeling makes my stomach go cold. Lots of stuff you see and hear in the hospital is gross, but not like this.

"Stop it!" A woman's voice cracks through the air. The boys jump. So do Nessa and I. We turn to see who's come to our rescue. Not a woman, Celina. Hood down, head high, face calm. No, more than calm. Commanding. "Get out of here, now."

Three of our tormentors scurry away. She ignores the remaining two, pushing past them and through the door to the boys' room. Nessa makes a noise between a gasp and a cheer. A moment later, Celina emerges with our stuff and a condescending glare for the football players. She gives Nessa her bag and hands me Phil, unscathed, thank God.

"Grow up, why don't you?" she tells the boys.

One of the players looks sheepish, but the other has his hands curled into fists. Celina sees it as well, stepping away from the door so she has more room, keeping her hands open but raising them so they're above the boy's.

"Mr. Young," a man comes up behind us. Mr. Thorne. "Don't you have somewhere to be?"

The boy glares at Celina for a long moment before smirking at

Mr. Thorne, obviously not intimidated by the guidance counselor. Then he points at me, like he's making a special note to remind himself who is to blame for all this.

With the boys gone, Mr. Thorne turns to us. "Are you ladies okay? Do you need to talk?"

We exchange glances and I can't help but giggle with relief. Nessa chimes in, and soon all three of us are laughing. "No, thank you, Mr. Thorne," Nessa says politely. "We're fine. C'mon, Celina."

We each link arms with Celina and continue to class. As soon as we're out of earshot of Mr. Thorne, Nessa says, "You were fantastic. Your mom would be so proud."

Celina's smile fades at the mention of her mom. Nessa looks abashed. "I'm sorry—"

"No," Celina says, thrusting her hands into the pockets of her hoodie. "Don't be. That's the nicest thing anyone ever said. Thanks."

I can't help it. I hate that I don't know what to say to make her feel better and can't do anything to help. So I drop Phil and give her a hug. It startles her and she winces. I let her go, sorry that I've embarrassed her. "Thanks, Celina. Maybe someday you can teach me how to do that thing with your voice. That was awesome."

"Yeah," Nessa says. "You can practice using it on Tony Carrera. Tony, stop it! No, I mean, don't stop! Oh, right there…" She makes kissing noises and we both break into giggles again.

But not Celina, I notice. She stops and stares down the hall. It's the tall football player. Keith Young. And he's watching her.

Blows her a kiss with his hand and waves good-bye. Like they have a date or something.

"We should tell Mr. Thorne," I say. The second bell rings. We're late.

"No," Celina answers. "Don't worry about me. I can take care of myself."

36

"here have you been?" Mom demands at lunch as I schlump into her office and drop down into the chair beside her desk. "I've been waiting."

I just shrug. I'm too busy worrying that, because of me, Celina is now a target of Mitch Kowlaski and his buddies to pay attention to Mom's familiar refrain of worry.

"You kids." Her voice is loud, too loud. Slowly it penetrates my foggy brain that she's upset. Which never, ever bodes well. "All I do all day long is try to help you and what do I get for my efforts? Disrespect. Disobedience. Defiance."

I jerk my chin up. Alliteration. This is bad. Very bad. "I'm sorry."

She doesn't even hear me. Instead, she's banging through her refrigerator, rattling bottles of insulin and other medication as she hauls out my lunch. She glowers and dumps it on the desk in front of me. "Eat."

Eating is the last thing I want to do. But I know better than to say anything when she's like this, so I meekly unscrew the lid off a jar of pureed pears and take a small spoonful. The baby's smiling face on the label reminds me of my questions about my twin—but clearly this isn't the time to ask Mom about a dead child. My dead brother.

Then it hits me. So hard that I almost sputter and choke on the pears. God, I'm so stupid.

He would have died less than a year after she and Dad were married. I've been so obsessed with thinking about how my dad felt that I hadn't done the math. How painful it must have been for her, to lose him. And then with me sick, to constantly worry about losing me.

Because of me she had to face that agony again, every day. Wondering when I'll drop dead. Like holding your breath through eternity.

I'm such an idiot. All the pain I've put her through. "I'm sorry."

This time she hears me. She stops her pacing, spins on her heel, stares at me as if thinking I'm mocking her, but her expression softens. She gives me a big sideways hug, smearing pears all over my chin, and sits down across from me in her desk chair.

"It's okay, sweetie. It's not your fault. But I'm going to talk to Mr. Thorne about getting you out of peer support. I don't think those kids are a good influence on you. I don't want you seeing them anymore."

Wait. Drop peer support? Where'd that come from?

"Besides," she continues, "you don't need counseling. You've got me to talk to."

Does that mean I can stay in school? Feeling like I'm tiptoeing across a high wire, I struggle to keep my voice nonchalant as I say, "I like Celina and Nessa and Jordan."

She shakes her head, looks sad. Pats my knee. What happened to treating me like an adult?

"You're so sheltered. You just don't understand."

What the hell does that mean? "Understand what?"

She doesn't answer. Instead, she spins out of her chair with new energy. "Oh. I've got something for you." She reaches to the top of the filing cabinet and takes down a thick three-inch binder bulging with papers. "I spent the morning copying your medical records and collating them for your biology project."

Thumping the heavy binder down on the desk in front of me, she sits back down, hands folded in her lap, leaning forward. Waiting.

I swallow a spoonful of pear. It tastes like white paste. "Thanks." Her smile falls. I wasn't enthusiastic enough. I make a show of thumbing through the pages, widening my eyes. "Wow. I can't believe this. Thanks, Mom!"

Perky enough. Good. Because I don't have the energy for more. Not today.

"You're welcome. Figured this would be easier for you and your lab partner to use than computer files." She pauses. "Who are you working with again?"

"Tony—Anthony Carrera." I'm surprised she can't remember but realize she's got a lot on her mind. If I'm healthy enough to stay in school, guess that means I'm one less thing for her to worry about.

She considers. "Nice boy. Good grades. Hasn't been in to see me for anything."

The last is the only negative thing she can find to say about Tony, so I figure I'm safe. I'm still puzzled by her sudden problems with Nessa, Celina, and Jordan. She was fine with Nessa and Jordan yesterday. Which left Celina. "You heard about the jocks. It wasn't Celina's fault."

"If you say so." Her tone is one of disbelief. "I'm glad you won't be associating with that girl anymore." She says it like it's now law, a constitutional amendment, commandment number eleven. "I don't think it's a surprise to anyone that that girl is severely troubled. No surprise at all. I'm afraid I'm just not going to be able to help her."

My mom giving up on a kid who needs her help? It doesn't make sense. Mom revels in lost causes like the Drama Queens we've met when I've been in the hospital. She thrives on the challenge of helping when no one else can.

"If you're going to blame anyone," I defend Celina, knowing there will be a price to pay, "blame me. They were upset because Mitch won't be able to play on Friday after what he did to me." I touched the right side of my hair, trimmed and pulled back with a barrette that Nessa loaned me.

"Mitch isn't playing because of me, not you," she tells me. "I went to Principal Beltzhoven and insisted on it. I will not stand for anyone treating my daughter with such disrespect. And then the way he talked to me—" She shakes her head at the memory. "Don't you worry about him. If I have anything to do with it, he won't be playing football ever again. Even if I have to sue the school district, force them into providing a safe haven for students here to learn."

I blink at her passion. I've heard her talk like that to doctors and nurses she disagreed with, fighting to get me the best care possible, but for the first time I'm realizing that Mom brings her crusading spirit to her work at school as well. Maybe that's why she and Celina can't get along—they're both heroes in their own way.

The bell rings, but before I leave for art, I can't resist giving Mom a hug. She looks surprised. "What's that for?"

"Just to thank you for taking care of me and all the other kids here."

She looks down to pick a stray piece of lint from her cardigan but can't hide her smile. "It's my job. Get going so you won't be late for class."

37

The rest of the afternoon goes by quickly. In art class, I try and fail to recreate my memory of my brother into a portrait. Then in world cultures, Mr. Thibodeaux drones on about Marie Antoinette while Nessa and I take turns doodling an elaborate ball gown that starts out like something Marie might wear but ends up more like a Lady Gaga costume.

Tony and I spend bio and Spanish talking family trees and our futures—well, his, not like I really have much of one. Turns out he's taking upper level bio because he wants to start taking college classes next year and get into med school.

I listen and do a lot of nodding—once he starts talking, I don't want to risk shutting him up. I've never met anyone who has their entire life planned out like Tony does. Most I ever planned ahead was the next test or surgery, and that was more like dreading than planning.

Tony's excited about the future, says the possibilities inspire him.

Inspired—I've never met anyone inspired before. The word feels powerful. As if he can breathe in the future, using it like oxygen to fuel his body.

He can't wait for tomorrow and the day, year, decade after.

Me, I'm just hoping I live long enough to see homecoming.

After Spanish, we walk together to my locker. It's kind of cool walking with someone as tall as Tony. He sees over most of the crowd and can steer us past any knots of students, avoiding the jostling and hip bumping. Plus, he carries Phil, so no constant looking behind me to make sure I'm not tripping anyone.

I actually feel like a normal girl, walking with a normal guy, like maybe we could be a normal couple.

Or so the fantasy goes. Of course, this is before I realize there are other reasons why I should've been looking over my shoulder.

A gaggle of cheerleaders and football players clusters around my row of lockers. They're giggling, so at first I smile, thinking there's something funny going on. Tony spots it first; I feel him tighten beside me.

The crowd parts and I see it. Blood-red ketchup covering my locker door. Dripping from sanitary napkins and unwrapped tampons, hanging by their strings.

I stop. It's just too gross for words. Who would think of such a thing—but of course, the answer to that is all too obvious.

The snickering gets louder. It buzzes around my head like a swarm of wasps. All I can think is that I have to clean it up before Jordan sees it. He's already been humiliated because of what I did in the cafeteria on Monday. I can't make things worse.

They've timed it so that's impossible. The entire school passes down this hallway to leave for the day. It feels like every one of them takes the time to stare at me, my locker, and laugh.

Tony stands beside me, waiting for my cue. But I have no idea what to do about this. Make some kind of joke—except I can't think of anything that won't make things worse. Maybe just clean it up? No, not while they're watching and laughing. Walk away? But then they win—and it would leave the mess for Jordan to deal with.

If I want to be an adult, I need to start by cleaning up my own mess.

Easier thought than done.

Jordan arrives before I can decide where to start. He surveys the damage in silence, glares at the onlookers, paying particular attention to the tall football player lounging against the wall across from us—the one from earlier, Keith Young—then he turns his gaze on Tony.

"Carrera," he says.

"Summers." They exchange an almost imperceptible nod, so I assume they're friends or at least not enemies. Tony hands me my backpack. "Need help?"

"No. We're cool," Jordan answers as he ignores the ketchup and twirls open the combination.

I almost miss the "we." Because they might be "cool," but I'm not. I'm freaking out.

Inside the locker, the swimsuit model is toast, having taken the brunt of the damage from the ketchup forced through the vents. There's ketchup on my dad's jacket, Jordan's gym bag, and his books.

A folded piece of paper flutters to the ground. I grab it before Jordan sees it. A note. Who's it for? Me or Jordan?

The football players gather closer, shouting catcalls of glee as we survey the damage. Mitch might be gone but his buddies clearly hold a grudge.

Both Jordan and Tony stretch themselves to their full heights, shifting their stance so they're between me and the jocks. They roll their shoulders back, and if they were gorillas, they'd be pounding their chests.

The world tilts around me and I feel like I'm floating, looking down from the ceiling—like I'm imagining all this. Or living someone else's life.

I mean, how the hell did I end up with not one but two white knights coming to my rescue?

I must be dreaming.

38

"I'm sorry about your stuff," I say to Jordan, not really knowing what to say but figuring that's a start.

"Don't worry about it." He hands me my jacket. "Doesn't look too bad. You can probably get it out in the wash."

"Hopefully before my dad sees it. It's his."

Tony is watching us and the crowd, which has diminished greatly. Escaping school for the day trumps witnessing our humiliation, I guess. "So," he says. "I'll call you later."

Jordan jerks his chin. Could he be jealous? Or just protective? Do the guys I meet fall under his peer-mentoring purview?

"Right. That'll be good." I'm trying to sound nonchalant about a boy calling me and failing miserably. I squeeze my fingernails into my palms to get myself to shut up before I say something even more lame.

Tony nods and leaves. If I hadn't been watching him, I never would have realized that a nod can mean both "hello" and "good-bye" in guy-talk. Kinda like Hawaiian, I guess.

"Oh my God, what happened?" No mistaking Nessa's meaning. She's shrieking as she pushes past the stream of students heading toward the door. "Who did this? Jordan, your stuff! Hey, it's not funny!" She yells the last to a pair of snickering cheerleaders strolling past.

Celina is behind her—I almost missed her, the way Nessa commands all of your attention and energy and focus. She would've made a great Diva. Unlike me, who works so hard to deflect people's attention.

Of course, that was before I crossed paths with Mitch Kowlaski.

Celina surprises me. She doesn't withdraw or hide inside her hoodie. Instead, she calmly observes the damage, takes the note from me, and opens it.

FREAKS DIE FIRST.

There's a lightning bolt piercing the words. It reminds me of the Nazi SS insignia. I can't help a shudder.

"They're jerks," Celina says. "They wouldn't dare actually hurt anyone."

"You really think so? Shouldn't we take it to the principal or something?" I ask.

"We'll just escalate things if we involve the authorities. Especially with no proof," Celina says. "But document it first."

"How do you know all this?" I ask her.

"Her mom was a cop," Nessa answers, taking the note from her and peering at it as if she could find DNA evidence with her gaze.

"*Is* a cop," Celina corrects. She shoves her hands deep into the pockets of her jacket. The way her tone drops, I'm surprised she hasn't pulled her hood up.

"Is a cop." Nessa's smile is uncertain, like she's not sure which way Celina is headed and wants to steer her right.

Nessa pulls out her phone and takes pictures of the note and the damage. Celina and I run to the restroom and grab a bunch of paper towels to mop everything up with. A few minutes later, the only traces that remain are the ketchup stains on our clothing.

Then I realize Jordan's vanished. "Where'd he go?"

"Guess he's had enough embarrassment for the day." Nessa's frown is back.

Celina stares down the now-empty hallway. "I worry about him sometimes."

"Being stuck with us isn't easy." Nessa sighs.

I close the now-empty locker, hugging my dad's jacket, ketchup stain turned inside.

"I have to get home," Celina says. "See you guys tomorrow."

Nessa and I walk Celina to the front doors where she runs and jumps on a bus. The same bus I'd be riding if I were normal.

When we go back inside, the school feels different. Ten minutes ago, it was swarming with students, voices bouncing from every surface, bodies jostling for position. And now? Empty except for the faint sound of music coming from the auditorium. Chorus or drama. Whichever it is, the music is low, creeping along the floors like fog through a graveyard.

If this were a movie, this is when the lights would go out and the killer would spring out from the shadows.

I take the opportunity to ask Nessa about Celina's mom. "You said Celina's mom is dying. What happened? Was she shot or something?"

In the movies and books, cops are always getting shot and coming back to work too soon. Then post-traumatic stress hits and they get drummed off the force until they prove themselves or become hard-boiled PIs or kick-ass vigilantes fighting vampires and demons…

Nessa interrupts my steamrolling imagination. "No, she didn't get shot. She got cancer."

We're passing the library and I pull up short. "Cancer?"

I'm regretting my flight of fantasy. Lacking in the basic social skills, that's what they'd say. If we were still in kindergarten. I'm reminded again of how much I've missed and need to catch up on—far more than schoolwork.

"She's in hospice care. Has been for a month. They keep saying it could be any time now and Celina keeps—well, anyway, it's a lot of ups and downs."

"I know how that is." We start moving again. I'm following Nessa's lead and realize she's brought me to the doors beside the gym. Through the windows, I see a blur of motion outside. My brain goes ker-klunk as I finally put the pieces together.

"Jordan went to fight the boys who vandalized our locker."

"Of course he did." Nessa's smiling as she reaches for the door handle. She enjoys having a Prince Charming fighting her battles, but I'm not so sure about the idea.

"Nessa, we have to stop them."

"No, we don't."

"Someone might get hurt."

"I guarantee it won't be Jordan. His dad is a police sergeant, works with Celina's mom. And his two big brothers are Marines. He knows what he's doing."

"But—"

"But nothing." She turns to face me, crossing her arms over her chest and blocking the door from me. "Say we go get your mom or a security guard or someone. They'll suspend everyone, including Jordan. Maybe even press criminal charges. All of which will go on his permanent record. Do you want that?"

"No, but—"

"Then after Jordan's suspended or arrested or grounded or whatever, do you think Mitch and Keith Young and their friends are going to magically make us their BFFs? No. It'll encourage them. They'll escalate things, only now we won't have Jordan to protect us."

"But it was just some ketchup—"

She's shaking her head, hard. "No. It wasn't. You and Jordan got the PMS treatment. You didn't hear what they did to Celina after lunch in gym class. They stole her clothes, shoved them in the toilet—an unflushed toilet. She had to wear her gym shorts and take her stuff to the home skills lab to wash them. And of course, the video is already all over school."

39

We burst through the doors and find five guys in front of the tiny alley where the equipment shed sits beside the gymnasium wall. At first I'm thinking it's a strange place for a fight, but then Jordan's head pops into view over the shoulders of the other boys, and I realize he's chosen this corner carefully: it puts his back to a wall and the opening is narrow enough the guys can't gang up on him.

There's the thud of someone hitting the ground. I cringe. Nessa cheers, so the someone couldn't have been Jordan. She pushes her way through the boys. I follow, my pack thumping over the uneven grass, wheels catching on clods of mud, half dreading what I'll see.

The boys watching are all wearing football practice uniforms. They jeer at us, but no one actually lays a hand on us. Nice to see they still have some civil manners. Or maybe we're simply beneath their notice. No threat.

We get to the front and I'm surprised to see Jordan isn't alone. Tony is with him, wrestling with his own football player, each trying to push the other's face into the mud. Jordan's opponent is down but not out. There's not much maneuvering room in the cramped space, but he manages to grab Jordan's leg and topple him to the ground.

I've been at the center of emergencies, but never before had to respond to one. Nothing in my life has prepared me for this. There's no sign of blood—not yet—and it seems to be more of a tussle than an actual fight, but as the crowd starts calling out encouragement, well, it's not hard to see where things are headed. Nessa isn't helping any, launching herself at Jordan's opponent when he throws mud in Jordan's eyes. Two of the other jocks pull her off, screaming.

I'm paralyzed. I have never been this close to violence in my life. My heart is thundering so it feels like a herd of horses stampeding inside my chest. My blood sings with adrenaline along with a hefty portion of fear that makes my stomach queasy and my mind slow to a drunken stumble. I stand there, clutching my pack with Phil inside. So much for carrying life-saving fashion accessories.

The crowd moves, ebbing and flowing with the combatants, pushing me along with them. It's a frightening feeling; any one of these boys is twice my size. I fight my way to the fringe of the crowd and catch my breath. One of the boys stands alone in the back. He's not watching the fight. He's watching me.

Keith Young. Mitch's buddy.

I lean on my pack's handle, gasping in a few deep breaths, clearing my head, and slowing my heart. I remember my cell phone and grab it. It's not as fancy as Nessa's, no video, but it does have a camera. I start to take pictures of everyone. At first I sneak the shots, palming my phone and aiming it. A few guys notice but do nothing, so I grow bolder. I hold the phone to my face. It feels like a shield or maybe a superhero's mask I can hide behind. Put some distance between me and the violence.

"Stop!" I shout, my voice cracking like a cheap tin whistle.

One guy tries to grab the phone, but I back away. "Don't you touch her," someone yells. I'm not sure if it's Tony or Jordan. But then Nessa's there, standing firm between me and the others. Suddenly so are Jordan and Tony, guarding my flank.

I'm out of breath even though all I did was snap a few pictures. "I think you'd better all leave now."

"What if we don't want to?" Keith says, finally pushing off the wall and sauntering to the front of the pack. "You show those photos to anyone and your friends here are toast." He extends a hand, palm up. "Give me the phone and no one gets hurt. At least not today."

The jocks rear up, hoping I'll call his bluff. It feels like the air is being sucked into a vortex as we wait. Time stretches to the breaking point.

I have no idea what to do—give up the phone and make all of us fair game for them tomorrow? Or stand my ground and risk getting hurt today? I remember Celina, the way she refused to back down.

I tighten my fingers around the phone. "No."

My voice still isn't back to normal, but it's less shrill.

Keith's pack of wildcats leans forward, ready to pounce, waiting for his command. Jordan and Tony tense on either side of me. Nessa reaches for my hand, her grip sweaty.

"What's going on here?" My mom is standing in the doorway. "You kids, go on now. You know you shouldn't be here."

Unlike my amped-up squeak of a voice, Mom's is just like the voice of the nurses in the hospital when they're calming down an angry patient or parent. When I see them like that, I always think of that scene in *To Kill a Mockingbird* when Atticus takes on the rabid dog, all calm and in control, and I wonder how grown-ups learn to do that. Or Celina—it was exactly the way she'd defused things earlier. Damn, she needs to teach me how she does it.

"Just go now." Mom uses that same, level, *don't be stupid* tone.

Keith Young nods, looking from me to Mom then back to me, his gaze lingering and making me feel like I need a shower.

He purses his lips as if whistling some invisible note only football players can hear. Whatever he's communicating, they listen. They pull back their shoulders, not to throw a punch but to salvage their pride, and pivot, heading off toward the playing fields like they're one organism with a bunch of hands and feet. And one brain: Keith's. They're even congratulating themselves, clapping each other on the back.

But a few look back over their shoulders to glare at me, still holding the phone containing the evidence that could damn them, and I know it's not over.

In fact, I'm pretty sure Nessa's right. By interfering, I've made things worse.

40

I'd like an explanation," Mom says.

We look at each other. Jordan speaks up. "It was just a misunderstanding, Mrs. Killian."

She glares at each of us in turn. Then she narrows her eyes at me. "Scarlet, I expected more from you. Nessa, I'll give you a ride home. Time to go." She doesn't wait for us but turns and leaves.

"We'll be right there," Nessa calls, waving a hand cheerily as the door closes behind Mom. I gaze at her in admiration, envious of her acting skills.

Mom didn't even bother to check my vitals. I'm glad, since she'd probably overreact to my racing heart and call an ambulance or something. But still, it's puzzling. And how did she even know we were here?

The others slowly relax. Not me. Me, I'm like a jack-in-the-box wound so tight I'm ready to launch into orbit. My hands shake so hard I drop the handle to my pack, letting it fall to the dirt. Would've dropped the phone as well, but Nessa takes it from me and slides it back into its pocket alongside Phil.

"What were you thinking?" Jordan says, whirling on me. His voice isn't loud but it feels loud. I recoil as if taking a blow.

"I was thinking it might be nice not to watch two of my friends get beaten up by a bunch of Neanderthals," I answer.

Nessa takes his side. "Nothing was going to happen. Those guys are all show. They'd never risk getting kicked off the team or missing the game Friday. Jordan had to stand up to them or things would only get worse."

"You don't know that."

"And you," Jordan says, "don't know half of what went on—"

"Nessa told me about Celina."

"You think what you did today is going to help Celina? Think you can waltz in, your first week here, and just fix everything? You have no idea." He spins on his heel and stalks off.

"Jordan, wait!" Nessa calls after him, but he just flicks his hand in our direction and keeps on going.

I watch him leave but have no idea what to say. Other than that he was right. I didn't know what the hell I was doing. Had no clue.

Tony stands beside me, his weight bouncing from one foot to the other as if he wants to run. He's plastered in mud and grass but doesn't seem to notice. "Guess I should get going," he finally says. "See you tomorrow?"

He leaves before I can answer. Nessa hauls my pack through the door, giving me the silent treatment. But she does hold the door open for me, even if she isn't meeting my eyes. Somehow I feel ashamed, like this is all my fault and I've done something horribly wrong, betrayed my friends, especially Celina.

My stomach is hollowed out with fear. My first week in school and I might have already lost the only friends I have.

"I'm sorry," I tell Nessa.

She looks over her shoulder to the door behind us then she gives me a hard look, like she's deciding something. Finally she turns her back on the door and shrugs. "C'mon, I've had enough of this place for one day."

That's when I realize that the other door, the one she turned to stare at, is the door leading into the gymnasium. Where her sister died.

41

Nessa lives in College Heights, one of Smithfield's older neighborhoods filled with sprawling maples and sycamores and big colonials. Compared to our street, it's pretty upscale. No Mercedes in the driveways, but Volvos and Audis instead of Fords and Subarus. Makes sense since her mom is a county commissioner and her dad teaches psychology at Smithfield College.

Mom pulls into the driveway of a white two-story with tall columns reaching from roof to ground in the front. The place feels different from its neighbors—yeah, the lawn is trimmed and leaves are raked, but there are no pots of mums or pansies, no wreath on the door, no signs of life.

"Is there anybody home?" Mom asks. She senses it as well. The house feels empty. Worse, it feels sad.

"Mom will be late—election in six weeks. But Dad's home."

When my dad comes home, the house feels bigger, brighter. He races to catch up with me and Mom, starts projects he never finishes (and forgets about by the next time he's home), loves to mess with the yard or garden or shrubs. This house doesn't look like a house where a dad is at home. Where anyone's at home.

Before either of us could say anything more, Nessa bounds out of the car and is halfway down the drive, waving good-bye.

Instead of driving away, Mom gets out of the car and follows her. I don't know what to do, so I get out as well. By the time Nessa reaches the front door, Mom is right behind her. A man is standing in the front hall when Nessa opens the door. He's not very tall, skin darker than Nessa's, and a little mustache that looks out of place on his moon-shaped face.

"Dr. Woodring," Mom says, pushing her way inside despite Nessa trying to block her. "I think we should talk."

His eyes go big then he turns to Nessa and me. "Why don't you girls wait in the kitchen? I think there are some snacks available." His tone is formal; his voice has a faint lilting accent to it. Nessa rolls her eyes, grabs my hand, and tugs me down the hallway.

Their kitchen is huge, twice the size of ours. Everything in their house is white: white walls, white tile floors, white countertops. The only color comes from Nessa as she tosses her crimson-colored wool coat over one of the white chairs.

"Shh," she whispers. "This way. We can hear everything."

"But—"

"No buts," she tells me. "They're talking about me. I have a right to hear what they're saying. Why's your mom got to be in everyone's business all the time, anyway?"

All I can do is shrug and follow her. She leads me to a door in the far corner of the house. The house is old enough that it has high ceilings and there are glass transoms above the doors. Nessa positions herself against the door under the open transom and motions for me to join her.

"Mrs. Killian," her dad is saying. His voice is deep, resonant, and with that lilting lullaby accent. I imagine if I was one of his patients, I'd fall asleep on his couch while he was psychoanalyzing me. "I know you have the best of intentions, but really I have everything under control."

"Like you did with Yvonne?" my mother fires back, using her *I'm the nurse and know best* tone that makes interns scramble. "I tried to warn you—"

"I know, I know." There's the sound of a couch or chair scraping against the wood floor. "We should have listened to you."

"If you had—" Mom's tone softens.

"If we had…" His voice trails off.

Beside me, Nessa squeezes my hand. A tear slips from her left eye and she doesn't bother to wipe it away.

"Have you told Vanessa why her sister died?"

"No. She's still coping with the trauma." He made Vonnie's suicide sound so clinical. "We didn't want to scare her."

"She has a right to know that Yvonne was bipolar."

Nessa jerks her hand away from mine. She pushes open the door before I can stop her, leaving me standing there as she rushes in. Her dad is sitting on a leather sofa, his face in his hands. My mom sits beside him, her hand on his arm, comforting him.

"Vonnie was not bipolar!" Nessa shouts at my mom. "You're not a doctor. You don't know anything."

To my surprise, my mom just sits there and takes it as Nessa screams at her. Swear words and insults I've never heard before, not even while sitting in the ER waiting room on a Saturday night. Finally she winds down, weeping.

It's not her father who gathers her in his arms. He stands and moves behind the sofa as if to barricade himself from her pain.

No. When she collapses onto her knees, it's not her father who comforts her. Instead, it's my mom. She gathers Nessa into her arms and rocks her like a baby. "It's okay," she says over and over again. "Everything is going to be okay."

Finally Nessa looks up over my mom's shoulder at her dad. "Is it true? Vonnie was sick?" He nods. Slowly. "Why didn't you get her help? You're a doctor; you should have helped her."

"We tried. She started meds just a few days before—" His voice breaks and he swallows hard.

"Then you should've tried harder," Nessa says, climbing to her feet, fists on her hips. She turns to my mom. "You knew, you saw she was sick—"

"And I told your parents. Right away. I'm sorry, sweetie. But you need to tell your dad about what you're doing. Before it's too late."

Nessa steps away from my mom like Mom's dangerous. "I just wanted to feel better—normal—again. That's all."

Her dad comes from around the sofa. "Vanessa. What have you done?"

Mom speaks for her. "She's been taking antidepressants. Her moods have been up and down; they might be making her manic."

I remember what Jordan told my mom yesterday. I should have put the pieces together myself—instead I let myself enjoy Nessa's jubilance, never questioning it or trying to help her. Shame makes me look away and I accidentally catch Dr. Woodring's gaze. His face flushes and I'm not sure if it's with anger or embarrassment. After all, it sounds like my mom has better diagnostic skills than he does. And twice now she's tried to save his daughters.

"You know better than to take medicine not prescribed—" her dad thunders at Nessa.

Nessa doesn't back down. "All that talking crap of yours wasn't doing a damn bit of good. It hurt; it still hurts. Every. Single. Day. Besides, they weren't even prescription. Just over the counter. Herbal. All natural. Supposed to be safe."

Dr. Woodring gathers his breath and instead of yelling at Nessa again, he grabs her into a bear hug that lifts her off her feet. Tears rush down his cheeks. "Oh, baby, my baby. I'm sorry, so very sorry."

She grabs hold of him like he's the last lifeline on the Titanic and starts to cry as well. Pride floods over me as I watch the scene, trying to stay out of the way. Sure, Mom can be a pain in my butt. But she's damned good at what she does.

Mom finally notices me and nods for us to leave.

"Are they going to be okay?" I whisper as we let ourselves out.

She closes the door behind us and stops to look at the house for a moment. "Yes. I think so. Come on, you must be starving."

We head back to the car.

"We should invite Vanessa over to dinner some Friday," Mom says as she backs out and turns us toward home. "Give her folks the night off, get her out of that lonely house. Your dad can make his lasagna."

"Everyone loves Dad's lasagna." His ancient "family" recipe

involves Prego, four kinds of cheese, and a secret ingredient: fennel. I relax. Everything is going to be just fine. Nessa will get the help she needs, I have friends I can invite over to dinner, and we'll figure out some way to help Celina.

"Why were you and Nessa with those boys behind the gym?" Mom asks, breaking into my good mood.

I exhale. I've been waiting for her to ask about the fight, but it seems like she's more worried about me hanging out with boys. That's something new. Part of me likes it. That I could be the kind of girl a mom worries about. It's almost, well, normal.

"Nothing," I answer, striving for a combo of ennui and mystery. "Just hanging out."

Mom makes a poof noise as she exhales. Like she's resigned herself that, just like any other girl my age, I'll have secrets from her. "If you say so."

And that's it. No grilling, no lecture, nothing.

I turn away in the darkness of the car and smile at my reflection in the mirror. Excitement simmers through my blood and I can't wait to get home and call Nessa or Celina or Tony or Jordan— someone, anyone to share this feeling with.

I've done it. I'm a normal girl despite my broken heart.

42

My triumph is short-lived. As soon as Mom gets out of the car and doesn't wait for me as she heads into the house, her posture rigid, I realize she's upset. Not just mad or annoyed. Upset, capital U. I rush after her, Phil bouncing against my leg.

Then I draw up short. What am I supposed to apologize for? Having friends? Standing up to bullies? Trying to be normal?

I hang up my coat while I try to figure out the answer. I've worked so hard to get here, to take control of some small part of my life. Why should that upset her so much?

We end up barely talking during dinner. She says she has a headache and is going to bed early.

Mom's headaches are always stress-related, and since I'm always the stress, I make her a cup of her favorite herbal tea and take it upstairs to her as a peace offering. I figure I owe it to her after she helped Nessa. Not to mention Nessa's dad.

She's lying in bed, right in the middle since Dad isn't coming home tonight, looking pale and small and dwarfed by the pillows surrounding her on the king-sized bed. She has the lights turned off except for one small reading lamp and the TV is on but muted. And she has those frown lines around her mouth that always mean trouble.

"I feel like I've failed you," she surprises me by saying.

"Mom…" I trail off, unbalanced and with no idea how to respond. It's my job to make her feel better, only fair since she spends so much of her time doing that for me, but I'm not sure what's wrong tonight. My going to school seems to have upset every routine we have—including how we communicate.

"I try so hard." She closes her eyes as if I'm painful to look at.

I set the cup of tea on the bedside table and hover. Suddenly I know what it must be like for her taking care of me, frustrated when she can't make everything better or take the pain away.

"It'll be fine." I tell her what she always says to me when I'm the one lying sick in bed. "You'll see. If I can make it through this week then I can make it through the month, and then—"

She flinches as if she knows something I don't. "Honey." Her eyes pop back open. "I can't stand to see you getting your hopes up like this. You know you can never live a normal life, no matter how much you try."

Is she reneging on our deal? I'm supposed to have all week to prove myself. And look at me, I've been doing great. "But—"

"You'll only break your heart, dreaming of what could be. After seeing what almost happened to Vanessa because no one told her the truth, I think we need to talk."

"Could those medicines really have hurt Nessa?" I'm changing the subject; at least I hope I am.

She nods. "Yes. But once they're out of her system, she'll be fine. And now her parents can get her the help she needs."

"It was really brave of you to go in there, talk with Dr.

Woodring." I'm realizing that most people would never get involved, would never care as much as Mom does. Not here in the real world outside of the hospital.

"You're old enough now. You need to act like an adult and face reality." She hauls in a breath, not looking me in the eye. Something Bad is coming. "You know that even with the defibrillator surgery, odds are you won't live long enough to graduate."

No. I didn't know that. No one ever said that—they just said the internal defibrillator *might* prevent a sudden cardiac event. My cheeks go cold and my hands open and shut, trying to squeeze my blood back through my veins. No one has ever given me a time frame for my death before…but, in my heart, I know she's right. Ever since this summer and my last Set Back, I've been feeling like time's running out.

"Then maybe that's all the more reason for me to try to live like a normal girl now," I whisper, afraid my words will scurry away and hide from her scrutiny. "I mean, if there's no time to waste…"

Her sigh fills the room. She closes her eyes again. "We'll see."

Her words haunt me. I've never seen her so tired before, no matter how sick I was or how much was going on at the hospital.

I know she's not lying about my heart running out of time. Just the opposite. Finally, someone is treating me like a grown-up, telling me the whole truth. No one has ever done that before. Not the doctors or nurses. Not Dad.

Know what? The truth sucks.

THURSDAY

43

The next morning, Mom is back to her usual self, the poised and confident Nurse Killian. Except she's barely speaking to me. Barely even looking at me. As if she's already declared me dead.

Me, I'm a mess. I didn't get any sleep last night, spent it researching the defibrillator surgery that I already spent all summer researching before I refused it. Nothing's changed; there is no new medical miracle that will make the operation less dangerous or more effective. The only reason I have to change my mind is that it would make Mom happy.

Can I do that? Risk my life with a dangerous operation just to make her happy? Especially since we both know the ticking bomb that is my heart is running out of time, with or without the defibrillator?

She's done so much to keep me alive. Shouldn't I do this one thing for her?

The question haunts me all morning. Then, after homeroom, on my way to lunch, I run into Jordan heading away from the cafeteria. "Where are you going?"

"No use causing trouble with the jocks." He pushes through the doors leading to the space outside the gym where the fight was yesterday. Today we're the only ones here. He drops his pack and grabs a sandwich from it, eats standing up, back to the brick wall. "Want some?"

"No, thanks." We stand there in silence. I know my mom is waiting for me to get my lunch, will come looking if I'm late, but it's my first chance to talk to Jordan in private. And I could really use a guy's point of view. "Why was Tony here yesterday? It was our locker trashed and Celina's clothes."

We both stare at the trampled grass beside the equipment shed. He doesn't answer right away. He chews and thinks, chews some more. Then, finally, just when I'm about to give up on him altogether, he says, "Maybe because if you hadn't come along, it would have been him getting the treatment from the jocks."

"Why? He seems so nice."

The look he gives me is pitying. I think about what I've just said and I'm not sure which he found more pathetic: the fact that I thought nice was a good thing in a guy or the fact that I was so naive.

Then his expression softens. "You're a lot like him, you know."

Is that a good thing or bad? I'm not sure what to say.

"You both walk around like this place isn't real—" He falters, takes a moment. "It's like, like you've created some other school in your minds, a Smithfield High that doesn't exist except the way you imagine it. For you, coming here is an escape from the hospital."

More than that, it's an escape from loneliness, but I don't correct him. I don't want him to stop talking. It feels so good the way he thinks and considers each word, not to see if they're right, but weighing their impact on me, seeing if they're right for *me*. No one has ever talked to me like this before.

"For Tony," he continues, "it's like, even though he's one of the few kids who actually loves being in school—and believe me, that alone is enough to make him a target—but it's like he's already gone. Off to college and med school. Leaving Smithfield and the rest of us behind. He's run ahead, so far ahead that none of us can ever catch up."

Wow. Jordan's a poet. The way he talks, he sees the world in ways the rest of us can't even imagine.

He finally notices I'm staring at him. His gaze jumps up to meet my eyes, flicks back down to the ground, then bobs up again. Seems like he's used up his quota of words for the day and all he does now is stare into my eyes.

Could he be jealous? Of me and Tony?

A sudden thrill shoots through me as the possibilities swirl through my brain. Suddenly I imagine myself dancing with Jordan—a slow dance, the kind where you have to hold your partner tight. Like we're meant to be together. Like we will be together.

My heart skips, thudding me back down to earth.

Okay, maybe we don't have long. But we can make what little time we have together count, really count for something.

How can I tell him any of this?

I can't. Instead, I just stand there, letting the brick wall hold me up as he munches his bologna and mustard on white. I watch the way his jaw moves and almost swoon when he licks a dab of mustard off his thumb. Twice I open my mouth to say something—anything—but thankfully I shut myself up before I say the wrong thing.

The door beside us bangs open as Nessa storms out. "You guys ditched me!"

"We didn't mean to," I jump to Jordan's defense.

"First Celina goes home early. Then *you* don't answer any of my texts. Oh, and your mom's looking for you. I think you're in big trouble." She says the last in a singsong voice.

She's been avoiding me all morning—embarrassed, I guess, about what happened with her dad last night. Nice to see she's still talking to me.

"I've got to go." I grab my pack and Nessa slides into my spot beside Jordan.

He slants his gaze at her as if he just noticed her arrival. "Celina get home okay?"

She nods, fingers skimming her Pandora necklace. Her comfort item, the nurses would call it. "Texted me to bring her chemistry assignment."

"Drop it by. I can do it."

I'm surprised at his volunteering. But Mom's waiting, so I have to leave them. As I head down to her office, I wonder about Jordan.

It doesn't seem like him, abandoning us to our own defenses during lunch. Even if it might mean trouble with Keith Young and the rest of Mitch's friends, wouldn't it make more sense for him to stay with us?

Suddenly my stomach bottoms out. And it has nothing to do with being hungry. How could I be so stupid? There is no me and Jordan, no us. Except in my warped imagination.

As I hurry past the cafeteria doors, dodging the pummeling noise coming from inside, I realize Jordan knew Celina wouldn't be at lunch. That's what freed him from guard duty.

A normal girl might think that was a compliment, that he thought me and Nessa could take care of ourselves.

But Jordan doesn't make me feel normal. Not at all.

44

After lunch, I leave Mom's office thoroughly confused. She doesn't even comment on my being late; all she does is hand me a vitamin and watch me swallow it; then we eat in silence.

Gym is next. I tug Phil through the door to the girls' locker room. It takes me three tries before I find an empty locker on the lower level and by then the room is swarming with female voices chatting and yelling and squealing, soprano echoes pinging from every surface. Someone has their tunes cranked up—Lady Gaga—adding to the cacophony.

I don't get to actually participate in gym, but the rules are, even if you're sitting out, you still have to change into bright orange shorts and a Wildcats T-shirt and watch and learn the rules of whatever game they're playing. Sounds boring. I'm hoping I can sneak a book in with me. Neither Nessa or Celina have gym this period, so I'm surrounded by strangers.

The girls crowded around me are in various stages of undress. A few stripped their shirts and jeans off immediately and parade around in their underwear, not bothering with their gym clothes as they shout to each other or sing into pretend microphones and dance in time with the music. Others hide behind their locker doors as they quickly change, tugging their shirts over too-big or too-small busts.

I'm not really shy about my body—you get over being embarrassed about being naked real fast when you've got dozens of doctors and interns and students examining you. So I get my gym clothes out and strip at a normal pace. It's not until I finish slipping out of my shirt that I realize people are staring.

"You a cutter?" one girl asks, pointing to the scars that line my belly.

"Shut up, Lynette," someone else hushes her. "She's the sick girl, the one who died."

Tuesday I was able to sneak in without anyone noticing, but I guess word has spread since then. The crowd draws closer. All staring. At me and my scars.

I'm used to doctors and nurses looking, but their clinical assessments are very different from this group whose eyes gleam with curiosity and excitement. Like I'm here for their entertainment.

"What's that one from?" The first girl points to a short scar under my left rib cage.

"Feeding tube. They call it a PEG."

"And that?" someone else calls out.

"Exploratory laparoscopy."

A murmur thrills through the crowd. I'm sweating and no place to hide it, standing there in my bra and panties.

"What about the one on your leg?"

"Oh, that one." I try to act nonchalant. "That was a nasty one. Intraosseous infusion site got infected. Flesh-eating bacteria."

The last is an exaggeration; it was only regular staph, but they don't know that.

"Did it hurt?" Her voice is tinged with awe.

"Yeah," I reply with a shrug. No one has ever admired my scars before. Much less thought about the pain behind them. "Nothing compared to this one though." I pull down the waistband of my panties, just enough to show the top of my hipbone, and turn so they can see. "Bone marrow aspiration. Had two of those."

Appreciative murmurs ripple through the crowd. As much as I hate being the center of attention, it's kind of cool finding a way that my freakiness can be used to my advantage. Maybe I'll even make some more new friends.

Feels like my plastic bubble might be expanding. The thought makes me smile.

A whistle screams. "Let's go, ladies! I want everyone out on the floor by the time I count to ten!"

45

After what happened to Celina yesterday, I worried that gym class would be awful, but it's actually fun. I keep score while girls play badminton and a few of them even talk to me. And the afternoon looks good because next comes biology with Tony—and no Mitch.

I'm actually humming, off-key of course, as I stroll into biology.

"Hey, freak!"

It's Mitch. I stop inside the door, stunned. Ms. Blakely is nowhere to be seen. Neither is Tony. The other kids are either gathered around Mitch, watching something on his phone, or working way too hard to ignore us.

Mitch licks his lips like he's getting ready to eat something tastier than lunch. "Little Miss Priss. Hear you like it rough. Show us those scars of yours."

I blink, start to say something, stutter to a stop, and can only stare.

He holds up his phone as the others around him snicker. There, in full color, is a picture of me—in my bra and panties. I'm looking over my shoulder, tugging the waistband over my hip. And smiling. I'm actually smiling—excited to be accepted.

Idiot. My mouth goes dry as my heart stumbles. How could I

have been so dumb? Thinking those girls were interested in me. It was all a setup.

"Thought you were suspended, Kowlaski," Tony says, coming up behind me.

"Not anymore. Coach needs me on the field tomorrow and I can't play if I'm suspended."

I'm still frozen, unable to look up from a spot on the linoleum where someone must have spilled potassium permanganate, staining it a violent purple. The odd-shaped blob is mesmerizing—I wish I could melt right into it.

Behind me, Tony sucks his breath in. He's seen the picture. I feel his heavy stare land on me. My ears and neck light on fire as sweat trickles between my breasts.

"Yeah, not much of a rack, but her ass isn't too bad if you like them bony," Mitch says.

Tony takes a step toward him but even I know that's a bad idea. I grab Tony's arm and steer him to an empty bench across the room just as Ms. Blakely comes in. "Okay people, let's get started."

I hunch over my notebook, scribbling Ms. Blakely's lesson on plasmids, working hard to ignore the giggling and note passing and furious texting going on all around me. Tony nudges me gently with his elbow and points with his pen to his notebook.

Ignore them. You're better than they are.

I turn my head away. Easy for him to say.

46

One thing you learn fast in a hospital is how to vanish. Not physically. Mentally.

Like when you're lying on your belly, naked from the waist down, and they're shoving needles into your pelvis, sucking out bone marrow like high-paid vampires. Or during MRIs, you can't move a muscle without messing up the scan and there's noise like jackhammers going off all around you, so you just...*poof*...leave it all behind. Go someplace else.

My someplace is walking on a beach. I've never been to one in real life, so I let my imagination fill in the blanks based on the movies and books I've read. My beach is nice and quiet, warm sand beneath my feet, a gentle breeze.

And no one in a white coat or with a needle or scalpel anywhere within a hundred miles.

As Ms. Blakely drones on, I try desperately to escape to my beach. And fail. Maybe because this kind of pain is different from physical pain.

It invades every crevice of my mind, making me question everything. I feel betrayed and ashamed and guilty—what have I done? I don't know, but the feeling is there and I can't deny it—and angry and stupid and scared and, and, and...alone.

I'm sitting in a crowd of people and am desperately alone. Exactly what I fought so hard to come to school to avoid.

Is this how Lacey felt when she collapsed in the hallway and died? Except she wasn't alone. I was there with her and the nurses and doctors were all trying to help her.

No one can help me now.

I squeeze my eyes tight, salt stinging them. But I don't cry. Instead, I wonder why the hell I wanted so desperately to come to school, to try to be normal.

Tony nudges me as Ms. Blakely breaks us up into our teams to work on our genetics presentations. "Did you get your medical records?"

I haul them out of Phil's pack. His eyes bug when he sees how much there is to go through. "This is all you?" He starts leafing through the pages. "Don't suppose you have them digital so I can cut and paste into our report?"

"I have them on my Dropbox, but haven't had a chance to organize them yet. My mom put those together." I'm reluctant to touch the binder. Somehow it feels like touching a jar filled with someone's ashes. "You can keep those and I'll email you the shared folder from my Dropbox account."

He's totally focused on the project, doesn't even notice my monotone or that I'm pretty much checked out, too busy ignoring the stares and whispers aimed at me. "That works. I can work up a PowerPoint tracing the mutation back—your family's been tested, right?"

"My mom died right after I was born and my dad hasn't been

tested yet. But I can get a family history from him tomorrow night when he's back in town."

"Tomorrow night?" His head jerked up at that, back in the real world. "Aren't you going to the football game?"

I grimace, nodding to Mitch and his buddies. "Probably not."

"Don't let those goons stop you. Besides, they'll be the ones on the field getting the snot knocked out of them. Isn't that worth watching?" He pauses, twirling his pen again but this time fumbling it. "I was kinda hoping you might want to, maybe, if you're in the mood, go with me?"

I'm stunned. Amazed. Elated. Defying gravity and spinning into outer space. My heart thumps yes, my mind shouts yes, my stomach shivers in anticipation.

"Scarlet?" Ms. Blakely is standing behind us, holding a piece of paper in her fingers. "You need to report to the principal's office. Immediately."

"But—" I look at Tony. I can't say yes in front of a teacher.

"Now." She scoops up Phil and hands him to me. I grab my notes and stand. Tony is staring at me—everyone's staring at me, but Tony is the only one I care about. "Let's go, Scarlet."

"Call me," I mouth to Tony who nods. I'm trembling with excitement about tomorrow and hope he sees that in my smile.

Then I turn to leave and see the look on Ms. Blakely's face. She looks worried.

And it's contagious.

47

Mom is waiting outside Mr. Beltzhoven's office. She doesn't look happy—her face is pulled into so many directions that it's done something unimaginable, twisting her movie-star good looks into something ugly. She sees me, pivots like a soldier, raps twice on the door, then enters without waiting for him to answer.

The principal's office is tinier than I imagined. No windows. No books. No vanity wall, which surprises me. The only decor is a few cheap motivational posters. *Courage happens by chance, not choice. Life is a bowl of lemons, so get squeezing.*

They don't even make any sense. Maybe that's why I'm having such a hard time fitting into Mr. Beltzhoven's school.

He's sitting behind his desk, a middle-aged man who might once have been handsome before he gained a belly fatter than Santa's. He stands to nod to Mom then sits back down, a barren wasteland of fake oak veneer stretching out between us and him. He turns his smile on me and his teeth show. There's a piece of spinach caught between them. Other than that, his smile could have been the same as Mitch's. Hungry. With me a tasty little tidbit being served up to him. *Yum yum.*

"Curtis, we need to take action on this immediately," Mom

says as she takes her seat. She sits on the edge, chin high, hands folded in her lap. Her posture conveys royalty and superiority. It takes me a second to realize Curtis is Mr. Beltzhoven.

Mr. Thorne enters behind us and suddenly the room is way too crowded. He and Mom exchange glares of mutual antipathy. As if she thinks this is all his fault.

"I think it might be best for Scarlet if she waits outside," Mr. Thorne says.

Mom bristles at that. He has no idea who he's dealing with. Things are going to get ugly. "I know what's best for my daughter. And after the way you mishandled Yvonne Woodring's suicide last year, I'm surprised Curtis allows you to handle anything." Mom purses her lips, cherry blossom lipstick feathering into wrinkles. Uh oh.

Thorne's impervious to her insults. "Behavior like this is quite worrisome."

"He's right, Cindy," Mr. Beltzhoven finally speaks up, earning a glare of his own from Mom. "We need to nip this in the bud."

"Nip it in the bud? You mean stopping any further harassment of my daughter before I file civil suit against the school district? You have read the new federal antibullying mandates, haven't you?"

Mr. Beltzhoven doesn't back down, to my surprise. Instead, he looks awake, like now he's finally interested. "Have you seen the photos in question?"

"Of course not. I don't—"

He swivels his computer monitor in Mom's direction. There

I am larger than life—well, not literally, but it feels like those images on the screen fill the entire room.

One of them is zoomed in far enough that you can see the scars on my belly. Not to mention how small my boobs are. Jeez. Why couldn't the zoom at least make them look bigger?

The whole thing's surreal. I'm floating again, heading off for a long walk on my beach, dissociating from what's going on here, barely hearing the grown-ups as they decide my fate.

What I think or say is meaningless, so why bother? Just like being back in the hospital.

Thorne says, "I've talked with several students present in the locker room at the time. They all say Scarlet posed voluntarily. And you can see for yourself she's smiling for the camera."

I never even saw the cameras. But I know better than to say anything, preempt my mom. I can't stop staring at the me on the screen—she does look happy.

Which is really pitiful when you think about it.

Should've never trusted those girls…but how do we know who to trust?

After all, I really know no one here at school other than my mom. Some people seem nice, but how can you tell who's a friend and who's an enemy?

Take Tony. Maybe he's acting like a friend just to get a good grade on our genetics project. After all, who better to partner with than a girl like me who comes complete with her own medical records and genetic freakiness? Or Celina, Jordan, Nessa—there's no reason for them to be my friends. We're just assigned to peer support together, prisoners sentenced to the same cell block.

At least in the hospital you didn't have to worry about being betrayed. Hurt, lied to, bored to tears…yes. But no one pretended to help you just to make you suffer for their amusement.

Maybe I was better off without friends. Maybe Mom was right. Should've just stayed home. Alone. Until I die.

But…that's not how I really feel.

I'm sure it's what Mom will tell me once we're alone, that I should have listened to her, that I don't need any of my friends. That all I need is her.

She loves it when she's right and the rest of the world is wrong.

But I really *do* like Tony and Jordan and Nessa and Celina. It feels unbelievably good having someone besides my mom to talk to and share my day with.

All those wonderful, exciting, thrilling things that happened to me this week—more than in my whole life. Well, unless you count almost dying. But that's not exciting. Anyway, it's merely what everyone expects from me.

I'm going to miss being a sophomore freak.

Closest to normal I'm ever gonna get.

Of course Mom isn't letting Thorne get away with tarnishing my reputation. Or hers. "So," she says, leaning forward to turn the computer monitor off, "you're suggesting that my daughter somehow posed for pictures she didn't even know existed and then sent them to the entire school?"

Mr. Beltzhoven answers, "We're still trying to track down who sent them." Then his smile widens and I brace myself for something bad. "So far all we've found is an email address. It belongs to a student, but of course, we need to verify—"

"Verify, schmarify," Mom scoffs. "Who is it? Who did this to my daughter? And why?"

The principal rocks back in his chair. "Maybe Scarlet can answer that. You see, the email belongs to Celina Price."

48

"Celina Price?" Mom's voice is shocked with outrage. Her face flushes red and the veins in her neck pop. I've never seen her like this before—not even when the allergist accused me of sneaking Bad Foods to cause a reaction and get attention, as if a seven-year-old would think that way.

Why would Celina do this to me? Besides, she went home before lunch—she couldn't have taken the pictures.

But anyone could have forwarded them to the entire school.

My heart squeezes, about to burst with the pain of Celina's treachery. Could someone I thought was a friend be so cruel? Why? What was the point?

Then I remember what Mitch's buddies did to Celina yesterday. I know she didn't do it. We're both being set up.

"I knew that girl was trouble." Mom's on her feet, leaning into Mr. Thorne's personal space so far that he backs up until he hits the wall. She whirls on the principal. "Curtis, I hope you're taking appropriate actions."

"Of course. We are, we are. There will be a full investigation."

"By someone other than Mr. Thorne." Mom narrows her eyes at him. "You were Celina's counselor. I hold you responsible."

"Me? I can't—"

"You, Mr. Thorne." She turns and grabs my arm. "I'm taking my daughter home now. She shouldn't have to endure such a negative atmosphere of harassment and bullying. I'll be back to consult further with you, Curtis, before the pep rally. By then, I'm sure you'll both have a plan of action prepared to ensure those involved are adequately punished."

I barely have a chance to grab Phil as she hauls me out of there. I practically have to jog to keep up with her.

She's muttering, never a good sign. "I tried to help that girl and this is how she repays me. As soon as we straighten this out with the school, I'm going to have a word with her mother." Anger laces through her words like arsenic.

"You can't. Mrs. Price has cancer; she's dying."

She nods to the security guard at the front door as we push through it. "Dying is no excuse to let your children run wild." She glances back at the school. "Curtis better have a damn good apology waiting when I get back. Or I'm going to sue, I swear I will."

Oh boy. Suing is Mom's ultimate weapon. I've lost track of how many doctors we've changed because they pissed her off and she threatened to sue them. Thankfully she never has—at least not as far as I know.

She beeps the car unlocked then looks at me across the hood as if she'd forgotten I even existed. "This little experiment of yours is over. You're not coming back here. Ever."

49

Mom drops me at home with strict instructions to take two extra stress vitamins and heads right back for another meeting with Principal Beltzhoven. I watch her drive away; she doesn't even wave at me, she's so focused on getting her lipstick right as she steers one-handed. Pulling out all the stops—even using her looks to make sure she gets what she wants.

I'm glad I'm not going with her. I've seen her rampages before. She gets so obsessed about the slightest little thing—a test needing to be repeated or a nurse late with meds or, her all-time pet peeve, doctors who make her wait and then don't listen to her. As if she doesn't know her own daughter better than they ever could.

But this is new territory for her and I can see she's excited by the challenge. Defending my honor on her home field, in *her* school. Before she's done, she'll launch a single-mom crusade against the school, the football team, the entire district.

Then it hits me.

Celina's going to get caught in the fallout. She'll be the one to pay for this mess, not me. I'll be locked up here alone at home, safely away from the taunting and teasing.

Mitch and his friends have to be the real guilty parties. Because

I can't believe Celina did this. It makes no sense. Or maybe I just don't want it to make sense. I like having real friends.

Standing there, Mom's car long gone, I try to decide what to do next. Because the other big thing that makes no sense and I still need to sort out is what happened to my brother.

Maybe Mom has his records somewhere? Or at least a baby book?

I need to know his name, see his face…it's like there's been this big black hole of emptiness inside of me and now I know what I need to fill it.

I finally close the front door, shutting out the outside world. The sound echoes through the empty house and I hug myself against the cold. The thermostat is set at sixty-eight and it's a lovely September day, at least sixty degrees outside. Doesn't matter. On the inside, I'm freezing.

Eyeing the stairs, I finally get the courage to climb up to Mom's room. If there's anything about my brother, she'd keep it in there.

I start up. My hand's clamped to the banister so hard it rocks in its brackets. Three steps up and I hit the creak that sounds like a banshee wailing. That's the one that always wakes me when anyone goes up or down at night. It's also a great early warning system when I'm on my iPad and need a second to hide it.

Four steps up. I can't believe I'm going to do this. Invade my mother's privacy. But don't I have a right to know my own twin brother?

Five steps up. Sweat slips under my bra, sticking it to my skin.

Six steps up.

Seven.

The doorbell shatters the silence. My heart lurches, landing in my throat as I gasp. I'm trembling so hard the banister shakes with me. I can't let go.

The bell rings again. I turn. Through the sidelight, I see a guy. He raps his knuckles against the glass. He can see me as well.

It's Tony.

50

Stumbling down the steps, I run to the door and open it.

"What are you doing here?" I gasp, my voice still throttled with fear. What if it had been Mom?

"I was worried about you, so I ditched." He's doing that bouncing thing again, shifting his weight from one foot to the other like he'd rather be running.

I wave him inside and shut the door. And it hits me. I'm alone inside my house with a guy. The thrill of it warms me up, brings a smile so wide I can feel the dimple in my cheek stretching. Funny thing. My heart isn't pounding hard and fast anymore. It's as if Tony is my own personal pacemaker, steadying me. "You ditched? For me?"

"Sure thing. Do it all the time." He's the one blushing now.

"Liar. You never ditched in your life."

He shrugs with one shoulder, his backpack sliding down to his elbow, and grins. "So, you're okay?"

My turn to shrug. I lean against the door. We haven't made it past the slate floor of the foyer. But I have no idea where we're going or what we're supposed to do when we get there, so that's okay.

"I guess. Mr. Thorne said the pictures came from Celina." No more smiling. "I don't think I believe him though. I mean, I thought she was my friend."

His face went serious. "That's what I came to tell you. I don't think it's Celina either."

"Why not?"

"First of all, I doubt she would open a Hotmail account under *CelinaPriceSexy69*."

"Yeah. That doesn't sound very smart." And if there's one thing that I know, it's that Celina is smart.

"Plus, when did she have time? Your mom told you what happened to Celina third period, right?"

I shake my head. "My mom doesn't tell me anything."

"Someone pushed Celina down the steps behind the auditorium."

"Is she all right? Who did it?"

"She was pretty banged up. Thankfully your mom was there. She patched her up and sent her home for the day. She was pushed from behind and no one saw who did it."

"Mitch. Or one of his friends."

"Could have been anyone." He scuffs his feet. "I'm glad she's all right, but I hope she stays out of school for a while. It's only going to get worse."

"Why? Why do they torment her like this?"

He blows his breath out, which seems to collapse him down to my size. We still don't go into the living room—too formal—instead, I lead him into the kitchen where we perch on barstools at the counter, side by side.

"It's because of her mother," he finally says. "Before she got sick, Mrs. Price arrested Mitch's father for dealing meth and stealing money from his work. Even after she was sick, she left the hospital to testify at his trial. Now he's in Rockview, serving three years."

"But she was just doing her job," I protest, angry on Celina's behalf. Not to mention her poor mom.

"Maybe. But Mitch and his brother didn't see it like that. They lost their house, had to move into his aunt's basement. To get back at her, his brother tried to rob and beat up Celina's father while he was working nights at Sheetz. Mitch was probably in the getaway car, but drove off before the cops got there. So now his brother is in jail. His trial is in a few weeks."

"Oh my God. And Celina's dad?"

"Fine. A customer called the police and—" He pauses, suddenly looking away and shifting in his seat. "Intervened."

Silence as I process everything. I might not be good with a crowd, but I'm pretty good reading people one on one. "That's why they're targeting you as well. You were the customer. You called the cops and helped Mr. Price. You and he are witnesses against Mitch's brother."

Still not looking at me, he nods his chin up and down in a single jerk. "I'm sorry you got caught in the crossfire."

A few silly pictures of me seem like nothing to worry about. Not compared to physical assaults and threats of violence. Which would only get worse as the trial date grew near. Now I understand what Jordan was talking about during lunch.

"Thanks for coming over." It seems empty; I should be offering him more than words, but I have a hard enough time even coming up with a few words.

"No problem. You're only a few blocks from school and I cut through the soccer fields, made it even shorter." He shifts in his seat. "I was going to walk over to Celina's and check on her, but I thought maybe—" He leaves it hanging. "She actually lives just around the corner—my house is down the block from hers. But if it's too far or you're tired or…"

Again, leaving it to me. I am tired, but not in the way he thinks. Mentally tired, not physically. Mom won't be home from the pep rally for another hour at least. But she has this habit of calling to check on me at the worst times—it's why I can never sneak out for walks or anything when I'm home alone.

"Mom might call. If I don't pick up, she'll flip." It sounds lame even to me.

"She calls on this line?" he asks, pulling the base unit close to him. "That shouldn't be a problem. You can forward it to your cell."

"I can?"

"Sure. I'll show you." I watch as he punches in a few buttons and adds my cell number.

A world of possibilities dangles before me. My umbilical cord finally cut.

"Tony, you're a genius." I slide off the stool and give him a hug. He tenses at first then squeezes back. Tentatively, as if he's as surprised as I am and not quite sure how to do this either. "Let's go."

51

A few of the hospitals I've been in have outside areas for the kids. My favorite is Children's Hospital of Pittsburgh. The whole hospital is brand new, built entirely with kids in mind, so no matter how sick you are, you can still be a kid. I love it there.

I'd sit outside watching the sun throw my shadow around and do nothing but breathe. Not air that's been sterilized and deodorized and purified. Real air.

Invariably I'd have a Set Back or Near Miss or Something Bad would happen and I'd end up tied to a hospital bed, stuck inside again. But those few moments outside, under the sun—that was the feeling I tried to recreate when I built my imaginary beach to escape to.

Now, thanks to Tony, I'm living it.

I have many words to describe how I feel but none of them are the right word. Maybe because I'm feeling too much.

Thrilled, terrified, trepidatious, tingly, thunderstruck…the alliteration is addictive. I want to take each feeling, every sensation, and taste it like a forbidden delicacy rolling across my tongue.

Excited. Elated. No. Exhilarated. That's the best of the bunch. The way I can't feel my feet actually hitting the ground and have to keep looking down to make sure I'm not floating. The feeling of being too big for all that is inside me, yet too small to contain it. Like some kind of emotional Zen koan.

Once when I was little, my dad took me to the park (one of our secrets from Mom) and we rode the teeter-totter. I scooted way back and he was forward far enough that at one point, with a lot of work, we balanced perfectly, both suspended, our legs dangling—his bent to keep his feet off the ground. We never found that magic tipping point again, but somehow for those few seconds, the world stopped long enough for me to see Everything. Not with my eyes, with my soul.

The universe sang to me. Yes, if you shift your weight and work hard enough, you can find the answer to anything. Everything is possible. Even a little girl who weighs next to nothing suspending her father in midair.

Then one of us shifted or exhaled or blinked and Dad was back on the ground, his weight holding me hostage.

But for that one moment…

That's how I feel now. Walking beside Tony, my cell phone in my pocket and Phil inside Tony's pack, the fresh scents of fall swirling around us, intoxicating.

Each breath leaves me dizzy.

Alive. That's the word I really want. For the first time in ages, I don't feel numb or distant or like I'm a disease instead of a girl.

I feel alive.

52

A re you okay?" Tony asks, breaking the spell.
I pull my gaze down. I'd been walking with my chin aimed up so I could watch the way the breeze makes the treetops rustle as if they're dancing a waltz. My mouth is hanging open because I'm breathing through it—the better to savor every smell and taste—making me look like a total dork, I'm sure.

Straightening my posture and trying to appear somewhat normal, I nod. "I'm fine. Why?"

"You just had a funny look on your face, that's all. Anyway, I was saying. About the bio project. I couldn't find your genetic test results in the folder your mom gave you."

"Hmmm…" I'm distracted by a squirrel in a neighbor's yard, busy taunting a cat pressed against a window. "Try the online files. And while you're at it, could you keep track of any mentions of my twin brother? I want to learn more about him."

He stops. I stop. "You have a brother? A twin?"

He glances back at my house as if expecting to see someone waving for help, locked up in the attic or something.

"He died." How can I sound so matter of fact? But it's hard to know what to feel when I can't remember him outside of my dreams. "When we were little. My father never told me about him. I guess he was trying to protect me. I don't even know his name."

His eyebrows draw together like they're trying to fight their way off his forehead. "Your twin brother died? And no one ever told you his name?" His tone makes me stop. All my life, I've been surrounded by death. In a way, I understand it better than life. But Tony's words make me realize how much I've lost.

Blinking hard and fast, I start walking away so he won't see my face. With his long legs, he catches up easily. He touches my arm, lets his hand slide down, and intertwines his fingers in mine. I didn't realize how cold my hand was until his flesh warms it.

"I'm sorry. I had no idea."

I take a deep breath and pull myself together. "Neither did I. Not until I began reading those records. Guess these past few days have had something good come from them." I glance at our hands. More than one thing good.

"You talk like you're not coming back."

We start walking again. I take my time, but there's no easy way to say it. "My mom says I have to stay home. No more school."

"Your mom says." He stops again. Faces me. "What do you say?"

I blink in surprise. No one ever asks me. What I want to do with my body, what I want to do with my life. But I know the answer. Without hesitation, I say, "I want to stay. I want to go to school. Most of all, I don't want Mitch and those guys to think they've won."

That coaxes a smile from him. "Then we'll just have to change your mom's mind."

Hah. He doesn't know Mom. But I don't ruin the moment by saying so. This magical stroll with Tony has taken me into the realm of fairy tales and daydreams; I'm in no rush to return to reality.

"So, you've met Celina's mom?" I'm asking more than that. Tony understands.

"She's pretty cool. You'd think with everything going on—worrying about Celina and Cari, that's Celina's sister, and their dad and the stress of her job and being sick and now, well knowing that she'll be gone and they'll have to figure stuff out without her—you'd think she'd be like emptied out with everything, but instead it's like she's shrunk on the outside but bigger on the inside." He shakes his head as if irritated he can't explain it. But I know exactly what he's talking about. It's how daring to leave the house with Tony makes me feel. "You'll see. I try to visit when I can—usually on weekends so I can help Mr. Price. He's pretty quiet. I'd say he's in shock, but he's been like that ever since I met him over the summer."

"You didn't know them before? I thought you were neighbors."

"I knew Celina—we've been in the same school since kindergarten. But I never met her dad or sister. Her mom came by the school a few times. Safety programs, stuff like that. I'd heard rumors about her sister. She's never been in the same school with us except for when we were in elementary school. Sad to say, but back then we teased Celina about having a retard as a sister. None of us understood about autism or thought about how she felt." He scuffed his foot against the sidewalk. "Once we were in junior high, we all pretty much forgot about Cari. Celina kinda, I don't know, blossomed. Got solos singing in the choir, was top of her class, won the science fair. But then when her mom got sick, well, it was like she was juggling but couldn't keep track of the balls any longer. Everything came crashing down."

We turn the corner, walking in unison, not saying anything. Still holding hands, which I am definitely enjoying. I like how Tony is usually so quiet, but when we're alone he opens up to me. It makes me feel special. If he's like this around other people, I don't want to know.

My phone rings, breaking the spell.

I have to let go of Tony's hand to fish the cell out of my pocket. It rings again. Not good. Mom expects me to pick up right away when she calls.

"Hello?" I answer just before it rings a third time.

"It's me," Mom says. I cup my hand over the microphone, hoping there's nothing that gives it away that I'm outside. "Wanted to let you know that I'm going to be late. Did you take your medicine?"

She's talking about the vitamins. Which I haven't taken since yesterday, much less the extra doses she told me to take. "Of course," I lie. "I'm going to take a nap, so no rush on dinner."

There are sounds of the band warming up. The pep rally must be getting started. "Eat without me. I need to talk to Curtis, and then I'm not sure. This is all so stressful. I might take you in to see Dr. Cho tomorrow. Maybe Monday. Do you think you can last that long?"

She talks like I'm dying. Well, I am—but I feel fine right now. I guess when any little stress usually throws me into a Set Back, she's conditioned to take no chances.

"I'm okay. Let's see how I do over the weekend." I know there's no sense denying her a trip to the doctor, no matter how unnecessary, so I try to deflect her. "I figured out that it wasn't Celina who sent the pictures."

"I did as well. I'm still not sure she didn't play some role in the matter, but after some checking around, I'm pretty sure I know who's behind it."

"Mitch Kowlaski." Whoops. I should know better than to act like I know more than she does. She hates that. "I'm guessing," I add hastily.

"Don't worry. I'll get to the bottom of this and take care of everything. No one is going to do this to us and get away with it. Trust me on that. You just take your medicine and rest."

She hangs up without saying good-bye. I stare at the phone. I'm used to Mom taking control of my life, but does she have to treat me like I'm still a baby?

"Your mom?" Tony asks.

"Yeah. She's trying to run my life for me." I sigh. "As usual."

"Sounds like my folks." He rolls his eyes. "Everything I do, they want to know all about it. And when I tell them, all they do is talk about what it was like when they were kids. Like the world hasn't changed in twenty-five years? Get real."

We stop in front of a large Victorian painted lavender-gray with a wide porch, complete with swing. A white picket fence and archway with a lovely trellis covered in vines leads to the walk up to the house. It reminds me of my bedroom—nothing fancy but a lot of love went into everything.

The lawn is filled with curving plant beds, purple and gold pansies blooming along the edges, and the porch steps are lined with pots of bright colored mums. It's the kind of house where you expect a grandma holding a tray of freshly baked cookies to greet you at the front door.

Only as we walk up to the front door, we hear screaming.

53

Despite lugging Phil, Tony makes it to the front door before I do—those long legs of his. He rings the bell then barges inside before anyone has a chance to answer. I get there a few seconds later.

The foyer opens onto a wide curving staircase with a large living room on the left and a dining room on the right. The screaming is still going on. Nonstop shrieks that make the hairs on my arms quiver.

It's coming from upstairs. I run up just in time to see Tony go through a door at the end of the hall.

I clutch my phone, ready to call 911, and follow him.

It's a small square room on the back corner of the house with wide windows on two walls reflecting light through hanging prisms, casting rainbows on the dove gray walls. There's a mattress on the floor in the corner and a beanbag chair. And that's it. No other furniture or decoration.

Tony stops inside the door. Inside are Nessa and Jordan. In the center of the floor, a girl with short dark hair is attacking Celina whose left arm is in a sling. But it's not Celina screaming bloody murder, despite the scratches on her neck. It's the girl.

She's whip-snake skinny. And fast, writhing out of Celina's

free hand and attacking her—no, not her, she's desperately clawing at the sling, seems terrified of it. Celina's trying to extricate herself from both the girl and the sling but has hopelessly tangled herself.

Jordan begins circling slowly, crooning a low song, until miraculously everything goes quiet.

The girl's head whips around as she forgets about Celina and tracks Jordan. He circles closer and closer, like a snake charmer, and ends up sitting Indian-style across from Celina. He holds his arms open wide, still humming, and the girl crawls off Celina and onto Jordan's lap. He hugs her tight—so tight it looks uncomfortable, but the girl's expression goes from panicked to calm as he rocks her and keeps humming.

He catches Celina's eye and nods slightly as the girl exhales a long, soulful sigh and closes her eyes.

This must be Celina's little sister. Caridad.

Tony helps Celina to her feet. She seems unaffected by the emotion that rocks the room. I can't imagine what it would be like to live with this intensity every day. Two minutes of it and I'm covered with sweat, my heart thudding. Then it skips a few beats and my vision goes dizzy. Last thing I need is to have a Close Call, not here, not in front of my friends.

I back out of the room and lean against the wall, gathering my breath and willing my heart to slow down. Tony left Phil downstairs by the door; should I try to make it down there so if I collapse I'll be closer? My vision is filled with an image of Tony and Jordan seeing me half-naked as they strip my top off and attach Phil's electrodes, my body writhing as electricity shoots through it.

No way. Not going to happen. I'd rather die. After a few seconds of deep breathing from my belly, my heart obeys and returns to a nice, steady rhythm. For now.

I hate it when Mom's right. She was worried about exactly something like this happening.

Nessa, Tony, and Celina follow me into the hall. Celina leads us down to another bedroom, this one furnished with bed, dresser, bookcases, desk, and bright yellow walls covered in Impressionist prints. She collapses on the bed. Tony grabs a tissue from the box on the dresser and pats the bleeding scratches on the side of her neck.

While Nessa whirls on me, hands on her hips, leaning forward, standing between me and Celina. "Come to spy for your mom, have you?"

54

I stand there, speechless—just like the first time I met Nessa. Tony takes a step forward, placing himself between us, as if he's expecting more than words from her.

"You have no right—" he starts.

Nessa whirls on him. Her hands are balled into tight fists. "Don't give me that crap. Her"—she jerks her chin at me— "mother is making Celina's life hell."

Emotions collide inside me, threatening to tumble me off balance. I lean against the doorjamb, trying to sort out what's going on. "Why are you so angry at my mother? All she's ever done is try to help."

"As if you don't know—"

Celina closes her eyes. "Stop it," she says, her voice not loud but carrying the impact of a slap. "Stop it, both of you." She opens her eyes again. "Tony, would you and Nessa check on my mom? I'd like a minute with Scarlet."

Nessa balks but Tony takes her arm and they head out together. She glances back at us, her face filled with anger and concern. I'm guessing the anger is for me.

"I'm sorry about your arm," I tell Celina, not sure what else to say.

"Broken collarbone. Just what I didn't need." She pauses. "I'm sorry about those pictures."

"Just what I didn't need." My joke fails. "I know you didn't send them."

She shakes her head and makes a noise that's half laugh, half sigh. "Mitch Kowlaski. Idiot."

"Maybe if they lose tomorrow night, they'll finally suspend him. Make life easier for you." I want to ask about my mom but have no idea where to start.

She slides over a bit and I sit down beside her on the bed. Unlike my pretty-in-pink room, Celina's room feels grown-up, sophisticated—no, elegant, that's the word. Cheerful and bright but not childish at all. The artwork is inexpensive but carefully chosen. The books are many of the same classics I'd read as an escape from the hospital and hours of boredom.

"Life won't be easier for you if Mitch is gone?" she surprises me by asking.

I shake my head. "Mom says I'm not going back to school." I sound like a whiny baby and hate it.

"About your mom—"

"Why were you so upset after she sent you home this morning?" I blurt out.

She doesn't look at me. Instead, she focuses on undoing the strap to her sling and easing her arm out of it. She's wearing a hoodie, of course, and unzips it, awkwardly sliding free of it using only one arm. Without the bulky sweat jacket, I see that she's not really as fat as I thought when we first met—she just has layers upon layers of thick clothing, as if she needs the extra bulk for protection.

I wonder for a moment if she's pregnant or trying to hide an eating disorder. I'd met girls at the hospital with anorexia who dress like Celina.

Under the hoodie is a crew neck sweatshirt. She slides her good arm out, pulls it over her head, then gritting her teeth, slides her injured arm free.

Beneath that is a flannel shirt, oversized. She pushes the left sleeve up. Her skin, that golden, flawless skin I'd so admired, is covered with bruises of various ugly colors: iridescent green, yellow, angry red, blue, purple. Between the bruises are scratches and scabs in various stages of healing.

I gasp. Even when I roomed with cancer patients who had poor healing and easy bruising, I'd never seen anything like this. Her arm looks like a crazed psycho killer is using her for his canvas of violence.

"The rest of me looks as bad." She's so calm, staring at me as if waiting for something.

"Celina." I gulp. This is obviously the secret my mother had discovered. "Who did this to you?"

"You're just like your mom. Jumping to conclusions. Assuming the worst."

"This isn't the worst?"

"Look. This is nothing. Not compared to what my folks have to deal with. But your mom won't believe me. She threatened to call Child Services, report us, have me removed, Cari committed to some hellhole."

That didn't seem like such a bad idea if it kept Celina from getting hurt. "Are you safe here?"

"Of course." Her tone made it clear that no amount of arguing would change her mind.

"Who takes care of Cari when you're at school?"

"She goes to a special daycare facility. That's why I can never stay late after school. They bring her home at three-thirty. Before she got sick, Mom used to pick her up, but now—"

Now everything's changed. I understand that, all too well.

"Is Cari always like that?" I nod toward the closed door beside us.

"Not usually. But since Mom's been home and moved into a room downstairs, hospice workers coming and going, all of Cari's routines have been upset. It's not her fault. She can't help it. Usually I can calm her down." She picks up the sling, dangles it before her like it's contaminated. "Until something like this freaks her out. She didn't even know who I was. My own sister can't recognize my face."

There are tears in her voice. She flings the sling across the room. It knocks against the globe on top of her bookcase, making it twirl and teeter.

If I hadn't seen it for myself, I never would have believed that a skinny twelve-year-old like Cari could inflict such damage. I look at her arm again. "But—do your folks know?"

"No. And we're keeping it that way. Which is why I need your mom to mind her own business."

I can't stop staring at her bruises. Was it really the best thing, not getting her and her family the help they needed?

Mom talks about that all the time. Her responsibilities as a mandated reporter. How hard it is to make a judgment call. Weighing the best interests for her patient and putting them first. She always goes to bed early with a headache and Dad pampers her extra when he's home after she's had to report an abuse case. Says it's the toughest part of her job.

Now I understand what she's talking about.

How do I know what's best for Celina or her family? I barely know her and don't know her folks at all.

She shakes off my silence, rolling her sleeve back down. "Fine. If you won't help me, I'll find another way. Your mom isn't the saint she makes herself out to be."

I jerk so hard the mattress bounces. "What are you talking about?"

She shrugs her good shoulder. "There's stuff I've heard. A guy she got bumped off the basketball team, telling him she heard a murmur and that he needed a heart workup. Coach benched him, and by the time the doctors all decided he was okay to play, the season was over. He lost his scholarship because of it."

"So my mom's a little overprotective of her patients. After dealing with me, surely that's understandable. Better safe than sorry."

There's pity in her eyes. "You really believe that, don't you?"

Before I can answer, the door bangs open. My mom is standing there. Glaring at both of us.

55

"Mom, what are you doing here?" My blood flees my face, cascading down in an icy waterfall all the way to my toes. Shit, shit, shit. How the heck am I going to get out of this?

"What are *you* doing here?" She isn't shouting. Which is very, very bad. "Conspiring with her?" Contempt drips from her voice as she glares at Celina.

"Conspiring?"

Celina steps forward. "You have no right being here. You need to leave. Now." Her voice sounds like a cop's voice. Steady and filled with command.

"Did you think I wouldn't know?" Mom asks me, holding up her cell phone, which has a map of Celina's street on it. "Your phone led me here."

"I can explain—"

"I don't care. You're coming with me." She yanks my arm and hauls me out to the landing. Nessa and Tony are at the bottom of the steps, gaping at us. "You," she points her finger at Celina, "might want to start packing. I'm making that call to Child Services."

"No," Celina and I protest simultaneously.

She pays us no mind, pulling me down the steps. We shove past Nessa and Tony, and are out the door before I can blink.

"Mom. You don't understand."

"No." She lets go of my arm and whirls on me. "You don't understand. You have no idea who you're dealing with, young lady. I always knew this day was coming, but—" She shakes her head as if her words have fled her and she can't find them.

Finally she gets into the car, which she left running in the driveway. I risk a last glance toward the house. Tony, Nessa, and Celina are all staring at me.

I wave good-bye, wondering if I'll ever see them again.

56

During the short drive home I try to explain, try to protest, try to apologize. Anything to breach the wall of silence.

I fail.

When she gets out of the car, she doesn't even look back at me as she stalks into the house. By the time I get inside, she's hung up her coat and is stomping up the steps. Leaving me at the bottom, standing silent in disgrace.

Less than a week at school and I've found and lost four friends, humiliated Jordan while making blood enemies of the entire football team, ruined Tony's biology grade, possibly destroyed Celina's life and her family's reputation, and alienated my own mother.

Where's my plastic bubble to hide in when I need it?

I stand there, self-pity and remorse and guilt washing over me, leaving me shivering as shadows darken the foyer. Looking up the stairs after my mother has long since disappeared.

In the hospital, I never had to make decisions. Everything was planned out for me. What I wore, what I ate and drank and when, where I went, who I saw.

Now, here in the real world with real people getting hurt, I feel like I'm hanging over a precipice, barely clinging to sanity. Is this how being a normal teenager is meant to feel? Like there's no clear right or wrong and every step you take, someone is going to be hurt or disappointed or angry with you?

If it is, maybe I don't want to be a normal girl. Maybe I want to crawl back into my safe hospital bed, pull the rails up so I can't accidentally tumble out, and huddle under the covers.

Let the grown-ups who know what they're doing make all the decisions. It's kept me alive so far.

57

I drag my backpack—now empty of Phil, but I can't even think about little details like that right now—into my room and curl up on my island of pink ruffles and try to decide what to do. Seems like anyone I could talk to wouldn't want to talk to me. And what could they do anyway?

I squint my eyes shut, trying to conjure my little dream boy, my twin...but he's not coming to my rescue either.

There's only one person who can fix all this. The same person who solves all of my problems for me. Mom.

I look around my room. My bubble is painted pink, I realize. This is the place I'll always run to when the rest of the world is too much to handle. And me, with my broken heart, I can only handle so much. I'm not meant for high school or the cruel real world. Far better to stay here safe and sound, surrounded by people who can take care of me.

Growing up, being normal—it's all highly overrated. And way too much work.

I could never do what Celina does. Much less handle a sister's death like Nessa has. Or watch over the three of us like Jordan. Hell, I can't even force myself to ask my Mom the questions I need answered for my biology assignment. Sorry, Tony, but it's not going to happen. My twin might always remain a mystery.

I'm finally learning my limits. They're bounded by fake wood paneling and pink lace curtains.

It's not so bad. Not really.

I climb out of bed and shuffle up the steps. Knock quietly on Mom's door, almost hoping she's already asleep.

"Come in," she answers. At least she's talking to me.

My hand trembles as I turn the knob. I push the door open and stand on the threshold. Mom has the lights off, but the TV's on, the volume turned low. She's snuggled in her favorite sweater, the dark green one Dad says matches her eyes, lying on the bed.

"I'm sorry." My words come out choked with tears. She keeps staring at the TV as if I'm not there. I take a deep breath and step inside. "Mom, please. I'm so sorry. You were right."

That gets her attention. She turns her face toward me, the TV throwing shadows of color across it. "Right about what?"

Her voice is so cold it makes me shiver. I cross my arms over my chest in an attempt to get warm again. I take another step; now I'm halfway to her bed. Swallow my fear and answer. "Everything. You were right about everything. I should never have tried to go to school. I should stay home."

She nods and waits expectantly.

I know what she wants to hear. I bite my lip, not sure I can go through with it. My heart is thudding like the cops on TV, trying to bust down a door, rescue a killer's victim, open up, open up!

"You were right about my surgery." There I said it. "I should get the defibrillator implanted."

Sealing my fate, tying my future to a machine shocking me from the inside out, satisfies her. She springs off the bed and gathers me in her arms like she's just rescued me from something awful. "Honey, I was so worried! You have no idea—I thought you'd die before we could help you. You'll see, it will change everything. We can buy some time for you, sweetheart. And I'll take care of you, just like I always have."

She's hugging and kissing me and I feel like a little kid again.

Mom's voice fades and all I hear is the sound of clowns cackling. I blink and look over her shoulder and realize it's only a stupid TV commercial.

"There's just one thing," I say. My tone is timid, pleading, but Mom goes rigid and draws back, holding me at arm's length, eyeing me suspiciously. "Could you please not call Child Services? Give Celina and her family a little more time? Her mom doesn't have very long."

Anger flashes across her face like summer heat lightning announcing a storm's arrival. But then she smiles—the fake smile she uses on doctors when she's not too happy with them, but right now I'll take any smile. "Of course, dear. Whatever you say."

She hugs me again. "I'll call Dr. Cho tomorrow and we'll schedule the surgery for Monday—I doubt he can operate over the weekend. Oh, wait until your father hears; he'll be so happy. I'm proud of you for realizing you were in over your head, Scarlet.

There are some decisions you need to trust your parents to make for you."

Problems solved, world back in balance, safe bubble of existence intact.

So why do I feel so empty inside?

58

Mom makes her version of a celebratory feast—egg-white omelets with spinach, feta cheese for her, no feta for me; I get tofu instead. I eat it, wishing my dad were already home, wishing he'd cooked—I can't eat his lasagna, but I love to smell it baking and watch the gleam of appreciation and enjoyment fill his face when he takes his first bite.

I think maybe the tofu has gone bad because everything tastes like metal and even after two glasses of water I can't get it out of my mouth.

Mom doesn't notice that I don't finish and dump half my omelet in the trash. She's too busy making her Lists.

Who to call: school, insurance, admissions coordinator, Dr. Cho's nurse, church (to start a prayer circle for me), stop the newspaper since we'll be gone a few days, hold the mail.

What to pack: clothes for three days for her, one day for me (I'll be in a hospital gown), nightgown, robe, toiletry, shower sandals (she thinks hospitals are filthy and honestly, she's not wrong), her laptop, cell phone and charger, address book (just in case Something Bad happens and all the friends and relatives need to be called on short notice), notebook and pens to record everything the doctors say, medical records (although the hospital already has everything), my vitamins, a list of Good Foods and Bad Foods.

"You're not on your period, are you?" she asks, gnawing on her pencil.

"Mom. No."

"Good. If something goes wrong, they might need to use your femoral artery for a cath."

I wish I hadn't eaten the little bit of omelet I had. My stomach churns enough acid that the metal taste is finally burned away. The last time I had a cardiac catheterization, the site bled like crazy and I had a bruise the size of a tennis ball—a hematoma, they called it. They almost had to take me into surgery to repair the site, said I must have loosened the pressure dressing and tore it open while I was asleep.

Thank God Mom was there. She stopped the bleeding and saved me from another surgery.

"Do you think that's a possibility?" I ask, crossing my fingers below the table where she can't see them.

"Sure. I want them to do EPS studies to make sure the defibrillator works properly. And I'll need to check my research from the summer—they might insert the electrodes through the femoral artery or maybe it's the jugular. I'll talk with Dr. Cho and let him know which approach I prefer."

The one with the least amount of scars and chance for things going horribly wrong is my vote. Not that I get a vote anymore. I've sacrificed that right in order to save Celina's family. It was worth it. I hope.

"I'm tired. I think I'd better go to bed," I mumble.

"Good night, sweetheart. Remember, you can sleep in tomorrow since you'll be staying home." She gives me an absent-minded kiss and returns to her list making.

I shuffle off to my bedroom feeling achy and sore as if I'd already had the surgery.

59

Curled up on my bed, I send my first text ever. It's to Nessa, since I doubt Celina is talking to me.

Asked Mom. No Child Svs. Tell C.

A few minutes later she sends: Great! CU at sch? Or game? XOXO

There's a good chance they'll never see me again. I roll my eyes at myself—could anyone be more self-pitying? Talk about wallowing.

Maybe.

But even as I send it, I know it's not true. There's no maybe. I'll never get to the game tomorrow night. Never get to any game.

My phone buzzes and this time it's Celina. She's sent a photo: a self-portrait of her grinning a big, fat goofy grin as she and Cari hold up a beautifully colored sign that says *Thank You!* Cari is smiling as well, even though she's not actually looking anywhere near where the camera is aimed.

I stare at the picture for a long time. It makes me feel warm and toasty inside. That I could make someone so happy, help them so much. It feels good in a way I've never felt before. Like I matter. No, like what I do matters.

I lock the photo so it can't be erased accidentally. I know I'll look at it again, especially come Monday when the doctors have me naked and shivering on their table, getting ready to cut.

A quiet tap at my window startles me. My room, since it used to be the den, has French doors leading out onto our back patio, but they're always locked and never open. The tap comes again.

I slide out of bed, one hand clutched to my chest. I feel silly, it's probably just the wind, but I'm scared and excited all at the same time. Because I really don't think it is the wind.

I pull back the curtain. It's Tony. He sees me, holds up Phil, and smiles. It takes me a few tries to unlatch the door and undo the deadbolt. But suddenly it's open and the night air rushes in, swirling around us both like invisible music.

"Thought you might miss this," he says.

His voice is louder than I'd like. Mom's room is upstairs and on the other side of the house, but still. "Come in."

Then he's inside and the door is closed and I have a guy in my bedroom.

Okay, calm down, calm down. What would a normal girl do?

I have no clue.

He hands me Phil, reminding me that I am in no way a normal girl. I'm a very abnormal girl. Abby Normal, my dad would joke. *Young Frankenstein* is one of his favorites.

Dad would *not* be happy to find Tony in my room.

"Thanks," I say. Lame! I stash Phil out of sight in my backpack like a thief hiding evidence.

"I'm sorry about what happened this afternoon." He looks around my room, eyes widening a little as he takes in the fifty-one flavors of pink. His gaze ends up back on me, head tilted a little as his weight shifts. He's watching me like he expects something, only I don't know what. "Want me to apologize to your mom? Tell her it was all my fault?"

I shake my head. Last person I want to be thinking of—or have Tony thinking of—right now is Mom. "No thanks. I took care of things. Everything is fine." Except for the part where I go in on Monday to be sliced and diced.

"Oh. Good." He looks down at the floor, notices his feet shuffling and focuses on them. They stop. End up pointed at me instead of the door. "Could I ask you a few questions? About our biology project. There's a few things that didn't make sense."

I appreciate the change of subject. And it's only fair that I help him salvage his grade since I won't be going back to bio. Of course, I don't tell him that. Not yet. I just can't. "Sure. That's the whole point of the assignment, right?"

"Great." He settles himself in the armchair with the pink fuzzy throw. Underneath it's an ugly orange tweed; it's Dad's old chair. "I finally found the lab tests. Your mom was wrong. You don't have the gene for Long QT."

I lean against the door, enjoying the cold glass window pressing against me. I feel so flushed every time Tony looks at me. Or talks. Or moves. "Are you sure?"

He nods. "But the doctor's note says thirty percent of patients don't have the gene. Said they were spontaneous mutations."

"Great. So now I'm a mutant grrrl." I claw my fingers and scratch at the air, trying to make a joke out of it.

"Don't worry. I don't think the villagers are going to torch this place."

Ah, so he's a *Frankenstein* fan as well. But his words haunt me—both the image of people rioting, like the kids chanting for a fight in the cafeteria Monday, and the fact that my mom screwed up. That never happens. And why does she take such delight in nagging my dad about getting tested? He already feels bad enough about not being around.

Oh. Maybe that *is* the point. She resents him. He's never had to deal with my illness, keep an eye on me, save me when I had a Near Miss…he has it so easy compared to Mom.

What the hell can I do about that? I don't want to be the cause of my parents' hurting each other. Once again I'm the rope caught in a tug-of-war not of my making. And I'm sick of it.

"What do your parents do?" I ask Tony, hoping to learn from a normal family.

He opens his mouth to say something. From his face, I'm guessing it's some kind of wisecrack. But then he shuts it again, shrinks his long body into the chair like a contortionist. "My dad's gone. A few years now. It's just me and my mom. She's a waitress at night and works days at a dry cleaners."

Sounded like that left just him. Alone most of the time. Maybe we have more in common than I thought.

"Do they—did they ever make you think like everything bad that happens between them is your fault?" I turn toward the window, looking out into the night. From the corner of my eye, I can see his reflection floating on the glass. Like he's still there with me, even when I'm turned away. For some reason, the thought makes me feel better. Less alone, less scared.

He shrugs. "That's what parents do. It's part of their job description or something."

He's being flippant. We both know the truth. Why bother putting it into words? It's too painful.

Silence.

I have the sudden urge to tell him I'm dying, that he shouldn't waste his time with me. Instead, I press my face to the cold window, kissing the glass. He can't see it, but my lips are tasting his reflection.

I feel like I'm saying good-bye. Like Monday is closer than three days away.

"Don't worry," he finally says. "We can still do the biology project." His voice is rushed, like he feels my pain—and thinks I'm worried about a stupid genetics assignment? Jordan was right; Tony does spend way too much time with his books.

"How?" I ask, turning back to face him. If talking about genes keeps him here in my room a few more minutes, I'm willing to indulge him. Better than waiting for Monday all alone.

"Well. If you're okay with it, we could research your brother's death. I mean, if you want to know. SIDS, sudden infant death, can run in families as well."

I frown and he squirms, finally getting to his feet. He's worried that he's upset me. But he hasn't. I just learned about my twin brother; it's too fresh and new and confusing for me to be mourning him. Instead, it almost feels like the death of a character in a story, one that makes me cry but doesn't change my life.

"They thought he might have Long QT as well."

"Not if you have a spontaneous mutation." Now his voice is back to normal. Mr. Scientist. "You're fraternal twins, not identical."

"Twins run in families too. We could study that." Somehow, I just can't see myself asking Mom about what really killed my brother. It would be cruel, bringing it up when she's so worried about me dying.

He brightens. "Yeah, we could. It's not as sexy—"

"Long QT and babies dying is sexy?" I challenge him.

He flushes, bobs his head in embarrassment. "From a scientific point of view." Shifts his feet again; this time they end up pointing toward the door. "Guess I'd better go back through those records again. You know, it's weird—there's no mention of your twin in the ones your mom gave you."

"I don't think she wants me to know." I hang my head low, trying to decide how much of my mixed-up life to share. I can't scare him off—not yet, please. "Too painful to talk about."

"Yeah, I get that." He scuffs his toe against the carpet, drawing a circle. "So, did you talk your mom into letting you come back tomorrow?"

I look away. Blink hard and fast. How can I tell him that there is no tomorrow for us? That I can be his genetic lab rat but not his lab partner?

Tears burn my cheeks. My face heats with embarrassment, but I'm helpless to stop the emotions overwhelming me. He stands there for an awkward moment as I sob, out of control.

I'm sure he's going to make a run for it. But he doesn't. Instead, he perches beside me, slowly wraps his arms around me, as if unsure of where to put his hands, like I might break.

As if I wasn't already broken. The thought makes me cry even harder. I rock against him, letting him support my weight as the tears empty out of me.

"It's okay," he says, his voice breaking with uncertainty. "Everything will be okay."

I want to believe him, but I know better.

"I'm not coming back to school," I finally choke out. "Not ever. Monday they're going to do surgery on my heart. I'm scared. I'm going to die, Tony. The doctors can't save me. No one can."

60

In the movies and books, first kisses are magical. They change lives. Promise the stars and moon and a bright future.

They don't taste of pepperoni. They don't end up with the other person's spit drying on your chin. They don't start with you both turning the same way at the same time and banging your nose on his cheekbone.

I wish I lived in a movie or a book.

Once I get my tears under control, Tony and I sit there, clinging to each other. Finally he seems to know what to do with his hands, rubbing my back, stroking my arm then softly threading his fingers through my hair as if exploring an unknown universe.

I rock back, watching him watch me. His gaze is intense, as if he's studying my every response. Then it drifts down to focus on my mouth and stays there.

He licks his lips. I don't think he even knows he did it. We both start breathing faster, harder. Then he moves in for the kill...er, kiss.

It all happens so fast. Instinctively, I arch back but then quickly change course when I realize what he's doing—and end up squashing my nose against his face, our lips nowhere in range of each other.

Things go downhill from there.

The fastest, wettest, clumsiest first kiss on record. Too bad we don't have the girls from gym class there to record it for posterity. I'm sure we'd win some kind of award—the booby prize for kisses.

"I'm sorry," I mumble as he pulls away and wipes the back of his hand over his mouth. Destroying any evidence I'd ever been there. "I've never—"

"No," he says gallantly, allowing me to salvage some of my pride. He climbs down off the bed. "It's my fault. I shouldn't have—I'll see you."

And he's out the door before I even catch my breath.

I fall back against my pillows, releasing a dust cloud of pink lace and ruffles, my face scorched with humiliation. I wish Monday were tomorrow and everything was just over and done with for good. Because being the clueless freak that I am sucks.

61

I finally fall asleep. My dreams are filled with Tony and our kiss, the little blond boy—who keeps crying even as he skips around poking his face between me and Tony and inserting himself into every dream sequence—and Cari's freak-out. Only in my dreams, it's me writhing around on the ground clawing and punching at nothing while everyone else stands around and watches, judging me, making comments on my technique and ineptness.

Just your typical night terrors.

I wake up gasping, trying to block out the dreams and the nasty taste they left in my psyche when I realize a noise I thought I'd dreamed was real.

Someone is on the stairs.

Of course it's Mom. It has to be Mom. But for some reason the sound of those footsteps hijacks my brain and I'm terrified.

In an instant, my vision fills with a dream I'd forgotten—the nightmare that's been haunting me these past few days, the crazy cartoon clowns trying to kill me.

I muffle my breathing with my hands and work to calm down. I can hear a person moving around in the kitchen.

Mom never, ever gets up in the middle of the night. She's the heaviest sleeper I've ever met. She can even sleep through a code blue or hospital alarms bleeping all through the night.

Something's wrong. My entire body feels it; I can smell the wrongness in the sweat pouring off of me.

I slide out of bed. Creep barefoot out my door and into the dining room. From here I can see into the kitchen while hiding in the shadows behind the china cabinet.

The kitchen light is on. It *is* Mom. She's dressed in her night-gown and bathrobe, smoking a cigarette! Did she get up in the middle of the night just to sneak a cigarette?

I feel vindicated. I've asked her about smoking many times, but she's always denied it. Made excuses for why she'd smell of tobacco, blamed my dad's occasional pipe, or said she was stand-ing in a crowded elevator with patients who'd been out smoking. And then she'd lecture me mercilessly on the evils of tobacco.

My mom, the smoker. My mom actually has a bad habit. She's not perfect after all.

I'm practically cheering as I watch, savoring the moment and thinking about when I'll take advantage of my newfound knowl-edge. I realize I should get a picture of this.

I tiptoe back into my room and grab my phone. When I get back to the dining room, Mom has left the kitchen. The door to the garage is just swinging shut and the lights are still on. She must usually smoke out there; otherwise, the house would reek of it.

Getting in position to catch her as she comes back in—and hoping she'll still have the cigarette in sight—I align myself in the tiny corner between the doorjamb and the china cabinet. Perfect.

She comes back inside so fast it surprises me, but I keep my finger on the camera button and just keep clicking. She's carrying a plastic sports bottle—one of the bright orange ones from school with the wildcat logo emblazoned across it. This one has a big black "K" scrawled on it. She sets the bottle down and starts rummaging through the junk drawer at the end of the counter.

As she works, she's humming and smoking and smiling. Her face looks so dreamy and faraway that I wonder if maybe the worry about my surgery has driven her to sleepwalking.

She pulls a small mallet from the drawer and carefully sets it beside the sports bottle. Next, she takes a box of plastic sandwich bags from the pantry and adds it to her pile. She goes to the cabinet up over the stove—the one where she keeps the cooking sherry—and takes a large stock bottle of my vitamins.

What is she doing? I snap a few more pictures, mainly hoping that they'll show something I'm missing with my own two eyes.

Then she puts everything into a trash bag and disappears back out the door to the garage. She returns empty-handed.

She finishes the cigarette with a satisfied sigh of pleasure, snuffs it out and tosses it down the garbage disposal, and smiles. She doesn't look anything like my mom—or Nurse Killian. Now I'm certain she's sleepwalking.

They say never wake a sleepwalker. What should I do?

She twirls around in a circle, her robe flying out like a ball gown, and hums a little louder. Her eyes are half-shut now and I wonder if she's going to fall back asleep right there on the kitchen floor. Should I guide her back up to bed?

She solves the problem for me. Dreamily, that strange smile still on her face, she glides through the kitchen, turns off the light, and starts up the stairs. I follow, keeping out of sight, but I want to make sure she gets back to bed all right.

I watch her climb the stairs, one hand dancing along the banister. I hold my breath, listening hard, and hear the door to her room shut. Safe and sound.

Wow. If Mom's been that worried about me, worried enough that she's sleepwalking, it explains a lot. No wonder she seems so tired and comes home and goes to bed right away without even talking with me. No wonder she's so stressed out about my trying school.

If the surgery goes well on Monday, maybe that will help.

But will it be enough? What if one night she sleepwalks her way right off the stairs and breaks her neck?

FRIDAY

62

I spend the rest of the night curled up at the top of the stairs just in case Mom gets up again. She doesn't. In fact, I hear her snoring most of the night. When her alarm goes off, I climb back down to my own bed.

I'm exhausted but who cares? Not like I have any place to go. I can sleep the entire day if I want. Just as soon as I see Mom safely off to work.

"Good morning," she chirps. Despite her extracurricular night-time activities, she doesn't seem tired at all. In fact, she seems more cheerful than she's been in a long time. "I'm calling Dr. Cho first thing. Tonight when your dad gets home, we'll celebrate."

"Uh-huh." I nod as I reach for my pillbox from the middle of the kitchen table. It has my doses divided by morning and night, but I notice she's placed three vitamins in each slot instead of one.

"Don't worry, vitamins are water-soluble. You'll just pee off the extra," she says when she sees me pick one of the horse pills up and look at it. "I want to make sure your immune system is at fighting strength before the surgery."

I say nothing. Should I tell her that I feel better without the extra vitamins?

"I know, I know." She laughs and kisses me on the top of my head. "You hate taking pills. But after Monday, you won't have to. Life will be different. Trust me."

Her hug takes me by surprise, a tight bear hug from behind. Mom's not a big hugger, but it feels good. I feel good, seeing her so happy.

I decide to continue lying about the vitamins, let her think she's helping. I gather the pills in my hand, hug her back, and go to get a glass of water, making a big show of gulping down my atenolol followed by the vitamins. While her back is turned, I shove the horse pills into my pocket.

What she doesn't know can't hurt her. Right?

63

After Mom leaves for work, I go back to bed. I feel achy, my stomach not too happy about my breakfast of steel-cut oatmeal that Mom made for me as a special treat. Usually I just grab a can of Ensure.

My sleep is feverish, filled with nightmares again. When I wake, the sun is streaming through the windows, filtered by pink lace curtains to give it an ethereal cast. A sticky sheen of sweat coats me and the bedclothes stink with it. My head is throbbing, I'm light-headed and nauseous. I crawl out of bed and slowly head into the shower.

Maybe I caught something at school. Most viruses need a few days to incubate, so the timing's right.

It'd be just my luck if Mom was right and going to school kills me.

I take my time in the shower; it hurts even to reach up and wash my hair. I hope Tony doesn't catch whatever I have. Poor guy, bad enough he wasted his time on me and probably is gonna ruin his biology grade because of me.

My mind keeps thrusting the image of our kiss front and center. I can't deal with that, not now. Too humiliating.

After drying off and climbing into some comfy old sweats, I

get a glass of orange juice, hoping the vitamin C will help me feel better. Mom made a fresh pitcher this morning, bless her, because I'm not sure if I have the strength to open a can and mix it up.

Maybe I should take a few of those vitamins. The extra niacin can hardly make me feel worse than I do already. But my throat's so achy, I balk at swallowing them. Even the orange juice tastes metallic and I throw it out after a few sips, change to tap water instead.

Then I hear a car in the driveway. A minute later, the garage door is opening and there's my dad.

"Honey, I'm home!" he calls out in his best Jack Nicholson.

My dad, he's always smiling. But it's a goofy smile, and you're never certain if he's smiling at something happening here and now or at something inside his head. And he loves to talk.

Mom, she has to talk as part of her job and dealing with the doctors and nurses. She can tell my entire life story, including surgeries, in under ninety seconds.

Not Dad. For Dad, talking is like taking a nice long walk in the woods. He enjoys meandering, taking unexpected paths, enjoying the scenery along the way.

Not at all like the way Jordan and Tony both seem compelled to hide both their words and emotions, as if it's classified information, might make them somehow weaker if it falls into enemy hands. They use their passivity as a mask: Tony to hide his passion and imagination, Jordan to shield the rest of us from his intensity.

As Dad pulls me into his arms for a welcome-home hug, not even noticing my fever sweat or flushed skin, it occurs to me for the first time ever that maybe my dad's absent grin is because he really is absent. He really doesn't know what's going on—all he knows is the version of our lives playing on the movie projector inside his head.

Who could blame him? Retreating into a world of make-believe instead of living in a world where your daughter is dying and you've already lost a son—not to mention a wife consumed with keeping your daughter alive. I get it.

Right now, I'm just happy to see him. Oblivious or not. He's my dad and he's here.

64

My dad grins his way through lunch. I barely finish my can of Ensure. But I do feel better after. He doesn't notice me skipping the vitamins Mom left behind, so I don't have to worry about faking or lying to him. For some reason, he's so much harder to lie to than Mom. Maybe because he's so trusting. He always expects the best of everyone.

"Your mom called me last night," he says as he's finishing his turkey sandwich. "Said we'd be celebrating tonight. Said it was a surprise. I know it's not my birthday, so care to fill me in?"

I shake my head. Leaving high school and agreeing to my surgery are no cause for celebration to me.

He wipes his mouth and leans back. "You sure? It doesn't have anything to do with a new arrival, does it?"

Is he talking about the defibrillator they'll be implanting in my heart? "Huh?"

His eyes go wide for a second and he looks flustered. "Never mind. How's school?"

Mom obviously didn't tell him about my quitting. Then I realize. This is my perfect chance to find out about my brother. "Okay. We're doing this big project on genetics. Mom's helping. She gave me copies of my medical records."

"She's the go-to person for stuff like that. Sure that's not cheating? Seems a bit unfair."

"Well, that's why I thought I'd interview you as my primary resource."

Now he's frowning. "Well, I'm not sure I know anything helpful."

"It's basic stuff. Like does anything run in your side of the family?"

He shrugs and shakes his head. "Nope. Everyone's healthy as a horse."

"Any twins?"

Now he's squirming. Then he blows his breath out. "So you know. Did your mom tell you?"

"No. It was in the medical records. But all it said was that I had a twin. And he died when he was little." His face goes wavy as I blink hard and fast. I have to swallow twice before I admit, "I don't even know his name."

He hides his eyes behind his hand, his thumb and index finger pressing the bridge of his nose. "Ashley. Ash, we called him."

65

Your mother—your biological mother—was a big *Gone with the Wind* fan, but she always thought Scarlet should have ended up with Ashley, not Rhett." He's not looking at me as he speaks. Instead, he's looking past me, out the window behind me. "I need to rake those leaves this weekend."

I pull him back to the here and now. "What happened?"

His breath makes a sound like a balloon losing air. "After your mother died, both you kids were sick all the time. The doctors said it was normal colds and flus, since you were in daycare and everything. Then your stepmom and I got together and she helped by watching you. You and Ash, you both did so well." His blink is in slow motion as if he's using the back of his eyelids as a movie screen. "Then one day Ash turned blue—we had no idea it was a heart condition. The doctors never found anything wrong, they did so many tests. But once, right there in the hospital, you did it too. Next thing they're talking reflux and aspiration, want to do surgery. I didn't understand any of it. Thank god your mom was there."

I wait him out. Beneath the table I'm balling the fabric of my sweatpants into a knot. But I try not to let him see how anxious I am for any information. Don't want to scare him off.

"I lost count of how many times your mom had to rush one of you to the hospital. It got to the point where she moved a cot into your room so she could watch over you at night. But then one night, she was just so exhausted. She fell asleep and when she woke up…" His Adam's apple jumps as he swallows. "Ash was gone."

We're both silent for a long minute. Then I ask, "What did he look like?"

He's long past smiling. His face is scrunched up, and for the first time ever, he looks old. "I kept some stuff. Want to see it?"

Without waiting for my answer, he trudges up the steps to their room and I follow.

"Please don't bring this up with your mom. Even though you kids aren't her own blood, she loves you so much. Losing him nearly killed her," he says as he pushes the door open. "Your mom was so upset that she tried—she almost—she accidentally took too many pills. I thought—I was so afraid that I'd be left alone again. I barely found her in time."

His words come out in a rush, his back turned to me as if that would make it easier for him to deny the truth.

I'm reeling. Not just from my headache and fever. My heart feels like it's skipping out of control, racing then skidding to a stop before resuming its pace at a slow stumble. Like it's as confused and overwhelmed by what he's telling me as I am.

He goes to the closet and gets a large shoebox down from the top shelf. Inside is a small book wrapped in blue silk. Ashley's baby book. We sit side by side on the bed as he opens it and turns the pages. I watch Ash grow from a scrawny red-faced newborn to a toddler with white hair and a mischievous grin.

My little blond boy. The boy from my dreams really was my best friend, my other half. No wonder my mind wouldn't let him go so easily.

"You two never let each other out of sight," Dad says as he turns past photos of our christening then our first Christmas, a Halloween where we're dressed as peas in a pod, barely able to waddle in the costumes. In every one, we're not looking at the camera. We're always looking at each other, sharing a secret smile as if we're in our own world.

"You were both late talkers—like you didn't need words. And half the time once you did start talking, it was to say what the other wanted, not yourself. Some days we felt like we had one kid with two bodies."

Hmmm…so I was a freak even as a baby?

But then he chuckles. "Used to drive your mom crazy. The tricks you two played on her."

"So we weren't sick all the time?"

"No. I guess not. Just enough to worry us. Not until after Ash passed and they realized you were sicker than anyone had imagined. Guess we should have paid better attention, but we wanted healthy, happy kids. Sometimes parents see what they need to see."

He says the last with such sorrow, as if asking for forgiveness. I hug him, hard enough for both myself and Ash. "It's okay, Dad."

He hugs me back. Then he turns to the final page, this time a photo of me and Ash getting our hair cut, or trying to—we're both obviously giggling and squirming too much for the poor hairdressers to do more than stand there holding their scissors and combs and laugh with us. Dad's smile comes back as he traces the picture with his fingers.

"Guess with you getting older, ready to move out on your own soon, it's no wonder your mom wants another one around."

"Another what?" I ask absently.

"Another baby. Didn't she tell you? We're adopting."

66

A dopting?" I almost drop the book.

"Sure. I could have sworn your mom said she was telling you this week. That's what we're celebrating tonight, isn't it? Our application getting approved."

I'm shaking my head in time with his words. "I had no idea."

"Oh, shoot. I've spoiled the surprise." He looks at me in dismay. "You're not upset, are you? If we get a baby, it will take some of your mom's attention away from you. But you're doing so much better—"

Do I break the news to him about the surgery Monday? Or the fact that Mom obviously hasn't told him—just like she kept it from me—that even with the surgery, my time is short?

I can't. I just can't. He's so excited about the chance to be a father again. I can't steal his smile away.

"No. I think it's great," I say. Even though it's obvious to me that Mom's set this up. Finding my replacement. What did Dad say? If it wasn't for me, she would have died after Ash? Guess she's preparing this time.

I don't know whether to feel angry or relieved. I've been dreading what would happen to Mom and Dad—but especially Mom, whose entire life is entwined with my illness and taking care of me—after I'm gone.

"What about your job?" I ask Dad.

"I'm being promoted. I'll be based at the office starting next month. No more travel for me."

Visions of him playing catch with a son are clearly dancing in his eyes. I smile at the thought. Imagine Ash as the one catching the ball.

Sadness fills me, but the void is smaller than it has been.

Dad glances at his watch. "Actually, that's why I'm home early today. I need to go in, get some paperwork done. Why don't you take these?" Dad says, handing me the shoebox. "Get to know your brother."

"Thanks, Dad. For everything."

He blushes as I kiss him on the cheek. We both stand up. "Okay if I take these to my room?"

"Of course. You know where to find me if you need me. I'm just a phone call away."

I head downstairs and close my door behind me. A few minutes later, I hear his car pull out. Ensconced in pink, I sit on my bed and open the lid on the box once more. I take out the baby book and set it to one side. Next is a lock of white hair, fine and silky, tied in a blue ribbon. I tickle my face with it; it's so soft.

Below that is the satin hem from a worn baby blanket, only a few inches left, clearly loved to rags. I hold it to my nose and inhale. Can practically smell baby powder and little boy on it.

A few loose photos, a paper from the hospital with Ash's baby footprints inked on it, and then the final item.

I stare at it, pain lancing through my chest. My heart has finally shattered, leaving only slivers as sharp as broken glass. A folded pillowcase. Orange with clown faces covering it. Laughing, smirking, killer clowns with bright red lips and flashing teeth ready to devour little boys and girls.

The clowns that have been chasing me in my dreams.

They're real. They're here.

67

Frozen, gasping for air as my heart stumbles back into a chaotic cadence, I can't do anything but sit and relive my nightmares.

Dreams? Or memories?

Maybe Mrs. Gentry's relaxation exercises worked better than anyone could imagine.

I find a photo of me and Ash in our beds, surrounded by clowns. Clowns on the walls, on the bright orange sheets we both have, painted onto the headboards. Maybe it's just a warped memory—I was upset about Ash leaving me and translated that into this irrational fear of being smothered by clowns.

That would explain the sound of the child crying in my dreams.

But what about the grown-up laughing? The woman telling someone "Hush, it's not your turn yet…"

I burrow under the covers, shivering uncontrollably.

A woman. With me and Ash. In our bedroom.

No. It can't be.

I skitter out of bed, almost tripping on the sheets as I lunge for my backpack and grab my iPad. I find the medical record of that first hospital visit for me.

Apparent life-threatening event in a twenty-two-month-
old white female, full-term product of a twin gestation...

Apparent Life Threatening Event. I Google the term. Near-miss
SIDS is the other name for it. A baby, usually less than a year
old, stops breathing for no obvious reason. Causes also include
gastro-esophageal reflux, infection, congenital heart disease, and
rarely, non-accidental injury.

Non-accidental injury? What the hell does that mean?

But I already have a pretty good idea. Doctor-speak for someone wanting to hurt someone else.

But it makes no sense. Why would anyone want to hurt—no,
not just anyone. My mother.

No. Stepmother. Not blood.

The room spins around me in a pink whirl as I fall to my knees.
My stomach is trying to claw its way up my throat but my heart
blocks its path. I can feel my pulse tap-dancing in my skull in
time with the black spots dancing before my eyes.

No. No. She's the one who Saved me. Who's always been there
for me. Without her I'd be dead.

Like Ash...

68

I barely make it to the toilet in time before I vomit. Kneeling on the cold tile, sandwiched between the tub and toilet, I lay my head on the side of the tub and force myself to just breathe. Deep, belly breaths. In and out. Nothing complicated, nothing scary, I've been doing it every day of my life.

It's something I shouldn't need to think about. But of course, now I can't stop thinking. The smell of laundry detergent and fabric softener mixed with fear. The feeling of being smothered.

That laughter haunting my dreams…my memories.

I still can't believe it. In fact, I decide I *won't* believe. I'll prove my crazy mixed-up mind wrong. Find proof of Mom's innocence.

That's exactly what I'll do.

Pushing myself to my feet, I stagger back out to the bedroom and find my cell phone. It's one eighteen; Tony should be just leaving biology. I call him, expecting it to go to voicemail since it's against the rules to use your phone in school, but he answers.

"Hey there," he says, his tone uncertain. "Are you okay?"

"I need your help." I sound melodramatic, something out of a dime-store novel, so I suck in my breath and try again. "Could you skip? Come over and help me with my medical records?"

"Well, I have AP chemistry next—"

He's taking life sciences and AP chemistry the same semester? He really is serious about getting out of here and into college early.

"No, I understand. That's okay." Already I'm regretting getting an outsider involved. What if my prying starts rumors flying about Mom? If anyone knows how dangerous that is, it's me.

"I'm on my way."

He hangs up before I can protest and tell him to not bother. I stand there, swaying, staring at the phone in my hand.

What have I done?

I get myself cleaned up and change into jeans and a sweater just in time for the doorbell to ring. Tony's using the front door this time—I'm not sure if that's good or bad.

I'm actually not sure of anything. Including what the hell we're going to be doing.

My mom didn't try to kill me.

The thought of explaining all this to Tony makes me nauseous again.

But I open the door anyway. Inviting disaster into my home.

69

Y"ou look awful." The first words out of Tony's mouth.

Guess we're not going to be kissing again anytime soon. But then he totally confuses me by giving me a hug. Not a guy-friend hug, it feels more like a real boyfriend hug.

But what do I know? I'm the crazy person who's spent the afternoon imagining her mother might be a monster.

"I need your help," I whisper into his shoulder before I let him go.

"Of course. I'm here. Anything."

We separate and I lead him into the dining room where we can use the computer and have room to spread out the medical records.

"Did you—" I can't even ask it without sounding nuts. "I mean, while you were looking through the medical records—" All of a sudden, they're no longer "my" records but "the" records. Like I've disowned my own life. "Were there any more discrepancies?"

He stands very, very still for a long moment. He's wearing jeans and a gray Wildcats sweatshirt and a corduroy jacket. Slowly he drops his pack, unbuttons the jacket, and takes it off, hanging it on the back of a chair. At least he hasn't run away. Yet.

Then he meets my gaze. "Why don't you sit down?"

The look in his face. Haunted. That's the only word I can think of.

The room wobbles as I lurch to a chair. I fall into it. "What did you find? Tell me everything."

I must be shivering—I don't know, I can't feel anything—because he drapes his jacket around my shoulders. He doesn't sit but rather squats beside me, holding my hand, stroking it as if trying to coax warmth back into it.

"What did you find?" he echoes my question back at me.

I can't. I just can't. I don't say anything, just squeeze my eyes shut and shake my head.

He releases my hand and sighs. Then stands and takes the notebook out of his pack. I open my eyes and he's got the records separated into sections piled across the table. Then he adds new pages of his own—computer printouts highlighted and covered in his handwriting.

"Last night, I noticed something weird in the electronic records compared to the written ones," he began. His voice sounds like a lot of the doctors I've had. Remote, clinical. Which right now works for me. "It's not just missing data like the genetic tests and the existence of your twin. The ones your mom printed out give a totally different version of your—er, sickness."

All I can do is nod and listen. My fingers wrap around the edge of the chair's seat, holding me in place and upright.

"I realized they'd been altered. Tailored to fit a certain ailment."

"I don't understand."

"When you were a baby, it was mostly breathing problems, right?"

"Yes, but those could be explained by Long QT—"

He's shaking his head. "They *were* explained by Long QT. The way they're described by your mother *now*. But if you read the original notes from back when you were a baby, the notes she didn't include in here"—he taps the binder Mom prepared—"it's a different story."

I'm totally lost. "You're saying she edited the version she gave me?"

"No. I'm saying she's edited every version she gave everyone. Look, here in the GI version—that's gastroenterology—"

"I know what GI means," I snap at him. My headache's back, full throttle. Even my eyes hurt.

"Right. Well, anyway, the history the first GI doctor records from your mother is that you had failure to thrive and episodes of vomiting ever since you were a baby. Apparently she described the classic symptoms of gastro-esophageal reflux, and despite a normal pH probe test, they try you on meds after she brings you in one more time with an Apparent Life Threatening Event."

"I know what that is," I say before he can explain it to me.

His expression has changed to pitying. "She keeps telling them the meds aren't working. She wants them to operate. Put in a feeding tube. Their notes indicate that they want to try new meds, because when they examine you, they just aren't finding anything wrong. Then there aren't any more notes from that doctor but a few months later you have a new doctor. This time she takes you there *with* the diagnosis of severe reflux. Their history says that the old doctors have already tried everything and wanted to operate but she doesn't want to subject you to that without a second opinion. Makes it sound so bad that the new doctors say yes, the first guys are right, we need to operate."

I look down. My fingers are tracing my feeding tube scar through my sweater. I can't feel them. I can't feel anything. "But that's pretty much the truth. Besides, just because a mother fights for the best medical care for their child doesn't make them wrong about what that care should be."

That's what my mom tells other moms at hospitals. Moms she thinks are wimping out, following the doctors blindly. She calls them sheep, says they need to learn to fight for their kids.

"Doctors don't know everything," I add. My mother's ultimate rebuttal. "But a mom sees her kid every day."

He's nodding in time with my words. Just like doctors do when they're politely listening to Mom's suggestions but are ready to ignore her. Anger coils inside me, making it hard to take a deep breath.

"I read everything, Scarlet. There are records and notes she's altered—to slant things her way before she passed the records on to the next doctor. Easy to do before electronic medical records. All she needed was a little white-out and a typewriter. But in the computer version of your records, she kept a copy of all of the originals. So they were there to compare."

Curling up in the chair, knees to my chest, hugging them, I'm trying my best to make myself a smaller target. To hide from his words. So they can't hurt me. Because everything he says hurts so bad—worse than anything I've ever felt in a hospital. Tears slide off my cheeks onto the knees of my jeans. I don't even notice. I like seeing the world blurred. It makes this all seem like it's not really happening.

Where's my beach? My lovely beach. It's gone. I can't get there. Not from here.

70

He leaves his notes—his precious evidence—and comes to me. He reaches out a hand but I shy away. It drops to his side. Empty.

Just like I am.

"I'm sorry," he whispers.

"Okay." I somehow find my voice again. "So she changed the records to convince doctors. That doesn't mean—that can't mean—"

He turns away. Like he can't even look at me. I'm that pathetic.

"She hurt you, Scarlet. You and, I think, your brother."

"You can't prove that!" Now I'm shouting, the rage that's built inside me exploding as if it has a will of its own.

He whirls back. "Why are you defending her?"

All I can do is stare. How can he even ask? What kind of boy is this that he doesn't know the answer?

I unfold myself and stand up. "Out. Get out of my house."

He stands firm. I try to push him. He doesn't move. "I want you gone. Go away!"

I pound on his chest with my fists, flailing and crying and screaming. He just stands there. When I quiet down, he says, "Think about it, Scarlet. Who saw? Who was the only person who ever saw anything?"

He wraps his arms around me, catching me before I can collapse, and holds me tight. "You know I'm right."

I do. I do. I do. I do. I do.

But that doesn't mean I believe. How can I believe what he's saying, what I'm thinking?

I'd have to be a monster to believe that. And monsters deserve to die—maybe that's what happened. My mom saw the monster inside me and knew that.

"It's all my fault." The words emerge in a gargle of tears. "All my fault."

"No." He holds me tighter.

All I can see is the gray of his shirt—now black with my tears. All I can smell is Tony. Musky, sweet, autumn leaves crushed underfoot—all Tony.

"It's not your fault," he keeps repeating. We stand like that for a long time. Long enough for my tears to stop and my heart to tumble into an oddball, almost-normal rhythm.

Then he says, "I stayed up all night trying to figure this out. Then today I went to the library and did some reading."

I brace myself. So far Tony's reading has only brought me pain.

"There's this…condition. Called Munchausen by proxy. People, usually moms, hurt kids so they can get attention from doctors and nurses or be treated like heroes when they 'miraculously' save them. I think that's why she did it."

Enough people do this that there's a name for it? I wonder at that. A sliver of hope chisels itself into the darkness. Maybe I'm not the monster, the crazy one. Maybe it's not all my fault.

My cell phone rings and the frayed thread of hope dissolves as reality intrudes.

I push away from Tony, wipe my nose on my sleeve, and grab my phone.

"You bitch!" Nessa's voice thunders through the receiver. "How could you?"

71

Tony yanks the phone from me before I can drop it, but I can still hear everything. "Nessa. This isn't a good time."

"What are you doing there? Never mind. Put Scarlet back on. I want to hear what she has to say."

"No. Really, whatever is going on, it will have to wait."

"It can't wait. That bitch ruined Celina's life. Her parents are with the cops and Child Services right now and they're taking Cari away and—"

Her words finally penetrate the ice block that's encased my senses. I've never felt so cold in my life and can't feel my fingers when I reach for the phone. Tony hesitates then hands it to me. I put it on speaker. "Nessa, slow down. What happened?"

I can't believe how calm I sound. It's as if my voice has been frozen along with the rest of my body.

"Your mother. Called Child Services. She and Thorne yanked Celina out of world cultures. But now Celina's gone, and it's all your fault." Her words are clipped and rapid-fire.

I understand what she's saying, but I can't put two words together to answer. One phone call, one broken promise, and my mother just destroyed a family. All I can think about is Mrs. Price, lying in pain, unable to see either of her daughters before she dies.

Monster.

The word ricochets through my brain.

"What do you mean Celina's gone?" Tony asks.

"She saw what was coming and took off. She's not answering her phone. I don't know where she is. I ran to her folks' house, but she's not there. It's a mess. I'm afraid of what she'll do."

"Do you think she'll go after Mrs. Killian?" Tony says.

"I don't know. Jordan's out looking for her. He's a wreck. I've never seen him like this. I think he's afraid she'll do something—like Vonnie did—something crazy. And I—I just don't know what to do." Her desperation crackles through the air.

I take the phone from Tony. "Nessa. It's okay." I'm lying. Just like my mom always lied to me when things went horribly wrong in the hospital. "Everything will be okay. Are you back at school?"

"Yeah. Everyone's still here because of the game tonight."

"Stay there. Keep looking. We'll figure something out and call you back." I hang up before she can realize how empty my words were.

Tony's way ahead of me. "Where's your mom?"

"I don't know. At school, I guess." I glance at the clock. School's been out for almost fifteen minutes. "Maybe on her way home. She and my dad were going out tonight, I think."

He nods to the phone in my hand. "Call her."

I almost drop it. "I can't. I can't talk to her."

"We need to know where she is. If she's anywhere Celina can find her, it's our best bet to find Celina."

"Do you really think? Celina would never—"

"Just make the call."

I start to but can't. So I do the next best thing. I call my dad.

"Hey, pumpkin." He sounds happier than he has in a long while.

Guilt twists through me like a red-hot poker. What I know—what I believe—will destroy his world.

"I was just about to call you," he continues, oblivious as always.

Anger tangles with the guilt. Why didn't Dad know? Why didn't he do something? Stop her?

Why did he bring her into our home to start with? He should have seen, should have protected us.

My throat chokes tight. Thankfully he does all the talking.

"Your mom has to stay at school for the game tonight. They need her on the sidelines or something. Anyway, some guys here at the office were going to take me out, celebrate my promotion. Your mom thought you'd be okay on your own. Said you'd probably only want Ensure for dinner anyway—what do you think?"

What do I think? He really, really, really does *not* want the answer to that question.

But then, that's Dad. He doesn't really want the answer to any question. Really doesn't want anything in his carefully balanced existence questioned at all.

"I'll be fine," I grit out, my jaw feeling bruised, I'm clenching it that tight.

"Okay, great. I'll see you later. Love ya." He hangs up.

I stand there, staring at the phone. The slideshow plays across the display. Celina and Cari smiling at me. The pictures of the football players during the fight. Then the pictures from last night of my mom.

"What's she doing?" Tony asks, watching over my shoulder.

"Sleepwalking." I replay the pictures. "At least, that's what I thought."

"What's that bottle? It looks like pills."

"My vitamins. She buys them in stock bottles because I go through them so fast."

"Show me."

I stare at him. "What do my vitamins have to do with anything?"

"Are they prescribed by your doctors?"

"No. They're just vitamins."

"Do you ever feel sick after taking them?"

I turn away, heading out to the kitchen so he can't see my face. My entire body feels like it's strung together with barbwire, pulled tight, sharp jabs everywhere as I realize how painful the truth can be.

"They're up there." I point a shaky finger toward the cabinet over the stove.

Tony's tall enough that he doesn't need to stand on tiptoe to reach. He rummages in the cabinet and brings out a bottle of vitamins and a spice container labeled sea salt.

"What's that doing up there? We don't keep the spices there. Mom says the steam from the stove ruins them."

He hands me the spice jar as he opens the vitamins. It's a new bottle, still sealed, and I breathe a sigh of relief. How warped is this? Actually thinking my mom was poisoning me and being relieved to see it's not true.

Maybe all she did was lie to the doctors. That's bad. I can't even begin to process the anger and betrayal I feel because of all the pain those lies cost me.

But she's not a killer.

I hang on to that fact with both hands as Tony breaks the seal and spills a handful of vitamins into his palm, examining them.

"I guess I was wrong." He hands me the pills. "Sorry."

I'm staring at the pills. Right color. Right size. Wrong markings.

"Tony." My voice is small and far away, a mouse scurrying to hide from danger. "These aren't the pills she's been giving me."

72

He spins so fast he knocks over the bottle, spraying vita-mins in every direction. They ping across the counter-top, ricochet against the backsplash, nosedive into the sink beside us.

Tony doesn't even notice. He grabs my arm. Gently, like he has to hold me up.

Maybe he does. Suddenly, I'm not quite sure which way really is up.

"Scarlet. We need to find out what she's been giving you."

His words hit my brain like it's a trampoline and bounce off again and again and again…until I finally get it.

Really get it.

"I have some. In my pocket. From this morning." It's a struggle to translate thoughts into words—there are just too many swirl-ing in my head. Instead I run to my room and rummage for my bathrobe. I think I remember hiding the pills in there…yes, there they are.

"I'll check on the computer." Tony and I head back to the dining room. My head is spinning. Not just with implications and realizations and accusations, but with feelings.

For the first time in years, I realize that what I thought I was feeling, what I thought were emotions, were really just the tiniest pinpricks compared to the real thing.

Maybe being numb wasn't such a bad thing after all.

I pace behind Tony as his fingers fly across the keyboard. I want my beach; I want my hiding place; I want my bubble.

I want to run away from my life.

"Got it!" He sounds excited. Then he makes a noise deep in his throat. A rumble that would make a pit bull back off.

I lean over him, read over his shoulder. "Exzyte? Bang her longer, harder, faster than ever before…it's an ED pill!"

"Herbal supplement for erectile dysfunction. Which means it's not regulated. But look at the side effects listed by this medical journal." He scrolls down. There's a bullet list.

- Abdominal pain
- Nausea and vomiting
- Metallic taste
- Dry mouth
- Myalgia
- Headache
- Flushing
- Dizziness
- Insomnia

"I have all of those. But you can get those same symptoms from vitamins," I'm compelled to add. "And none of them are life-threatening."

"It gets worse." He clicks on a case report. "A man taking Exzyte herbal preparation presented to an emergency room with Long QT syndrome. Doctors said it couldn't be distinguished from the real disease. And it's just as deadly."

I'm clinging to the back of his chair, fighting to stay on my feet. "Is it—is it permanent? The heart damage?"

My own heart zigzags into a flutter rhythm as I wait for his answer.

He keeps reading. My vision is too blurry to read the screen. Maybe if I can't see it, it can't be real.

"No." He blows out his breath, the tension releasing from his posture. "As soon as the drug is out of the system in a day or so, the symptoms resolve themselves."

"Tony, I haven't taken any vitamins since Wednesday."

"Good. That's great."

"No." I shake my head. "No, it's not. Because I feel worse today than ever."

73

Tony turns to me, puts his palm on my cheeks and forehead as if testing for fever. "Maybe we should get you to a doctor."

"And tell them what? That we think maybe my mom poisoned me and that some of the best specialists in the country are wrong and I'm really not sick at all and here's the proof…except we don't actually have any proof, do we?"

"We have the pills."

"That doesn't prove anything. They'll say it was a mix-up. A mistake."

"But we can't risk it. What if you get worse? You could—"

I put my hand up. I can't handle him saying the words out loud.

"Tell me more about this Munchausen thing. Seems like they wouldn't want to kill the kid because that takes away their little drama, right?"

Suddenly I'm lumping my mother—Mom—in with an anonymous group of crazy ladies. I feel like I've wandered into some surreal movie, like *Suspicion* or *Spellbound* where Hitchcock plays with the audience's minds, convincing them of one thing when the reality is very different.

My life as a movie. I can handle that, observing it from a distance, so much easier than actually living it.

"Some of the moms actually enjoy the attention they get when the kids die. There was one lady in Philly who killed ten of her kids."

"Ten?" Holy hell, this is warped. I still can't believe we're talking about this. Maybe I really am on a beach somewhere and this is all a hallucination. Then it hits me. "But she still had other kids. So it could start all over again."

He catches my gaze and holds it gently, slowly nodding. "Your brother. That's why she let your brother die."

I can't answer. I'm floating, far away from Tony, from my body, from my life. I've almost convinced myself that this isn't real, it's just another nightmare, when my heart starts to flutter kick. The pain of it beating out of control is nothing compared to the pain of the truth pulling me back to earth.

I sway and Tony settles me gently onto a chair. He squeezes my hands in his. "But you don't have any other brothers or sisters, so she's not really trying to kill you. She needs you. She just needs you to be sick. Right? So you'll be okay."

I shake my head. My breath is coming fast and shallow and I feel light-headed, like someone's sucked all the oxygen out of the room. I'm not sure if what I'm feeling is fear and anger and betrayal and disbelief or if it's really my heart galloping into a Near Miss. I close my eyes and press my knuckles into them, focus on my breathing. That's real. I can trust that. Slowly my heart steadies.

"My dad came home early today. To celebrate." I swallow. Twice. My throat burns with acid and fear. "They're adopting a baby."

He stands there, still holding my hands. The entire house holds its breath. Like we're not part of the real world outside where birds are singing and kids are playing and real moms are cooking dinner for real dads coming home to real families.

Not my family. My family doesn't exist. It's all a lie.

Tony drops my hand and spins away, grabbing my cell phone again. He looks at the pictures of Mom from last night. "She took the pills with her this morning. Must be planning to grind them up with the mallet. Maybe she's done it before." He heads into the kitchen. "What has she been feeding you?"

I follow him, still a little woozy. Remember the spice jar and grab it. It's labeled "sea salt" but it doesn't look like salt. No crystals, just beige powder. "The tofu. It tasted funny. And so did the oatmeal this morning."

He has the fridge open. "There's no tofu left. What else?"

"Orange juice. She made it."

He grabs the pitcher and sets it on the counter. "Anything else?"

I think back to when I was thirteen. The Year of Nothing Good. How I lived on Ensure and vitaminwater. Until I almost died.

But Mom was there to save me.

"Ensure. But that's sealed in cans."

He takes the package of Ensure out. We buy it in bulk—it's not even real Ensure, it's a generic version. It comes in cans with a small foil seal over the drinking hole.

Tony sets them on the kitchen table and examines a can from every angle.

"Nothing." He frowns and grabs a can, shaking it hard and turning it upside down, rolling it between his palms.

A single white drop falls onto the table. Bounces, quivers, then dies.

"The seal has been broken," he says. "She probably used a small needle and syringe. Too small to see. But—" He gives the can another hard shake and a second drop flies free.

"Maybe she just wanted to make me sick enough that the doctors wouldn't argue about the heart surgery on Monday." It sounds lame even to me.

"Or maybe she wanted you to die before the surgery. Think of the attention. Such a tragic story. If the doctors had only listened to her, done the surgery sooner—"

"Stop it!" My scream echoes through the empty house.

Tony straightens. Jerks himself as if only now realizing this is *my* life, not a science experiment. He sets the can down carefully and approaches me. He wants to hug me. I back away. Right now, I don't want him touching me.

"I'm sorry," he whispers. "I'm so sorry."

My phone rings. I edge past him and go into the dining room to catch it on the third ring.

"Did you find Celina?" Nessa asks, shouting to be heard over the noise of a crowd. "Tell me you found her."

Shit. I've totally forgotten about Celina. "No. Not yet. But my mom's at the football game. That might be a good place to start."

"I'm *at* the game. I can't find anyone!"

"Don't worry. We're on our way. We'll meet you at—" I flounder. I've never been to a football game before. The stadium is just on the other side of the gym though. "We'll meet where the fight was. Outside the gym. Okay?"

"Okay. But hurry."

74

I grab my coat and Phil. Habit, pure habit. "Maybe I don't need it?"

Tony opens his pack and drops Phil inside. "We're not taking any chances." He hesitates. "You should stay. But I don't want to leave you here alone. We could—"

I open the door and step through it, ignoring him.

"Okay." He closes the door behind me. It's already dark. That weird twilight blue-black dark that happens when the sun is just starting to set. And chilly. I'm glad for my coat.

We walk together in silence for the first few minutes. I can't remember the last time I was outside at night like this other than to be bundled into an ambulance.

I've never strolled through my neighborhood after dark. It's kinda weird. Walking past houses with their warm lights, cozy families snugged inside, me on the outside, hiding in the shadows.

Freak.

Mitch and the others. They sensed it as soon as they laid eyes on me. Herd instinct, Darwin at work, I don't know. But now I know they were right.

Tony takes my hand in his. I'm glad he's there, but it doesn't really help me feel better. Not now. Not after knowing what I know. Nothing can ever make me feel better.

"What's the plan?" he asks.

I'm supposed to have a plan? No. That's not the way things work. Everyone always has a plan for me: another doctor's visit, another surgery, another pill to swallow…suddenly I'm supposed to be in charge?

Fear breathes down the back of my neck. I can feel it, pushing me away from my home, my safe haven, my plastic bubble of pinkness.

It's laughing. Knows I'm clueless about how things work out here in the real world. It's ready to snap me up, chew me up, and spit me out when I fail.

"I don't know," I finally admit. "Find my mom and—" What? Confront her? We have no evidence. This isn't like *CSI* where we can drop off a can of Ensure and have it tested for some internet herbal penile enhancement drug and get results in thirty seconds before a commercial.

"Jordan," Tony says. "His dad's a cop. He'll listen to us." He glances back over his shoulder toward my house. "Maybe I should have grabbed one of those bottles. Evidence. Because if your mom comes back and sees everything—"

"So we need to find her first." I sound more certain than I feel. Last thing I want is to actually see my mom. Ever. Again.

"Why do you suppose she took all that stuff last night?" he asks. "If she really wanted to get rid of the evidence, she'd have taken the spice jar too."

My jumbled mind is trying to put pieces together—somehow

everything fits, but I'm just not sure how. I pull out my cell phone. I've used it more in one day than in the year I've had it. I call Nessa. "Did you find Celina?"

"No. Jordan's here, helping me."

"We're almost there." I can see the lights of the stadium as we turn the corner. "How did my mom know about Celina's injuries in the first place?"

"I don't know. Gym class? Or maybe when she checked Celina after she fell?"

I'd forgotten about Celina's fall. "If Mitch pushed Celina and that was why her secret was exposed, could she blame him as well?"

"Shit," Nessa says. "Now we need to find Mitch too."

"We know where he'll be—in the locker room. Tell Jordan to keep an eye on him. We're almost there." I hang up.

Tony's frowning. "Your mom was pretty pissed off when Mitch got off scot-free after sending those pictures of you."

"Oh yeah. She hates when anyone defies her—" I break off. "You think she's going after him, not Celina?"

"That sports bottle in the pictures. Have you ever seen your mom use one like that before?"

"No."

"Maybe the 'K' wasn't for Killian. It was for Kowlaski."

Suddenly the pieces fall into place. So typical of my mom. Nobody crosses her and gets away with it. And she promised that she'd take care of Mitch. She just didn't say how. "She's going to poison Mitch. And frame Celina for it."

75

Tony leads me across the playing fields. They're on the other side of the gym from the football stadium, but we can hear the bands warming up and the murmur of the crowd. We make it to the equipment shed where Nessa's waiting.

"Where's Jordan? Is he with Mitch?" I ask.

Nessa leads us inside the school—she's blocked the door open with a rock. The school is dark except for a few lights. And so empty our footsteps echo in weird ways that make me want to keep looking over my shoulder. The locker rooms are on the other side of the gym so we can't see them from here. "He's standing guard outside the locker room, watching for Celina."

"Tell him to watch for my mom as well. Don't let her into the locker room."

"Why not?"

Tony answers for me. Thank God, because I'm not sure I can say the words out loud. "We think she's going to poison Mitch's water bottle and frame Celina for it."

Nessa blinks hard then grabs her phone. "Your mom would do that?"

I look away.

"Can you get us into Celina's locker?" I ask when she hangs up from Jordan. "We can see if there's anything suspicious inside. Grab it if there is."

"This way."

Nessa leads us back to the main corridor then down a side hall to where Celina's locker is. Someone, probably Mitch since it's misspelled, has scrawled "Purvert" on it in red marker. I guess the rumor has morphed from Celina being a victim to her being an abuser.

Nessa spins the lock and opens it. Inside, there's a plastic bag with white powder labeled: *JWH-018, not for human consumption.*

"What's that?" I ask, reaching for it.

Tony stops me. "Synthetic marijuana. Kids have died from it. Acts like PCP." He points to a second bag, smaller and labeled with flowers. "That one is bath salts. Will also make you go nuts—like that face-eating crazy guy down in Florida."

Nessa grabs both bags, shielding her hand in her coat sleeve to preserve any fingerprints, and carries them to the next row of lockers. She tosses them on top of the lockers where they skid out of sight. "Now we can find them if we need to, but no one can pin it on Celina."

We're staring at her in admiration. She brushes her hands together. "Hey, my two best friends are the kids of cops, what did you expect?"

"Let's find Mitch before my mother does."

We start down the next hallway, circling around to the other side of the gym. "What would happen if you add the JWH-018 and bath salts to the Exzyte?" I ask Tony.

He considers. "The perfect way to mask a heart attack as a drug overdose."

At least he didn't say "the perfect murder." But that's what we're all thinking.

76

We meet up with Jordan outside the boys' locker room. He looks haggard. "Did you find her?"

"No." Nessa fills him in on what's going on.

Jordan's expression morphs from worry to anger.

"Jordan, we'll find her. It will be all right." I try to touch his arm and he flinches.

"You can't know that." He straightens, shoulders back, ready for a fight. He can barely look at me. I know he blames me for all this. "What the hell is going on with your mother? Do you really think she's trying to kill Mitch and blame Celina? Like destroying Celina's family wasn't enough?"

Tony fills him in while I stare at my shoes, shame coloring my vision. Nessa makes a small gasp of surprise when Tony explains about my brother and my symptoms, but Jordan's silent until he finishes.

Then Jordan smashes the heel of his hand into a locker so hard the metal buckles. "Damn it to hell, I trusted her. I told her everything. How could she?" He turns to me, fists bunched at his sides. "What if your mom isn't satisfied with trying to frame her? What if she's done something to Celina? Maybe poisoned her as well? She could be hurt, lying somewhere—" His voice trails off.

A loud rumble, forty pairs of stomping feet, interrupts him. The door to the locker room shakes and then everything goes quiet.

"The team's run onto the field," Tony says. "What should we do?"

Jordan answers, "I'm calling my dad. Then I'm going out there and getting your mother to tell me what she's done to Celina."

"Tony, go with him. Try to convince Coach to get Mitch off that playing field."

"What are you going to do?"

"Nessa and I will search Mitch's locker. See if the water bottle is in there."

"You can't go in there," he protests.

Nessa doesn't wait. She pushes through the door. We follow her. The guys head out to the field while Nessa and I start looking for Mitch's locker.

"Do you really think your mom might have hurt Celina?" Nessa asks. I don't answer—all my answers fled with the lies that were my life.

We find Mitch's locker, emblazoned with his number and name. It has a padlock on it, but it's not locked, just hanging there.

"There's one place we haven't looked for Celina." She hesitates. I undo the padlock and open Mitch's locker. There's a wad of clothing shoved into the bottom. Spare toiletries on the shelf above. A dirty jockstrap hanging from one of the hooks.

"Where?" I can't find the water bottle. Did he take it with him?

"Her office."

I straighten. The nurse's office has a set of large cupboards with locks, a big closet, lots of nooks and crannies. Plenty of places to hold someone captive. "Go. I'll let the guys know the bottle isn't here."

Nessa rushes out.

Suddenly there's silence. Not just the room, but inside my head also. Like all the crazy thoughts and feelings have canceled themselves out, leaving just me.

I close my eyes. Breathe in. Breathe out.

Try to remember my life before this nightmare began.

It's a blur.

But I can see some things clearly. Nessa's smile welcoming me in the library. Jordan's touch that first morning. Celina's bashful offer of help. Tony's hazel eyes as he invited me to partner with him.

I can't lose these memories. Not like I lost Ashley.

I'm still not sure what the truth of my life really is. But I'm willing to fight to find out.

"Hey, it's the freak!" A man's voice blasts through the silence.

I open my eyes. It's Mitch Kowlaski. With Keith Young hard on his heels.

Both rushing toward me.

77

Before I can blink, Mitch slams me into the locker beside his. With his football pads on, he seems twice as big as normal.

"You snooping in my locker, bitch?" he screams into my face.

His skin is flushed; he's so angry that each word is accompanied by a stream of saliva. His hand presses against my throat and I can't answer. I can't even breathe.

With strength that amazes me, he uses one hand to lift me off my feet. I'm dangling in the air, choking to death. Panic colors my vision. I kick and pound my fists against him, but he doesn't even notice. He's smiling—no, not smiling, more like the uneven gaping grin of a jack-o-lantern the week after Halloween.

Then he laughs and grinds his body against mine, pinning me between him and the locker. He's enjoying this.

A rushing noise fills my head. The world goes dim. I don't have any strength left to fight.

"Stop it! Mitch, get off her!"

Keith's words penetrate the haze that's drowning me. Suddenly I'm falling. I hit the bench and roll onto the floor, gasping. My neck is sore, I can't even try to swallow, every breath scorches.

"Coach sent you in here to cool down, not screw around. You nearly took that receiver's head off."

I blink away the red spots dancing in my vision and see Keith holding Mitch from behind in a quasi-choke hold. Hard to do with all the pads they're both wearing.

Scrambling back, putting as much distance between me and Mitch as possible, I finally find my voice. "Mitch, did you drink from your water bottle?"

Keith looks at me like I'm nuts. But Mitch says, "Of course I did. My rally girl left it for me with a special treat. She scored some Four Loko."

Great. Caffeine and alcohol on top of the psycho-marijuana substitute and bath salts. Not to mention the Exzyte. And two hundred pounds of raging hormones to start with.

I struggle to my feet. "Mitch," I keep my voice low and calm. "I think your water bottle was drugged. Are you feeling funny? Chest pain? Heart racing?"

He's staring at me, eyes bugging out. His chin juts forward and with a roar worthy of the Incredible Hulk, he slams Keith back against the lockers, breaking free of his grasp.

Keith cracks his head so hard I can hear it. Blood streaks down the locker door as he slides to the floor.

Mitch charges me. "You did this! You bitch! What did you do to me?"

I turn and run. Have no idea where I'm running to, just searching for any escape.

Then I see an exit sign. Mitch seems blind to the obstacles between him and me—he's tripping over the benches and gear strewn around the locker room floor. Which slows him just enough that I have a chance. I sprint toward the door, my own heart pounding so hard and fast I'm waiting for it to just give up and skid to a stop.

Push through the doors and find myself on a path walled in by chain-link fences heading below the bleachers and out to the field. The roar of the crowd drowns out my screams for help. There's an empty police car parked on the other side of the fence but I can't see anyone near it.

Mitch bellows incoherently as he slams through the doors. He's gaining ground. All I can do is head for people, hope someone can stop him before he reaches me.

I keep running, my feet pounding against the cement. Up ahead, coming from the field, I see a group of figures. A little closer and I see it's Jordan. He's got his hands behind his back, a cop at his side, like he's under arrest. Behind them is Tony.

They stop when they see me—or more likely when they see Mitch charging like a bull in heat. The cop pushes Jordan down and out of the way and takes a stand, hand on his weapon but not drawing. All he sees is a football player chasing a girl. He has no idea what's going on.

Tony and Jordan are shouting at the officer. Before they can do anything, Mitch tackles me from behind. I go skidding face first along the path, bouncing off a cement support beam below the bleachers.

"I'm gonna kill you, freak!"

I roll over and see Mitch's fist in the air, aimed at my face.

"Stop!" the policeman shouts.

To my amazement, Mitch stops. And he climbs off me. My jaw creaks as I draw in a breath. There's blood on my knees, my jeans are torn, and my palms are scraped up. But other than that, I'm okay.

Tony rushes to my side and helps me up. Mitch is walking toward the officer, hands out, palms up, saying, "Officer, this is just a misunderstanding between me and my girl."

"Don't listen to him," Tony yells.

"Watch out!" Jordan shouts as he's struggling to his feet. I realize he's handcuffed.

The crowd is roaring, stamping their feet on the bleachers, and the officer doesn't have a chance to respond. Not before Mitch launches himself at him, aiming low, throwing him up and over his shoulder. The officer ends up in a crumbled heap beside Jordan while Mitch keeps running.

We rush after him. He pushes his way past the cheerleaders and launches himself onto the field in the middle of a play. Two guys from Bellefonte try to tackle him, but he's too fast. He brings one down with a clothes-hook move and kicks the other in the face mask. Then he's up again and running.

The crowd is on their feet. Everyone is screaming. The refs are blowing their whistles and throwing yellow handkerchiefs. Both teams are running around. Not sure if they should go after Mitch or the ball.

Tony and I get to the edge of the field just in time to see Mitch collapse.

78

Tony and I run onto the field, pushing our way through the players standing around Mitch. He's gasping, hands pressed to his chest. I kneel beside him and find his pulse. It's skipping erratically like a kid playing chopsticks.

The crowd separates and Mom arrives, accompanied by Mr. Beltzhoven and Coach. She throws a bag to the ground and grabs her stethoscope.

"He's been drugged," I tell the coach.

He doesn't hear me. Too many people talking at once. Mr. Beltzhoven does though, glaring at me like I'm the one who gave Mitch the OD. "Stand aside, young lady. Let your mother work."

Mom kneels beside Mitch on one side, me on the other. I grab his wrist again and feel for his pulse. Nothing!

I start CPR, pushing my weight against Mitch's bulk and getting nowhere fast. Tony quickly drops his backpack and takes over for me.

"Epi," Mom snaps, pulling the stethoscope from her ears. "Get me the epinephrine from the med kit."

Coach opens the medical bag and rummages through it.

Maybe I know nothing about living life as a normal girl,

but I know a lot about medicine. Including everything about Long QT.

"Stop!" I shout. "Don't let her give the epi."

"Scarlet, you need to let me do my job." Mom's tone is a knife, cutting through the noise, aimed at me.

I know that tone. You do not mess with Mom when she uses that tone. That tone means: *obey or suffer the consequences.*

Not this time. I know better now.

"You're the one who gave Mitch the drugs," I yell loud enough for everyone huddled around us to hear. Now all eyes are on me. Including Mr. Thorne's and two referees who have joined us. "If she gives him that epi, it will kill him."

Tony pauses long enough to say, "Scarlet's right. Listen to her."

Then he goes back to pounding on Mitch's chest. He's sweating, panting as he pumps. Mr. Thorne spells him while I tear open Tony's backpack and pull Phil out. I pop open Phil's front and grab the electrodes that need to be placed on Mitch's chest. If we get him hooked up fast enough, we can save him.

Tony struggles to unfasten Mitch's pads without getting in Mr. Thorne's way. "We need a knife or pair of scissors to cut these off."

"Help me attach these," I plead to the adults crowded around us.

"Nonsense," Mom says. "Give me that epinephrine. Now."

Coach hands her the epi. I hesitate, almost back down, until I see her smile. No one else is in position to see it; it's aimed at me and me alone. More than a smile, a smirk. Victorious, gleeful, powerful. In her glory.

Ready to kill.

Tony lunges for her arm, knocking the syringe of epinephrine away. Coach and two players grab him, hauling him off Mom.

I take advantage of the distraction, pull up Mitch's shirt, and get one electrode stuck to his belly. Now I just need to get the other one placed with his heart between the two.

Mr. Beltzhoven scrambles in the grass and finds the syringe. He hands it to Mom.

"Stop!" I try one last time. "She'll kill him."

"You two." He points to two football players. "Restrain that girl."

"No!"

Now both Tony and I are squirming in the grasp of football players.

"I think we should listen to Scarlet," Mr. Thorne says, sweat dripping from his forehead as he keeps pumping on Mitch's chest. He's huffing and puffing and the compressions aren't doing much good as he wears out.

Mitch is turning blue; he doesn't have any time left. Mom snaps the cap off the epi.

"Halt," a man calls. I glance over. Another police officer. Jordan's with him but no longer in cuffs. Behind them are Nessa and Celina. "Don't touch him."

Jordan twists the syringe from Mom's grasp. The football players are shocked and confused. I squirm from their grasp and return to Mitch's side. Jordan crouches beside me. "Scarlet, what do you need?"

"Get this on his skin across from his heart. On the right side of his chest or back, wherever you can put it as fast as possible."

The entire stadium is watching us. Jordan, Celina, and Nessa join me and Tony on the ground. He yanks Mitch's jersey and pads out of the way, sliding the electrode in place. Beyond us the adults are shouting at each other.

"No one should touch the patient. Analyzing," Phil tells me once the electrode is in place.

Come on, come on. The words stampede through my brain. What if we're too late?

"Shock advised. Stay clear of patient." Phil's voice is so calm. Wish I felt that way.

"Get back everyone," Tony says.

"Push the flashing orange button now," Phil instructs. "Deliver shock now."

Electricity jolts through Mitch's body. His back arches and hands jerk up. Then he bounces back against the ground.

"Shock delivered. Be sure to call emergency medical personnel. It is now safe to touch the patient," Phil announces. Do I detect a note of satisfaction in his tone? Probably not but I reach for Mitch's pulse and it's strong and steady. His eyes flicker open and he moans.

The medics arrive and we scramble back to make room for them. "What's going on?" one asks.

Mom is still arguing with the cop, so I give the report. "Seventeen-year-old white male, no past medical history, suspected Exzyte, synthetic marijuana, and bath salt overdose complicated by recent ingestion of alcohol and caffeine. Patient was running and collapsed, went pulseless. CPR was begun as the AED was applied. Shocked out of it with good pulse and capillary refill. Respirations normal, still altered level of consciousness."

"Good work, we'll take it from here."

They quickly package Mitch for transport and run him off the field onboard their stretcher. Leaving me to face Mom.

But this time I'm not alone. I have my friends to back me up.

79

Mom spots me and breaks free of her argument with the police officer. She takes the three steps needed to reach me. Her chest heaves and her cheeks are puffing with every breath. I've never seen her this angry. Never. Every wrinkle on her face is etched into her skin as her muscles contort with fury.

"How dare you!" She slaps me so hard I would have fallen if Jordan and Tony hadn't caught me.

Oblivious to the gasps of the crowd, she reaches her arm back, ready to haul off and hit me again.

Too late. Mr. Police Officer, who from the stripes on his sleeve I'm guessing is Jordan's dad, yanks her arm down, twists it behind her, and has her in cuffs before she can sputter a protest.

"Let's go. All of you. We're going down to the station and straighten all of this out." He begins to walk my mom through the crowd of stunned players. "Now!"

We fall in line behind him.

Tony reaches for my hand and suddenly I don't really care what happens next. I know it's not going to be easy and there's a good chance Mom will convince the cops she's innocent. I'll deal with that when it comes. At least the people who count, my friends, know the truth.

"What happened to you?" I ask Celina as we straggle off the field.

Thousands of eyes are on us but the crowd is eerily quiet as if they realize they've witnessed something remarkable, even though they have no idea what happened. Celina is leaning heavily on Jordan's arm; there's blood on the collar of her shirt.

"She"—she nods at Mom—"hit me on the head and locked me in a cupboard."

"Had her gagged with duct tape, hands and feet too," Nessa put in. "Good thing I thought to look there. She could have suffocated."

"No, I couldn't have. In fact, I was almost free when you got there. Had most of the tape scraped off my face and wrists."

"And how were you going to get out of a locked cabinet without me finding the key?" Nessa shot back.

"Thank you, Nessa," Jordan says, using his free hand to pull Nessa to him and kissing her on the top of her head without ever letting Celina go. He nudges Celina.

"Yes, thank you, Nessa."

"You're so very welcome," Nessa says with a hop turned into a curtsy.

Jordan's dad leads us through the maze under the bleachers and we end up at his squad car parked alongside two others. Leaning against one is the first officer—the one who had Jordan in cuffs before Mitch knocked him down. He's looking a bit sheepish.

"Sorry about that, kid," he tells Jordan. "But you know, I have to take any report of assault seriously."

I glance at Jordan, raising an eyebrow to encourage him to

explain, but he simply nods to the officer and shakes his hand. "Of course, sir, I understand."

Tony whispers, "He was about ready to knock your mom off the bleachers to get her to tell him where Celina was, but your mom started screaming before he even touched her. Cop didn't believe Jordan or me, was gonna lock him up."

"Guess we're lucky his dad was on duty."

He nods. We sort ourselves out between the three cars. Mom alone in the back of one. Tony and me in another. And Nessa, Jordan, and Celina in Jordan's dad's. The officer driving us tells us not to say anything until we get to the station. He says it in a way that makes me think he's doing us a favor.

I've never been near a police car before. They're not as glamorous as you'd think from the movies. The rear seat is hard plastic and stinks of vomit and pee. It's pretty claustrophobic back there with the steel mesh on the windows and between you and the driver. Worse than an MRI machine.

But not so bad with a guy like Tony holding your hand the whole time.

Then we get to the station and they separate us all. I end up sitting in a room by myself for what feels like hours. It's got blank cinderblock walls, no windows, nothing but two chairs and a table. Finally, I end up folding my arms on the table and falling asleep.

No clowns or laughing women chase me in my dreams. No crying little boys. In fact, for the first time in a long time, I don't dream at all.

80

Scarlet. Scarlet, honey. Wake up."

I blink and open my eyes. It's my dad. Maybe I was dreaming, maybe this entire day has been a dream. Who knows? Maybe my entire life.

Dad doesn't look happy. Behind him stands a man in a suit who also looks very unhappy.

No dream.

I jerk upright. Suspicious. Does he believe me? Or Mom? Is he going to make me go back home with her?

"What's going on?" I ask.

At least Mom's not here—which I hope means she hasn't talked her way out of everything yet. I'm betting on her doing just that. After all, anyone savvy enough to manipulate world-class doctors for years can probably handle a bunch of small-town cops.

"Scarlet, this is Mr. Anderson. There was an emergency hearing and he's been appointed your guardian *ad litem*." Dad squirms. He obviously wants to say more.

"Thank you, Mr. Killian. I'll take it from here." Mr. Anderson steps forward, between Dad and me. "I believe the detectives are waiting for your statement?"

Dad heaves in a breath. Holds it for a long moment then lets it escape. He nods and says nothing, but does stop to kiss me on the cheek before leaving. I touch my finger to the warm spot left by his kiss.

The door closes behind him and I suddenly feel like I'm adrift, floating on a sea of uncertainty.

"Why isn't my dad my guardian?"

"The district attorney thought this best. This way everyone's interests are represented."

Even I can read between the lines of his legal mumbo-jumbo. "He wasn't involved."

I think. I hope.

"Can you prove that?" He doesn't wait for my answer. Good thing, because I don't have one. Instead, he pulls out a legal pad, uncaps an expensive-looking pen, and sets a digital recorder between us. "How about if you tell me everything? From the beginning."

81

It's been an amazing month.

Turns out I'm not really allergic to anything. Me, Nessa, and Celina have been trying every kind of food out there just to see what I like and don't like. And guess what? I like it all! Except raw sushi and oysters. But everything else, even sardines and artichokes and weird little fruits that are the ugliest thing you've ever seen—Jordan found me those, left them in our locker wrapped in a big purple bow.

I haven't seen my mom since the police took her after the family court judge found her guilty. Not guilty of everything—not yet. She still faces assault and attempted murder charges because of Mitch and Celina. But that's criminal court, which takes a lot longer.

Living without her hasn't been as hard as I thought it might be. Not that it's easy either.

Dad lets me do anything I want. Sometimes I take advantage of his guilt, but Nessa says that makes me normal, so I don't feel so awful about it. And sometimes I tell myself he owes me. What do I want from him as payback, I'm not sure…maybe my childhood back?

The judge made Dad and me go to counseling, alone and together, and he's going to decide in another month or so if my dad gets to keep me or not. He has a hard time believing someone as smart as my father could have been so clueless for so long. But hell, even I was clueless. We were all so busy trying to make Mom happy, we forgot to take a look at what was really going on around us.

The shrink the judge sent me to is a woman, about Mom's age. I think he did that on purpose, just to torture me or something. At first all I did was sit in silence, dissecting her every word and gesture, trying to uncover the hidden meaning behind them, certain she's manipulating me, just like Mom did. Whatever she asked me to do, I did the opposite.

If she asked me to be honest, I lied. If she asked me to express my feelings, I shut down. If she tried to help me relax, I blew up in anger—that was the breakthrough, I guess you could call it. Finally, no, not finally, for the first time ever, I let myself get angry at my mom, at my dad, at my life.

After that, no one else wanted to be around me for days. Anything set me off—Nessa called it PMS on steroids—but I was like an addict; once I started feeling things for real, I couldn't stop.

Tony and I talk a lot. But we also spend a lot of time not talking. We'll go to the park and play like we're little kids. My old favorite, the teeter-totter, which isn't quite as much fun now that I'm tall enough to touch the ground with my toes. The swings are my new favorite, especially when I sit on his lap and we pump together, our bodies moving in unison. And the tilt-o-whirl. I'll lie in the middle and he'll run around the edge, spinning it as I stare up at the sky and clouds and trees overhead, breathing in the clean, fresh air of my new world.

We even figured out how to kiss finally. I go right and he goes left. I always start things, control how long, how hard—I need that right now. Sometimes he gets frustrated with it, sometimes even angry. I don't understand guys and I can tease him without meaning to. But we're both learning.

Even when we fight, it's okay. Another lesson I needed to learn, probably should have learned way back in kindergarten.

He has a way of letting me know, even when he's mad at me, that he still cares. He touches his finger to his lips then turns it over, like he's releasing a kiss into the wind, sending it my way. Telling me that he wants *me*. The abby-normal girl, the extra-ordinary girl, the broken girl who almost died.

When he does that, it's like the whole world stops.

Nessa laughed when I told her that, said it's just hormones, which is probably true, but I don't care. Knowing why something happens doesn't make it any less fantastic.

My counselor says I'm "blossoming." Sounds lame, but inside I know she's right. For the first time, my clothes actually fit. When I look in the mirror, I see a real girl, someone with a life ahead of her, not a half-dead girl.

Jordan's helped too, even though he still doesn't say a lot. I've watched him play soccer and he's so intense, rips around that field like it's a canvas of mud and grass and he's an exuberant kindergartner who gets to finger-paint with it all. He doesn't get angry when they lose. I think maybe because he puts his heart and soul into playing and just has fun.

I want to live that way. Not necessarily happy all the time, but appreciating all the possibilities that surround us in every moment and taking full advantage of them. *Carpe diem,* Celina's mom calls it. She's like Jordan. Doesn't talk much, but when she does, it's well worth listening to.

Live for the day.

Which makes this morning all the more painful.

Dad pulls the car up behind a gray sedan and we get out. Neither of us says anything. Me because it's too much work just to keep from crying or screaming or lashing out at him.

Him? I'm not sure why he isn't talking. He used to be such a big talker, but I'm finally realizing all those words were just a smokescreen. Hiding the fact that he never really said anything.

My legs feel stiff with the cold. I'm wearing jeans that are finally looking broken-in, a State Police SWAT sweatshirt Celina gave me—it's too big but makes me feel strong; it used to be her mom's—and a Juicy Couture hoodie Nessa lent me. She sent the matching pants as well, but as much as it'd be fun to make my dad go nuts by wearing them, I can't lower myself to providing free advertising to a company by wearing tight-fitting pants with "juicy" written across my backside. Talk about demeaning.

I might be not-so-normal, but I have my pride. It's newly found and hard won. And I have the scars to prove it.

The leaves are off the trees and the mountainside is bare to the wind. We're back in Jeanette. Where we lived when I was young.

Where Ash died.

Where he was killed.

Which is why we're here. It's taken this long to get an exhumation order. Mom's lawyers fought it every step of the way. But when the DA in our county found that no autopsy or toxicology screen had been done by the Jeanette coroner (a funeral director who admitted that Mom talked him out of the autopsy, and that even if he had wanted, he hadn't had the budget to do a complete investigation) and the State Police detectives learned Mom had gotten a prescription for liquid codeine (for a toothache—she'd gotten her dentist to call it in for her) filled the day before Ash died, the judge signed the order.

And here we are. Sun barely up over the mountains in the distance, no birds singing, not around the graveyard at least, only the sound of a backhoe digging through the dirt.

Dad and I watch in silence, our hands almost but not quite touching.

"I didn't know," he whispers. Mainly to himself, because I've heard it before and I'm not listening anymore.

At first I forgave him. It was scary enough facing life without Mom around; I couldn't bear to lose Dad as well. But funny thing is, he's even more terrified of not having Mom around than I am. Like he needed her in some warped way.

My life depended on her—literally. But from the way he keeps turning to me to make decisions, plan our future, seems like his did as well.

I don't have the words to describe how angry—no, furious, no, something beyond fury—that makes me feel. At him, at her, at myself.

The only innocent in all of this is Ash.

My fingernails bite into my palms as they raise the cement container that holds his casket. It's a big hole but such a tiny gray box.

The detective overseeing things nods to us. The workers stop, the container resting on the grass beside Ash's headstone. They step back and give us space.

Dad doesn't move. He tries—one aborted step forward that leaves him grasping the top of a tombstone for balance. He slumps, turns his head away, but not before I spot his tears, glistening in the dawn-slanted rays of the sun.

I walk to Ash. As I do, the birds start singing again. I imagine my little blond dream boy bobbing his head around a headstone and grinning at me, as if he's playing hide-and-seek and wants me to join in on the fun.

And what fun we would have had, me and Ash. I might not remember any of our life together, but my imagination is plenty good enough to fill in the blanks about what could have been.

What will never be.

I place my palm flat on the concrete slab holding Ash's coffin. It's chilly but not as cold as I feared. Clods of dirt cling to it. I scoop some into my fist, molding it into a small ball.

Just like we used to make dough balls for fishing. A stray memory hits me like a sunbeam. Me and Ash fishing from the side of a stream, tiny bamboo rods clutched in our hands.

Laughter.

His and mine.

And Dad's.

Tears spark my vision as I look up. The little boy is there. He waves at me and blows me a kiss good-bye. As if he's given me this memory as a going-away present.

I don't want him to leave. It feels like part of my insides have been ripped away, tearing me in two as he fades from sight.

Dad places his hand on my shoulder. Turns me to him.

The workers return to remove Ash. Dad and I cry together, clinging to each other for support. The dirt in my hand crumbles and slides beneath my fingers, dribbling to the ground.

Finally I step away from Dad. "Let's go home."

As we drive over the mountains and back to Smithfield, I think about what I'm going to tell the judge. He's given me the option of leaving Smithfield—and Dad—for good if I want. Said he'd let me live with my aunt, Dad's sister, in Harrisburg. I've only seen her maybe half a dozen times my entire life.

Living with a stranger. Or living as a stranger.

Those are my options.

By the time we get into Smithfield and drive past the high school, I have my decision.

It's scary. Terrifying.

Which is exactly why the new me, the contrarian me, wants to do it. Just because I can.

Hell, I think I am going to do it.

Stay here. With my dad. With the gossip and stares and bullies at school.

With my friends.

Because let's face it. Life's too damn short to leave the people you love behind.

Q & A WITH CJ LYONS

Q: Is Long QT a real disease?
CJ: Yes. As a pediatrician, I diagnosed my niece with Long QT Syndrome when she was born. Her heart specialists believe she's the youngest person in the world diagnosed with Long QT. She's had to take medicine every day of her life and can't ever skip a day. So far, that's added up to over ten thousand pills taken.

You know that feeling you get when you've run as hard and fast as you can and you stop but your heart keeps galloping along? And you wonder for a second if maybe it's not going to stop, but will keep galloping out of control? But then of course it settles back down. For people with Long QT, their heart doesn't change gears well, going from regular to galloping and back again. So they have to avoid anything that would make their heart race.

No sports or aerobic exercise. No horror films. No roller coaster rides. No jumping into cold water on a hot summer's day.

But that doesn't have to stop someone with Long QT like my niece from having a great life. Today she is a brilliant, active fourteen-year-old who gets straight As, enjoys horseback riding, archery, reading, and breeding Rottweilers, and who wants to grow up to be either a fashion designer or President of the United States. Her main fashion accessory is her portable defibrillator,

Phil, who goes with her everywhere, including camping, to the beach, and recently to her first Broadway show.

Broken is dedicated to her fearless approach to life where out-witting Death is simply part of her daily routine.

Q: And Munchausen by proxy is real as well?

CJ: Sad to say, but yes. I've been involved in diagnosing several cases, including one where we suspected a mother of killing three of her children. Thankfully, it is an extremely rare disease—in fact, some experts believe that there are more people falsely accused of Munchausen by proxy than those who actually have it. I don't think that's the case. After seventeen years of working in pediatrics and in the ER, I've seen way too many warped people who think it's okay to treat kids like objects rather than people.

But the important thing to understand is that just like bullying or any kind of abuse, it's okay to tell. If you don't feel comfortable talking with your parents or the adults you're living with, find a police officer, teacher, doctor, or, yes, even the school nurse or guidance counselor, and tell them what's happening.

Tell the truth. That's the best way to help them help you. You don't have to make things up or twist things around because you're worried they won't believe you. Just tell them what happened.

The best way to end any kind of abuse is to break the silence.

Q: What about the rest of the medicine in *Broken*? Could any of that actually happen?

CJ: Yes. I've seen kids die of heart attacks from taking drugs like the bath salts and synthetic marijuana mentioned in *Broken*. The most common drug use I've seen that can literally cause someone to just "drop dead" is huffing—it actually creates an abnormal heart rhythm that is just like Long QT. There have also been recent reports of kids dying from so-called "energy" drinks.

Also, kids taking antidepressants, even the herbal over-the-counter ones like Nessa took, can have severe symptoms, including signs of mania. This doesn't always mean that you have bipolar disease though, because these drugs are very complicated and people respond to them in unique ways. This is also why it is very important if a doctor has you on an antidepressant (sometimes used not for depression but other things like headaches, PMS, etc.) that you never stop it abruptly—skipping doses can create unexpected side effects and be quite dangerous. If you're having problems and think it's because of a medication you're taking, talk to your doctor—don't just quit taking it.

Q: What was it like working in an ER? Is it like on TV?
CJ: Definitely nothing like *Grey's Anatomy*, but the first few seasons of *ER* get it right. Working in the ER is basically about learning how to control (and live with) chaos, the art of listening, and how to quickly decide what's the most important thing you need to tackle next.

I worked three jobs to put myself through medical school and one of them was waitressing at a very busy family restaurant. Honestly, that was the best preparation I ever could have had for life in the ER.

Q: Why did you leave medicine to write books?

CJ: I've been a storyteller all my life—a fact that used to get me placed in time-out a lot as a kid. But writing stories has always been my way of making sense of the chaos that goes on in the world around us. I wrote my first novel in college and wrote two more science-fiction novels in medical school.

Then, while I was an intern at Children's Hospital of Pittsburgh, one of my close friends was murdered. Dealing with that grief and trauma while still working seventy hours a week and trying to save lives—I wasn't prepared for that. So I turned to my writing and that's when I wrote my first thriller. I never thought about actually making a career of it until years later when friends who were published authors encouraged me to enter a national writing contest and I became a finalist. This led to several publishing contracts and I realized that as much as I loved being a doctor, here was a chance for a second dream come true: being a full-time writer.

It was a huge leap of faith leaving my job (and my patients—I missed them a lot!) but I've always believed that if you're going to dream, you should dream big, so I went for it. Since then I've published twenty books, hit #2 on the *New York Times* bestseller list, won awards for my writing, and, most importantly, have had the chance to impact millions of people through my novels. Talk about a dream come true!

Q: What's your best advice for someone who wants to be a writer?

CJ: Never surrender, never give up. Writing is hard work; it takes years to master the craft, so you need to stick with it. And read, read, read…pay attention to what makes the books you like work as well as why the books you don't like fail. You never stop learning in this job, but that's also what makes it so much fun.

Learn more about CJ's Thrillers with Heart at www.CJLyons.net and everything she knows about being a bestseller at www.No RulesJustWRITE.com.

ACKNOWLEDGMENTS

No book is brought to life without three things: Vision, Passion, and Commitment.

Broken is no exception. I had a vision: a book unlike any I'd ever written, unlike any that I'd ever read, about a disease so unlikely that experts debate its existence. Without my agent Barbara Poelle's passion for this project, *Broken* might have never been written, much less finished. The final magic ingredient came from my editor Leah Hultenschmidt and her fantastic team at Sourcebooks who brought *Broken* to life.

Thank you all!

HE SEES EVERYTHING

DON'T MISS
CJ LYONS'

WATCHED

"It is not light that we need, but fire; it is not the gentle shower, but thunder. We need the storm, the whirlwind, and the earth-quake."

—Frederick Douglass

cap·ping [kap-ing] *Verb, Slang:*
1. The act of shooting or killing someone with a gun.
2. The practice of capturing covert screenshots, usually of under-age girls and boys, and then using them to coerce the subjects into performing sexual acts on video. (See also: *capper*, noun, slang)

cap·per [kap-er] *Noun, Slang:*
1. An informer.
2. A person who captures covert screenshots for the purpose of blackmail, bullying, sexual gratification, or to trade among online communities.

1

Some guys think fire is sexy.

Watching the abandoned house burn, I spot a few of those in the crowd. While firefighters like my uncle are hard at work, these guys are hanging out, staring, licking their lips, one hand shoved deep down the front pocket of their jeans. Pyros.

That's not me. I don't love fire. I hate it. I envy it.

I *need* it.

I didn't start this fire, but I understand whoever did: the joy of creating something so beautiful. The temptation to give it freedom, let it take control, destroying everything in its path.

One spark is all it takes.

You think you can control it. You know it's wrong, but you don't know what else to do. You're trapped, a flame dancing along a match, running out of time, nowhere to go.

You figure you can stop. That you only need it just this once. Then everything will be okay and you won't ever, ever do it again. You won't have to, because you're in control.

At least that's what you think.

But sparks breathe and grow into flames. Flames surge into a full-blown blaze. You try to smother them, but it burns, hurts so bad you pull back. Lose control.

If you ever even had it to begin with.

That's life. My life.

Some days I want to burn the world to ashes. Let the flames loose to scour the filth and dirt, devour the pain—my pain—and start fresh and new again.

But fire never keeps its promise. You can never give it its freedom—just like I can never let my feelings escape, never tell anyone the truth.

If I did, my whole world would burn like the house in front of me.

It's mesmerizing, watching the well-rehearsed movements of the men attacking the flames. There's no one inside the two-story frame house on Pine Street, so they're coordinating an exterior attack. A few of the guys nod or wave at me. Most of them are grinning as they lean against the water gushing through their hoses—and they don't even know it. In their own way, they love fire as much as the pyros do.

I wish I could love anything that much. Most days I just feel numb. Others, there's this rage burning inside me, consuming me, until it takes all my energy to keep it from escaping like the flames curling through the house's busted windows.

Dave, the engineer, checks the gauges on the side of the pumper truck—lime green, emblazoned with the Smithfield, PA Fire Department insignia—then joins me.

"You guys need anything?" I yell over the riotous clamor of water, engines, men shouting, the house groaning and moaning. Fires are noisy places. Most people don't realize that.

Or appreciate the stench. Not like a wood fire you build on a cold winter's night, safe at home. House fires mean all sorts of shit going up in smoke: carpet and plastic and clothing and insulation. The smell is the main reason the crowd stays back, not heat or fear.

It always amazes me how little fear civilians have—if they could get close, they would. Their faces light up, eyes reflecting the flames, and if it weren't for guys like my uncle and Dave keeping them back at a safe distance, they'd walk right into danger, like they're in a trance or something.

I guess we all have a love-hate relationship with fire. Some more than others.

"I can make a run to Sheetz, grab some sodas," I tell Dave. Fighting fire is thirsty work. And these guys will be here for a while, long after the last flame is doused. Putting out the fire is the fun part; the real work comes during the cleanup.

"Thanks, Jesse," he says. "But we're covered." We stand side by side in front of the pumper, arms crossed over our chests, and watch the fire's dying throes. "No signs of a meth lab or any hazmat shit, thank God. She was a bitch, but your uncle, he grabbed her by the throat and throttled her good."

Firemen talk like that, like fires are women, like conquering a fire is better than sex.

It's not PC, but if you've ever been inside a building, smoke so black even the strongest light can't penetrate it, thick with poisonous chemicals that would kill you if you weren't breathing through a mask, your heart pounding in your head as you inch your way forward, desperate not to get lost or fall through the floor and drown in the water your brothers-in-arms are pouring into the flames...if you've ever been there, you'd talk like that too.

I've never told my uncle or any of the other guys at the station, but fire isn't a "she" to me. Fire *is* me, like the blood in my veins or the electricity that jump-starts my nerves.

It's the fury that wakes me with its acid burn every morning, the pain that curdles my insides until I clench every muscle, trying to regain control. Fire is the part of me I can never show the rest of the world, but sometimes I have to let it out or I'll spontaneously combust.

We watched a video in health class last year. It was about not hurting yourself—drinking and driving, eating disorders, killing yourself, whatever. On it, a girl talked about cutting.

She said seeing her blood was like wrapping a chain around her heart, anchoring her to the real world. Without the blood, she'd just float away into nothing. Only by tearing into her own flesh, allowing the blood to escape, could she release the pain building up inside.

I'll never forget that girl. She's me—before they locked her up and fed her drugs and turned her into a zombie telling other kids, *don't worry; be happy.*

Yeah right. Sometimes adults are so clueless, I wonder if they even live in the same universe as me. There are so many things going on right in front of them, inside their own homes even, and they're so damn oblivious. Wandering around in the dark, never seeing—or maybe they choose not to see. Which, in my book, is even worse.

Doesn't matter. All you can do is figure out what works for you. For that girl, it was cutting. For me, it's keeping my mouth shut and lighting my fires.

"Come summer, it'll be you," Dave says, giving the dying blaze a nod. I turned sixteen a few months ago; now I can join the department as a junior firefighter. Everyone assumes I'll follow in my uncle's footsteps, so I guess that's what will happen. No one ever asks me.

"Was it our guy?" We're far enough away from the civilians I don't have to worry about being overheard. Few outside the fire department and the cops know there's a serial arsonist at work in Smithfield.

"Yeah. Sixth one. Same signature."

"You think he's a bug?" Firefighters call people like me, who start fires out of compulsion, firebugs. I hate the term, although I have to admit that when the need strikes, I do feel like a worm, unable to crawl away from it—lower than low, belly rubbing the dirt.

Then I light a fire, bring it to life, and I feel almost human again.

"No. This guy's a pro. Cops are trying to follow the money trail, but it'll take time." Dave shrugs. Catching the guy isn't his job—putting out the fires left in his wake is.

"They came around last night, talked to my uncle. At the house." My uncle is assistant chief, in charge of personnel. Smithfield's a small city made smaller by the recession, and firefighters don't make much despite the risks they take to protect civilians. The temptation to earn extra money burning down empty buildings so owners can cash out puts even firefighting heroes at the top of the cops' suspect list.

"I'll bet he gave them an earful."

"Kicked them out. Said to get a court record for the personnel files, they want them so bad."

He looks at me, frowning. The lights flash across his face, red, white, red, white. "Jesse, you know anything about these fires?"

I shake my head. "No."

It's the truth. I can never lose control, let my fires enjoy a taste of freedom like this guy's. If I did, I'd destroy everything: my life, my family, everything. "I'm just worried about my uncle, is all." That part's also true, but not the way he takes it.

"Don't worry. He can take care of himself. Now you'd best get out of here before he sees you. He won't like you out this late on a school night."

I nod and head down the block toward my pickup truck, making my way through the lookie loos. Like most of Smithfield, this street is a roller coaster of steep hills, old-fashioned cobble-stones poking through worn-out macadam.

Sometimes it feels like Smithfield never left the first Great Depression behind. With its coal-stained frame and brick houses huddled against the wind whipping down from the Allegheny mountains that surround it, it hasn't changed much since my mom and uncle grew up here. Except the problems Smithfield faces today are a lot different than they were in the last century.

Meth, heroin, oxy—infecting both parents and their kids. And plenty more bad things going on in the dark behind closed doors. The lousy economy isn't helping any. Smithfield is set in some of the most beautiful countryside imaginable, but you tend to forget that when you live here and all you see is the broken-down concrete at your feet.

It's past ten on a Sunday night, but the block is crowded with men slouched against the shadows, using the spectacle of the fire as a chance to make a few bucks selling drugs. Dark hoodies hide their faces, but their hands give them away: fast moving, hand to pocket, money to hand, hands meet in exchange, nod of the head, hands back in pockets, saunter away.

I don't know why they even bother hiding in the shadows; anyone can tell what they're doing. No one seems to care. It's that kind of neighborhood…becoming that kind of city if things don't pick up soon.

Women gather with babies and young children, holding them tightly, talking to each other as they watch the destruction. One more drug house gone. No thanks to the city. They seem to think the arsonist is some kind of modern-day Robin Hood. They chat about planting a garden or having a new place for the kids to play since the house was on a large corner lot.

Wait until they see how long it takes the city to clean away the debris. Until then, the blackened, skeletonized remains of the house will beckon to their kids, daring them to risk falling into the gaping basement filled with soot and mud and water, climbing cracked timbers, combing through the ashes searching for treasure. Just last month my uncle's crew had to rescue a little boy from an old coal chute he'd fallen through after a similar fire buried it from sight.

I stop as the roof on the burning house falls in, releasing black smoke and flames to swirl into the night. The crowd pulls back with a cry of terror followed by cheers. My uncle and his men lunge forward, their grins wider than ever. This is the final battle, the last of the fun part. Then comes cleanup—smoking cigarettes while raking through the ashes, dousing any smoldering embers.

The crowd applauds the firefighters as the blaze surrenders. They don't understand what's really going on inside the fire or the kind of men who run toward an inferno instead of away from it.

They don't know fire like I do.

They don't want to.

Lighting a blaze, breathing life into the sparks, watching the flames come alive then die, leaving behind ashes of despair... Every fire I start is a new beginning, a second chance—a way to release the pain and find the courage to go on living.

Without my fires, I would have killed myself long ago.

With my fires, I can imagine hope.

———

Sunday, five hours later...

Miranda's fingers flew over her keyboards—both of them—as she followed the boy's trail from the streaming video. Looked like the kid in front of the webcam was in a normal bedroom in a normal house—no one would ever believe what he was doing at three in the morning. She was certain none of it was his idea. Just like her being here watching wasn't exactly how she wanted to spend a Sunday night either.

She couldn't believe her luck, finally tracking down one of the Creep's private live feeds. She couldn't close in on the Creep himself; he was much too careful. But his client, the perv from Tokyo, was an amateur at covering his tracks, giving Miranda the chance to trace the kid back to his home ISP.

If she could pull this off, the kid would be okay—they'd all be okay. At least that's what she kept telling herself, typing furiously, seeing lines of code glowing against the back of her eyelids with each blink. She was exhausted, but it was worth it. She'd seen the kid before in the Creep's glitzy teaser ads—movie trailers aimed at an audience with sick and twisted minds—but this was her first chance to track him to where he lived in the real world.

Occasionally she had to glance at the other screen—the one with the live action—to check the time code. 3:18 a.m. EST, 4:18 p.m. Tokyo. If they logged off before she finished, she'd lose the kid. Maybe forever.

She tried hard not to notice what was actually happening, what Tokyo perv was making the kid do, but then realized it was important that she pay attention. Not to the action playing out but to the kid. His face.

JohnBoy was his screen name. Not his real one, of course. Just like Miranda wasn't hers.

He could be any of them—he could be her. She had to bear

witness, not treat him as a disposable commodity, used and tossed away, like the Creep and his clients did.

It was important. It was why she did what she did.

Except now she was running out of time. In a few days, the Creep would win. Everything. Unless…JohnBoy…maybe he was the one. Magic Thirteen.

He was a year or two older than her, sixteen or seventeen. He looked strong enough, nice muscles, tall—as tall as her dad, even. So many of the others she'd found, they'd already been broken, damaged beyond repair. You could tell it by their eyes: dead and dull, staring at nothing.

Not JohnBoy. Despite the fake smile for the perv halfway around the world, she caught a spark of defiance in his eyes, hidden behind each blink. More than defiance. Hope.

As if he knew she was there, searching for him. As if he needed her as much as she needed him.

Shoulders tight, carrying a burden much too heavy for a skinny fourteen-year-old girl barely five feet tall, she hunched over her keyboard, fingers pounding the keys so hard shockwaves raced up her arms.

Hang on, JohnBoy. I'll find you. I promise.

2

Thursday, four days later…

Who the hell was William the Conqueror? I stare so hard at my exam paper my vision blurs. I know he's important, but was he before or after all those Henrys? Somewhere in the middle? I can't think I'm so exhausted. After I got home from another fire last night, King woke me for a live-streaming session with one of his clients.

Some days I get home from school and stand inside the door, unable to remember if I'm coming or going or anything about the day or if I even went to school. So much for education being the path to freedom.

Maybe some of us never find a way out. We end up trapped forever—like all those peasants and serfs used as cannon fodder by William and the Henrys and every egomaniacal dictator who came after them.

My phone buzzes in my pocket. Talk about your egomaniacal dictators. No phones in school, definitely not while taking a test. Those are the rules. But this is the phone King gave me. The one I must never, ever turn off or not answer.

I stretch to cover my movement as I slide it under the desk, typing with one hand.

JB: Can't talk.

King: Client wants JohnBoy. Now.

JB: Can't. Test. Gotta go.

King: Get out of it.

JB: Can't. Teacher.

King: I don't care. Five minutes. Live feed or else.

I stare down at my hand, at the words filling the screen. My mouth is dry; I can't get enough spit together to swallow. *Or else.*

Two words more frightening than anything the teacher can throw at me. I glance up at her. She's marking papers, clueless.

Not me. I know too much—learned it all when I was twelve, real-world stuff, true shit, not lies written by the conquerors for the history books. I know what King's "or else" can mean. The Spanish Inquisition has nothing on him when it comes to devising new and cruel ways to torture. King's torture doesn't leave a mark or bruise—his weapon of choice is the Internet and he uses it to reach anyone, anywhere, anytime he chooses.

I accidentally pissed him off a while back when the battery died in my cell and I missed his call. He punished me by setting my mom up on a blind date with a psycho she thought was a guy from the church choir. She was so excited, changed her dress three times—it was her first date since my dad walked out on us. Mom juggles two part-time jobs plus taking care of my little sister, Janey, so she doesn't have time or energy to meet nice guys, much less date. I'll never forget the smile she had as she ran to answer the door when he rang—I hadn't seen that smile in years, not since my dad. It lit up her entire being, like she'd swallowed a piece of heaven.

Haven't seen her smile like that since either. Her "choirboy" cornered me after he brought her home and told me exactly what he'd do to her if I ever kept King waiting again. Then he walked out of Mom's life, and she went back to being overworked, underpaid, and overwhelmed.

That's King's idea of "or else." Hard to care about a history test when your life is already over.

Pocketing the phone, I turn my paper over, lay my pencil on top, and walk up to the teacher. She glances up, startled. "What is it, Jesse?"

"Can I please use the boys' room, Mrs. Henderson?" I'm always extra polite with teachers. Best way to get them to do what I need them to do.

She looks disappointed in me. It's a look I get a lot. I'm used to it. Before King, it would have bothered me. I was always one of those kids who tried hard to be the best at everything. But that was a long, long time ago. Long before Mrs. Henderson ever met me. But every now and then, an adult like Mrs. Henderson realizes I'm not fulfilling my potential. Some kind of instinct makes them wonder why I'm such a loser.

Can't they see? I'm not a loser. I'm the Energizer Bunny, running a triple-A life fueled by anger, adrenaline, and anxiety.

But they can't see it. They don't *want* to see it. No one does.

"You know the rules, Jesse. You can't leave during a test."

Class only started ten minutes ago, so no way will she believe I'm already finished. But no way can I finish, not with worrying about the price I'll pay if I keep King waiting.

"I feel sick." It's the truth. Nothing new. I've felt sick, worse than sick—a dirty, queasy, constant burning in the pit of my belly—ever since I met King. Or rather, when he met me. I was twelve then. I'm sixteen now. The feeling hasn't gone away, gets worse every day.

Her frown deepens. I've used the sick excuse too often with her. Shame, really, since I love history. All those stories of far-off lands and adventure. It's the last class I'd ever skip if I had a say. But of course I don't. I have no say in anything. My life doesn't belong to me. It belongs to King.

"I'm sorry, Jesse. If you think you need to go down to the nurse, you'll get a zero for your test grade unless she can confirm that you're really sick."

I look down at my size twelves then up at the clock above her head, ticking away my precious five minutes. I nod. "I understand."

She scratches out a hall pass to take to the nurse. I grab my backpack and leave. As soon as the door closes behind me, I slide my phone free.

"Why aren't you live?" King answers.

"On my way—" The phone is yanked from my grasp. It's Mr.

Walker, the vice principal. He's always sneaking around the halls when class is in session.

Stupid. I should've been more careful.

"I'll take that, Mr. Alexander," he says triumphantly, as if he'd just single-handedly disarmed a suicide bomber.

Little does he know he actually does hold my life in his hands.

"Please, Mr. Walker—" I slouch, trying to make myself smaller than my six one. Don't want to intimidate Walker, who's only five eight with lifts in his shoes. He has short-man syndrome big time.

He arches an eyebrow at me then hangs up the phone. Hangs up on King.

Shit. Shit, shit, shit. The acid churning through my gut makes it all the way up to the back of my throat. Tastes like burning rubber. King is going to be furious. And I'll be the one to pay the price.

"That's my emergency phone. I was calling to let my mom know I'm sick and headed to the nurse's office." Over the past three years, I've learned how to act better than any of those pretty boys in Hollywood. I can see he's wavering, hold up the hall pass to convince him.

Unfortunately, Mrs. Henderson chooses that moment to come out and see what's going on. Two minutes later, my phone's confiscated after Walker sees I wasn't really talking to my mom, I'm back at my desk scratching doodles on my test paper (because who can think when they're imagining things far worse than any atrocities good ole Willie the Conqueror ever could have performed?), and I'm ordered to detention after school.

Most kids would be whining about how life sucks or how unfair it all is. Not me. I couldn't care less about my grade or detention or graduating.

If I had my way, I'd be gone already. Enlist in the Marines or Army, get my GED, have Uncle Sam pay for college. Wouldn't even care if they sent me to a battlefield, shit getting blown up, bullets flying.

That kind of war would be heaven. At least I'd have a fighting chance.

Not like now. Now, with King in my life, I don't have a chance in hell.

I stare at the closed classroom door. My phone is down the hall with Walker, waiting for me to pick it up after detention. By then it will be too late.

King is going to kill me.